Kruger's Milli

By

Damian P.O'C

GW00838595

Chapter 1

Kuruman

Bechuanaland Protectorate, South Africa.

Gold is never very far from Ragwasi's mind. Gold and diamonds and silver and cash and shares and bonds and IOUs, small change, peppercorn rents, windfalls and legacies; in fact, any sort of money or scheme for getting more of it is his abiding obsession. He simply cannot get enough of the stuff. The dream of untold wealth easily come by is Ragwasi's abiding passion - and it is also his Achilles Heel.

If Ragwasi has a flaw in his character then it is a tendency to avarice – and I am *not* saying that he *does* have such a flaw, if you understand me, because he is *ma bru*, my chief and also a Prince of the Tswana (I promoted him personally back in 1879), but some people less charitable than me *might* make a passing comment on such a flaw, *if* indeed he did have it. Don't get me wrong though; he has never been a miser or tight fisted and he always holds up his end when it comes to shared expenses and the like. *Ag*, he is so open handed where his family and friends are concerned that sometimes he will act like a spendthrift, splashing out on lavish celebrations and buying presents here, there and everywhere for all and sundry.

It is something of a mystery to me that he wants more than we already have though, for we are more than amply provided for; but when the itch for more is on him particularly strongly, it runs through our conversations like a seam in a gold mine, twisting and turning, sometimes fattening into a great lode of one grand scheme or other, sometimes petering out into a foolish dream, but always it is there and I have come to dread this itch of his because of the trouble he inevitably gets into because of it. Ragwasi has a lot of commercial acumen when it comes to the transport business, buying and selling hides or salt or anything to do with cattle, but it would only be fair to say that he has not yet mastered the intricacies of trading shares on the Johannesburg Stock Exchange fully. Recently, he has been going back and forward to Johannesburg more often, on the excuse that he must sell a diamond to improve his cash flow. This, I know for certain, is not the full truth because in fact, he has been fleeced every time he has dabbled because he cannot be brought to accept the wisdom that to make money one must buy a share when it is *low* and sell it when it is *high*.

'uPelly,' he says, frowning. 'What kind of a fool would buy a cheap and tawdry share when there are very fine and expensive ones for sale too?' Shortly afterwards, he comes back and says: 'I must sell these shares because they have lost their value and are no good anymore, uPelly. They are like an old and stringy cow. Only a fool would want them now.'

Ja, this is his logic.

Of all the multitude of his schemes for the getting of wealth, one particular idea has long lodged in Ragwasi's head. He believes that there are pots of gold buried here and there about the place just waiting to be dug up and carried to the bank and he cannot have enough of talk of buried treasure. In this belief, he is partially justified because our present wealth was acquired by stumbling on a river bed full of diamonds out in the Namib Desert, but despite this being a remarkable and unique and once in a lifetime thing, he cannot be brought to believe that our good fortune cannot be duplicated in some other place and at some other time. Indeed, with the benefit of all this thinking, he has come to the conclusion that those diamonds that we had found were somehow part of a long-forgotten royal hoard and that it is entirely possible – *probable* even – that one day, we will trip over another.

'All kings and queens who rule and who are vanquished leave valuable treasure behind them, hidden for the day when they will come back and need them again,' he says. 'I do not think that any king or queen would be any different or they would be thought to be very foolish and not worthy of being a king or a queen.'

We were sitting on my *stoep*, Ragwasi and I, back in the winter of 1899, smoking our cheroots and chugging surreptitiously at a bottle of Cape Smoke that our wives had forbidden us to have on account of our being drunk last night and falling over in the pumpkin patch, when he returned to the subject once more.

'Tell me uPelly, do you ever think of those fine but empty houses called Zimbabwe?'

'The ancient home of the Queen of Sheba,' I replied, proud to display my knowledge. There had been much discussion of the ruins of Great Zimbabwe recently in the newspapers. 'That is what Cecil Rhodes thinks, anyway.'

'And she was a rich and powerful queen with many cows and indeed elephants?'

'So it says in the Bible,' I agreed.

'And where is she now, uPelly?'

'Ah, she is only a legend now.'

'Correct: and her palace is in ruins and now belongs to uCecil Rhodoss,' replied Ragwasi, with satisfaction and a burp. 'And what does Rhodoss want more than anything in the world? That is right,' he said, answering his own question. 'Gold and diamonds. So he is looking for her hidden gold and diamonds. That is why he is rooting around in those rocks like a porcupine.'

'And why does he want more gold and diamonds, Ragwasi?' I asked. 'Don't you think that both you and he have enough already?'

He looked at me as though I was mad.

'Rhodoss will need gold and diamonds for the war that is coming with the Boers,' he said, plucking the bottle from my hands. There was a lot of war talk in the newspapers and everyone knew that a war between the British and the Boers would break out soon and though Rhodes was no longer calling the shots, for Ragwasi, Cecil Rhodes *was* the British government and he could not be dissuaded otherwise. 'War is *very* expensive, uPelly. You must have very many things if you are to go to war in this modern age, uPelly, and Rhodoss will need gold and diamonds to buy all these things. Do you not know this? Why else should we make this unpleasant and unwelcome journey to Johannesburg tomorrow?'

'Tomorrow?' I said, startled. 'I thought we were going next week.'

'Why should we wait until next week when we can get this unpleasant but necessary job done tomorrow?' he replied.

'Because you need to sell a diamond to improve your cash flow?'

'How can you say such a thing, uPelly,' he replied, taking a very long and very guilty slug from the bottle. 'Do we not have a very long shopping list of things to get for our wives so that we may be prepared for this war?'

In this I had to accept he was right. Preparing for when a war is coming is a difficult thing to do and it is much more difficult than just sitting on the stoep waiting for the stars to come out, which I like to do. Of course, it is always wise to lay in a few extra sacks of corn and coffee and sugar and to make sure that you are well supplied with Bovril and tins of things that your wife will miss if they are not available, but this shopping list included cases and cases of the things that my wife Tepo and Ragwasi's Chief Wife Boitumela wanted, which were mainly preserved foods, including Colman's Mustard, jam, camp coffee and a disgusting thing called Boiled Mutton which came all the way from New Zealand in a tin and should have been sent straight back. What was wrong with good Karoo lamb I could never work out, but our wives were going through a phase of preferring all things Imperial to anything African; it was not something I could fathom but we knew we would have to buy these things anyway if we did not want to have permanently ragged ears.

Actually, if I was to be in charge of preparing a country for war the first thing I would do is find out what were the favourite things of the wife of my enemy and then buy them all up from the store because when the wife of my enemy cannot get a Cadbury's chocolate bar or some Pear's soap, she will soon nag him into giving up all thought of a war. However, I was not in charge, so it still meant going to Johannesburg with a very long shopping list with lots of things on it but, I noticed, no Cape Smoke. That was easy to remedy though. We would buy a lot of tea in big sacks and conceal in them a lot of Cape Smoke in big bottles, just in case people came to their senses and did not have a war and Ragwasi could go off to root around in the ruins of Great Zimbabwe; but we also had to agree with the strict instructions of our wives to visit a chemist shop and buy a lot of bandages, antiseptic soap, a balm of comfrey and aloe vera, in case people did not come to their senses and started a war anyway.

What made all these preparations amidst uncertainty even more complicated was the letter I got in September of that year which came all the way from South America on a boat, then up from Cape Town on a train and then from Kimberley in the saddle bag of my son, Joseph, who I had sent to buy some ammunition and who Tepo had sent to buy some Cadbury's Chocolate. He rode up through the heat haze and red dust at a fair clip and I took pride that he was on the way to being a good horseman - if only he would let those stirrups down a little more and not pretend he was a jockey at the races.

Leaping out of the saddle with more bounce than I'd ever had, he presented the letter with a flourish.

'It is from Montevideo,' he said. 'Which is the capital of Argentina, the Land of Silver.'

'Montevideo is the capital city of Uruguay,' I said. Sometimes Joseph could be a little too big for his boots, having been to school and grown to think that he knew more than his old man. 'And it means *The Mountain That I Can See* in the Latin language. Now pass it to me.'

The envelope was a little yellowed but the paper was thick and of good quality and correctly addressed to me in a ball and chain handwriting that told me the person who had written it was educated and very possibly a woman. I felt it in my hands before opening it because I had come to believe that sometimes you can tell whether a letter contains good news or bad news just by feeling it. It is as though the thoughts that have gone into it have seeped out from the ink and got into the paper; I knew a chap who would never open a letter on the day he got it for fear that if it was bad news then it would be the end of him and he would therefore have one last day of peace before it came; he often would come and beg a bottle of Cape Smoke from me then – but I only ever gave him *mampoer*, which is a lot stronger and gives a thicker head and so when he woke up in the morning, the letter would be a relief for him however bad the news it contained. On that day, I should have followed his example and set the letter aside and helped myself to the mampoer; but I suppose it would have made no difference in the end. In fact, I did follow his advice in the matter of the mampoer, but only after I had opened the letter.

I opened it; it was from my sister, Hattie, and this was a real coincidence because Ragwasi and I had only been talking about her the other day in the context of my most recent visit to England. She lived in Bath, and as I had had a desire to see this city and to make her acquaintance anew, as I had not seen her since my exile to Africa, I had paid her an impromptu and unannounced surprise visit. Indeed, it was such an impromptu and unannounced surprise visit that she was not at home but instead had gone to help her husband build a railway in Argentina, he being an engineer by profession. No matter; I had read Miss Austen's *Pride and Prejudice* on the boat coming to England, having nothing better to do, and so occupied myself by looking about the town, which was impressive, but which I gather she thought was not. I think she must have been a very finickity sort of woman because it has some very fine old architecture from the time of the last George and before and is built out of Bath stone, which is dug out of the quarries at Coombe Down and is a wonderful warm honey colour, like the pelt of a lion, though not its dark mane. The terraces and crescents are also very fine and grand; the people who live in them have their reception rooms on the first floor which is very strange but I suppose they like the advantages of having a better view through being higher. To me though, after becoming used to the wide spaces of Africa, the place made me feel cramped up because there were so many tall, narrow buildings and hurrying people and I walked about with my shoulders hunched up as though squeezed like I did in Johannesburg. The air was thick too; I had forgotten that people burn coal to keep warm in England and this has a very different smell to it than a wood fire out in the open and gives off a dirty sort of smoke. Perhaps this is what Miss Austen really objected too. If so, I can see her point but she could really have made it with a lot fewer words in my opinion but then women do like to talk a lot more than men. I gather her other books have lots of words in them too.

Ragwasi did not think much of Miss Austen either after I had explained the main lines of the plot of that book *Pride and Prejudice*. He said there was not very much action, no elephants and how any rich chief like Lord uDarcy could hold his head up high after being cheeked by a slip of a girl like Missy Elizabeth was beyond him. He did, however, have a passing admiration for that Wickham chap who he said was a proper man and he would have liked to have seen how he would have fared with us at the Battle of Khambula. We are not very literate fellows, I will admit, but we do like a good story such as that one called *King Solomon's Mines*, which has a bit of a bearing on the adventure that I am about to relate to you when Ragwasi hands back that bottle.

So much for Miss Austen; Ragwasi was much more interested in the warm springs that fill the old Roman baths that are to be found next door to the Abbey and questioned me closely about when they were built and by whom. Necessarily, the details that I could provide were somewhat sketchy and it is to my shame that perhaps not all of them were accurate in their entirety and where the gaps in my knowledge were too great to be bridged by an admission of ignorance, I admit that I took a leaf out of Ragwasi's own book and made up what I did not know. He seemed pleased with my exposition though.

'It is a good thing to have a wash in warm water when it is cold, uPelly,' he said, putting his head back and blowing smoke at the clear stars of the night. 'Especially if you have many cattle to manage. But tell me more about these *amaRoma* who were such great warriors and builders.'

I told him what little I could remember from my history books of Julius Caesar and Julius Agricola and the Emperor Constantine, which was not very much, but again, he seemed pleased with the knowledge.

'And you say that these *amaRoma* disappeared into legend, leaving only ruins behind to mark the passing of their empire,' he said, and I caught that sideways ambivalent look he has when making a sly point.

'You think the British Empire will go the same way?' I asked. 'Surely not?'

'All good things come to an end,' he said, emitting a large fart of disapproval. 'This is the same for everything but tell me, uPelly, have you been digging in those ruins for gold? No? You have missed a big opportunity and it is not good to miss big opportunities where gold that has been left behind by emperors is concerned, uPelly. I am disappointed in you.'

Anyway, this is a digression but sometimes Ragwasi likes to go around the houses a bit and I think I have caught this habit of his, so you must just forgive me. Paths through the bush rarely run straight.

Hattie was my sister and her husband was a railway engineer in Argentina, which I think I have told you already, but if I haven't it does not really matter one way or the other. The only thing that made Ragwasi interested in her in the first place was the mention of *Argentina*

– the *Land of Silver* and I had some difficulty in explaining to him that this was not a literal description of the place and he only accepted my explanation when I asked him how on earth anyone could grow mealies on metal if the country of Argentina was made literally of silver. So back to the letter.

Dear Nicholas,

I hope this letter finds you well. I am well.

Whenever anyone starts a letter like this, it means trouble; it means that they have some bad news to tell you but do not really want to tell you.

I read on. It did not get better. The use of words and phrases like *uncharacteristic lapse* and *unfortunate misunderstanding* virtually guarantee that a letter does not just contain trouble, but that it contains a lot of it; and when you add in *let us not fly to judgement* and *inconsistencies in the case for the prosecution*, you just know that you have hit the bulls eye of trouble.

'Bring me the mampoer,' I said, pushing my hat back on my head and casting an imploring look at the sky.

'Will Mama allow it at this time, so early?' said Joseph.

'Mama does not need to know,' I replied. 'About either the mampoer or the letter, for the time being.'

'What is the matter, Papa?'

'It seems that I have a very stupid boy for a nephew,' I said. 'Now bring the mampoer, for all heaven's sake.'

The letter was from my sister, Hattie, and in a very long, roundabout way which needed re-reading several times and then reading again, this time between the lines, told me that her eldest son had somehow *got steamed up* and *gone off the rails* (she used a lot of railway terms) in the matter of a packet of diamonds that did not belong *entirely* to him but which had been found in his possession – or rather in the possession of a certain woman who was not *entirely* a Countess ('There uPelly! I told you! Is not a Countess like a queen who has lost her throne and must hide diamonds for when she returns?') - in a hotel room that the police had raided, *probably* by mistake, but which had been registered in his name; again this was *obviously* an oversight on the part of the hotel management. Not being *entirely* confident in being able to *be afforded the opportunity to clear his name* under the judicial arrangements then existing in the Republic of Uruguay which *did not approach the standards of our own Dear Empire*, the boy had shown the Peelers a clean pair of heels and jumped ship for South Africa, where he was now holed up under a name which was not *entirely* the name he had been christened with. Rather than Edgar Smithfield, he was now signing his communications as Stamford John Holtzhausen.

And could I help find him?

Now, the Cape Colony is roughly one thousand miles wide and four hundred miles deep; add to that the Orange Free State, which has a dimension of roughly three hundred by one hundred and fifty miles; the Transvaal, whose dimensions are roughly four hundred and fifty miles by four hundred; the Bechuanaland Protectorate (where we live) which is about five hundred miles by four hundred and fifty; and then…well, I shall not bother you with the vast emptiness of German South West Africa or Matabeleland or Rhodesia or Basutoland or Swaziland or any of the other thousand places where a man with a false name who did not want to be caught could be looked for without being found; and of course, this needle would have to be sought in a haystack thrown into turmoil by the great threshing machine of an approaching war.

The answer to the question of whether I could help find him was, of course, *yes*. Given that the circumstances that had brought me to Africa were not so different, how could I refuse? This was family and my stupidity as a boy had cost my family dearly. It was the least that I could do to make restitution.

First of all, though, we had to go to Johannesburg and so, on a peaceful morning during that August of 1899, we put on our thick woollens and tied blankets across our shoulders against the cold wind and set out with the wagon for the big city to sell a diamond so that Ragwasi could rescue his investment plans by throwing good money after bad and then buy all the things that Boitumela and Tepo had told us to buy, plus the things that we had added to that list on our own account (Cape Smoke and cheroots).

*

One of the reasons why Ragwasi was convinced that he would one day find a pile of buried treasure was down to the mining discoveries that had been made in South Africa during the last thirty years. First, in 1873, there had been the discovery of diamonds at Kimberley and then in 1886, gold had been found on the Witwatersrand. That such wealth could come out of a hole in the ground twice in his lifetime was proof incontrovertible to him that he too would make a second lucky strike.

Mind you, back then, at the time, we did not think that the discovery of diamonds at Kimberley was such a boon. Back then, we had been firm in our belief that the diamond mines at Kimberley were responsible for all the ills of South Africa because the desire for wealth had drawn too many ruffians and freebooters to Africa; and because the mine owners had paid the African labourers in guns and they had gone home as warriors eager to fight; and because rivalry for work had led to a worsening of the racial feeling between black and white; and because the desire to control the diamond wealth had led to war and strife between Boer, Bantu and Briton. We Tswana had lost a great deal of our land to the Boers because of this war and strife and so when gold was found on the Witwatersrand in 1886, just after the end of the war between the Boers and the Tswana, we were not pleased. The last thing we wanted was another Kimberley but that is just exactly what we got.

From a few hopeful prospectors panning for nuggets on a dribble of a river, a brand new town called Johannesburg had shot up from the middle of the veldt to become the wealthiest city in Africa almost overnight and the same old troubles reared their ugly heads once more. The first thing that happened when news got out about the gold was that a great rush of people from all over Africa and Australia and Europe and America, and just about everywhere you could think of, descended on the Witwatersrand like a plague of locusts. It was far worse than Kimberley because when Kimberley was discovered there were no railways to make the journey up from the Cape easy, but now anyone could land in Table Bay and be up in Kimberley within two days and Johannesburg by the end of the week. Of course, the first man there was Cecil Rhodes which could only mean trouble and the second man there was Paul Kruger, which guaranteed it. African men started to work for money to buy guns once more; racial feeling got worse; the Boers hated the influx of the English and other foreigners – *Uitlanders,* they called them – and hated the black people even more and then Cecil Rhodes decided to try and grab the mines for himself at gunpoint by sending in a column of freebooters and ruffians led by his crony Starr Jameson. The whole thing was botched, the freebooters rounded up and arrested, and he would have been a better man than he was if Kruger came to hate the British any less. He started using the money he raised from the gold mines to buy guns from Germany, which just made matters a whole lot worse, because although the British government in London distrusted Cecil Rhodes, they distrusted the Germans even more and because Kruger had looked to the Germans, the government in London decided it was time for Kruger to go and for the Boers to be taught their place properly. Everybody knew war was coming from that moment on. It was history repeating itself before our eyes; to the Sodom of Kimberley was added the Gomorrah of Johannesburg. Diamonds and gold; they caused more trouble in South Africa than ever they were worth.

At the beginning, Ragwasi and I had decided to make a pact to stay away from Johannesburg because we had been hypocrites in the matter of Kimberley; we had despised the devil of the place and all its works but we had made good business supplying meat and salt to it and we thought that God and the ancestors might forgive us once for our hypocrisy, but not twice, so we stayed away from Johannesburg for this reason. This was not such a big sacrifice because, as I have already told you, we had ample money and it is easy not to be a hypocrite if you have money; I know that in the bible it says that it is almost impossible for a rich man to get into heaven but I have become convinced that the Eye of the Needle is easy to pass through if you can grease it by giving money to Reverend Mackenzie for the building of a church in Kuruman.

Over the years though, we began to break our pact more and more, by mutual consent, of course, because it was hard to ignore a new place which promised all sorts of new things for Boitumela and Tepo to buy, but mainly because Ragwasi's desire to make money overcame his reservations. He grew more convinced than ever that there was a second pot of gold waiting for him out there, buried in the workings of the Johannesburg Stock Exchange.

'One day, I will find it,' he would insist, wagging his finger and tugging at the bottle. 'And then you will see.'

Of course the other thing we had to consider as we rolled across the veldt during those bright days of skies far, high and wide, was whether we would have to play some part in this approaching war. Neither Ragwasi nor I were spring chickens. I was approaching my forty-fifth year and although I was not a broken down old crock ready for the knackers yard yet, still I was beginning not to feel that I was thirty-five anymore. I did not seem to be losing the little spare ring of padding that grew around my tummy so easily whenever I was back from a hunting trip and feasting on Tepo's mealies which she sweetened with sugar. In fact, I had noticed that it was not disappearing at all but for some reason gradually increasing. Worse was the fact that if I took a trifling injury of some sort, it seemed to take longer and longer to heal; I shall say nothing about the little bit of grey at my temples. Tepo says I look distinguished, so I am happy with this; and my eldest boy, Joseph is almost taller than me – *almost*.

As for Ragwasi, well, he is some years older than me anyway and it would not be too much to say that he had grown rather corpulent and could do to lose a few pounds. That day, the horses thought so too and when he mounted up, the saddle creaked like a wheezy old man. He also had snow on the roof; Boitumela once said he should make a headring and wear it to cover it up; he got a little bit angry at this and spent the next week in his newest wife's hut. It was clear though that we both should be prepared to go to war because we knew from experience that whenever the British Army goes to war in South Africa they come looking for riders who know the country to act as guides and as extra cavalry which they call 'Light Horse' or 'Rangers' or some such thing; in fact they were just like the Boer Kommandos and advancing age was no disqualification for being pressed into service.

'It is the pitilessness of war that I am afraid of, Ragwasi,' I said, the first night that we camped on our way to Johannesburg. We had not spoken much during the day for when war is approaching, a man's head is filled with many thoughts and he needs a lot of time to get them in order, sort through them and then think hard on them. 'I have shot men down in battle, as well you know, but when I have thought about the men that I have killed, I don't regret my actions in killing them at the time, but I do regret killing them. And over the years these regrets have piled up and piled up like storm clouds in October until now I do not know if I can raise up my pitilessness again to shoot down more men. Does this make sense to you?'

Ragwasi did not answer straight away and I was afraid that he might not have heard me, or that the things that I had said were still in my head and I had yet to say them, for this is another thing about travelling in silence when a war is about to begin; sometimes the conversations in your head sound as loud as a shout in a canyon. So I took in the scent of the grass and heard the crunch of the grazing mules and looked up at the stars, which were bright and clear and cold, and waited. From the corner of my eye, I watched him as he chewed on a bit of biltong and looked anxious and it came to me then that in the past few days and weeks he had not really been himself at all in anything. He seemed changed, uncertain, not exactly unbalanced but some days his mood was not as predictable as it mostly was; some days he seemed to drink his mampoer reluctantly, half-heartedly, as though the joy had gone out of it. Of course, we were all worried about the war and it is also true that Ragwasi had managed to acquire as contrary a collection of wives as it seemed possible to get and that they gave him grief in greater or lesser measure all the time, but there was something else, something deeper, something that made him sit at the top of the hill in the early mornings and in the evening and look eastwards back towards the mountains of the Drakensberg. He could be snappish too and oft times, he would be jovial one minute and sharp the next. Tepo had remarked that his children seemed to be getting a few more slaps more often than they deserved, even though most of the time they *did* deserve them, little hellhounds that they were, and that some of his wives were grumbling, especially the most recent one who did not have a baby yet. Presently though, throwing a handful of sticks on the fire, he sat back against the wheel of the wagon and let out a long sigh.

'It is always the start of the war when an old man's troubles are worse,' he said, his voice no more than a mumble. 'The young men will not be restrained and will run off and get themselves killed to show how brave they are. The inexperienced try to fight only half-heartedly, as if war can be won with a slap rather than the stab that is needed and so the heavy, crushing blows that might end a war quickly are not given and the war drags on and on to everyone's loss. And us old men must sit and watch it all happen and can do nothing about it. You fear you cannot leave your pity behind in your house this time, uPelly. I fear this too, for I am as old, if not even a little bit older - but not much - than you. My fear, uPelly is a long war when every meanness can flourish, when every messenger that approaches a quiet lolwapa is longed for and dreaded in equal measure and at the end of it, no deal or treaty that an honest man can agree to, and so guarantee that it will be necessary to do it all over again. And the young men who survive become the old men like us, who fear and can do nothing, and no hillside is left without a grave.'

'We should have more sense, Ragwasi,' I replied. 'We should become politicians and see if we can do better.'

'Pah!' he spat. 'Do you think the great control the things that are done by them?' He took another log and tossed it onto the orange fire and gazed into it for a long moment. He was looking tired, more tired than even the hard work of a long day with a difficult mule in a frayed harness could make him. Ragwasi did not like mules at the best of times but even though they were standing asleep under the shelter rigged to the side of the wagon against the frost that would come down tonight, it was not this that was troubling him. 'They do not, uPelly. They are at the mercy of the world as we are. Do you think Kruger or Rhodoss can make up his mind as he wishes? He cannot; for he must do what his people want him to do or he will be removed and put into a comfortable lolwapa and told to eat biltong quietly and someone else will do the things that will be done. Do you remember the Zulu Chief, Cetshwayo, who we fought against? Were his warriors not eager for war with the British? Do you think they would have slept quietly if Cetshwayo had not allowed them to wash their spears? Do you think the Boers will go quietly back to their farms if Kruger allows the *uitlanders* in Johannesburg to move into his council and tell him what he should do?'

'I do not want a war, Ragwasi,' I said.

'But you do want the peace and plenty that can only be had when the disputes of men are settled,' he replied, irritably. 'And sometimes these disputes can only be settled by war whether this is a foolish way to settle disputes or not. A chief and his people are connected, uPelly, and they must do each other's bidding. There will be war uPelly, and our sons will be in it and become old men.'

11

This was not a comforting thought and it was made less comfortable by being on my mind all the way from Kuruman and nagging like a toothache but in my stomach, if you understand. My eldest, Joseph, was perhaps a little young to go to war but he was growing adamant that he would join up in some capacity and would not be persuaded otherwise. In truth, I did not try very hard to dissuade him because it is a man's duty to fight for his country when he is called; it is the basis of any tribe; if you will not fight for the tribe when the Elders decide in their wisdom that it is time to fight, why should the tribe fight for you when you decide in your own wisdom that you want the tribe to fight for *you*? I have read in the newspapers about people who do not believe this but I give them no time; they are stupid people who think that the world is full of reasonable people who just want to sit down and eat beef and do not want war. They should have seen what happened to the Herero people when they went to be reasonable with the Kaiser of Germany; or us Tswana, for that matter, when the Boers came. So I decided I would allow my son to enlist in whatever unit he thought suitable on the one condition that it was not the same one that I might join. I know that some men prefer to have their sons ride with them so that they could keep an eye on them, but I did not want the possibility to arise that I would see him shot or injured, or him me; also, sometimes men can be frightened into cowardice during a battle and though very often they regain their manhood soon after, I did not want my son to see me taking to my heels, as I have done on occasion.

Some of Ragwasi's sons were much older than Joseph and had ridden with us to battle before; indeed Seretse had ridden with us against cattle rustlers when he was perhaps younger even than Joseph and he now had his own sons in his own lolwapa, but there were others who were now of an age to fight who were also clamouring to go to war and Ragwasi had the devil of a time calming them down. In the end, he ruled that some must form part of a sort of Town Guard, others would be permitted to join a unit but only of Ragwasi's choosing and others must stay at home until they were taller than a mark that he made in a tree. There was a lot of dispute about this and it was not aided by some of his wives who did not respect custom and practice in this regard by allowing Ragwasi's judgement to go unchallenged. One of them took a panga and cut a mark in a yellowwood tree that was clear seven feet from the ground; perhaps she was one of these National Peace Council people from the newspapers; mind you, Boitumela put her straight. She too had seen what the Boers had done to the Tswana. *Eesh!* I heard her shouting from the far side of a bottle of mampoer. It sounded like a steam whistle in a train smash and went on for a very long time.

*

To all these considerations was now added that of my nephew, Edgar Smithfield – or Stamford John Holtzhausen as I must now learn to call him - who I was expected to help find even though he might be anywhere on the continent. As we rode on the wagon on the last leg into Johannesburg, I put my mind to thinking about this task as a way to keep my thoughts away from my sons and the coming war and as the wagon squeaked and creaked and rattled away with the mules complaining at every turn and Ragwasi huffing and puffing alongside them, the main thought that came to me was that it was an impossible task for me to complete. How could I find someone who I did not know at all? I had not seen my sister in twenty five years, had never met her husband and had never set so much as a single flicker of

12

an eyelid on the boy. There was no photograph or sketch to tell me what he must look like and the only clue as to his description was that *he is a good boy who takes after his mother in all the important things* which is exactly what every single mother in the world says about her blue-eyed boy, even if he does not have blue eyes and is instead a black sheep; *especially* if he is a black sheep.

'Of course, you will recognise him as soon as you see him,' said Ragwasi. 'Does not a cow know her own calf?'

'I hardly think that is a very helpful piece of advice,' I replied, as we approached the suburbs. 'If a cow has never seen his calf, how can he know it?'

'A cow is a *she*, uPelly,' replied Ragwasi. 'Is that him?'

Ragwasi pointed to a young hayseed, barefoot, wearing dungarees and a wide brimmed hat, leaning against a fence. 'Why don't you ask him? You are a very lucky man, uPelly, and this might be a lucky day for you.'

I gave a sigh and decided to indulge him.

'Hey *laaite*,' I called. 'Is your name Stamford John Holzhausen, by any chance?'

The boy stared back but did not answer. We rode on. I decided that I would stick to my plan of posting letters to my agent in Cape Town, old Mijnheer Cronjie, and to the bank manager and solicitor in Kimberley to look out for my nephew, if by any chance they came across him, which was not very likely admittedly, but what else could I do apart from asking everyone in Johannesburg their name and hoping for the best? Ragwasi, however, thought differently and called out every now and then to one stranger or another as we went further into the city, asking if they were Stamford John Holzhausen, and if not, did they know of him? He did it just to vex me, I am sure, and he succeeded because before long, I was looking into faces and imagining I could see my sister's features in them, which was doubly foolish because I had not seen those features since they belonged to nothing but a slip of a girl.

As we entered the city proper, that old uncomfortable feeling came upon me just as it does when I am in any town. I cannot help but think of ant colonies when I see any big town, but even so, Johannesburg, it has to be admitted, was a very impressive place. Around the market place the only indication that this had once just been a scrappy mining camp full of tents and corrugated iron sheds was a sole malingering ruffian leaning on a pick and smoking a pipe through a fat moustache, who eyed us with suspicion. Now it was all strict order (there were two jails), sanitary arrangements, government offices and a gas works; there were parks, open spaces and a football ground; a railway and a reservoir; a fine market square where the ox wagons brought in bales of wool piled six feet high and the quality trotted about in mule carts or arrived hot foot and dusty off the stagecoach checking their pocket watches against the clock towers; ornamental cast iron balustrades above fine arcades allowed loungers and loafers to smoke cheroots and look down on us *hoi polloi* from the balconies; many buildings had Doric columns and quoins that would have been at home in Newmarket or Colchester; there was plenty of good brick gothic too, all laid out in a grid system that completely confused us, being used to either the open veldt or the winding streets of an English town. Actually, at night it was *not* all order but rather a very big lot of *disorder* because there were a lot of bawdy houses doing better than all the boozers, barbers, tailors, flower sellers, pedlars and what not at taking money off the miners; boy! It could be wild! What would you expect when four fifths of the population was made up of young men? Anyway, I shall spare your blushes as you are probably a very respectable person who does not want to know about this sort of behaviour and so the less said about it the better. It does no-one any credit, I can tell you, and cannot be dwelt upon with honest profit; you can read all about it in the newspapers. Anyway, Joburg was a very wealthy town with a lot of good business too; Oliver & Co had a drapery sale on, Markhams windows were full of the latest fashions, while the pins, French chalk and tape measures of Rosenbaum ('Fit and Style Guaranteed'), Lawrence (High Class) and Rosenthal's (Gentleman's Hosier, Livery and Breeches Maker) were all flying like there was no tomorrow. Amms New Grocery and Hardware store down by the library was stuffed to the gunnels, Campbell's had a *Grand Display of Season's Novelties*, and I bought a copy of *Johannesburg Faces and Places* magazine to scan the adverts while Ragwasi queued up outside Hart's Rand Tobacconists. As for language, it was a real Babel; the streets buzzed with excited talk about progress and development and the possibility of war, which was a strange mixture I can tell you, and there were people of every nationality, every colour; Indian, Natal, Mozambique, Tswana, Zulu, Xhosa, American, Dutch, German, French, Chinese, Italian; but strangely enough, to my eyes the people looked to be mainly English, or certainly more English than anything Africa had seen before because their fashions were English; straw boaters, tweed waistcoats, impressive moustaches and plus-fours - of course, many of them were newly arrived from England; the Boers were mainly farmers and did not really take to the city and the black people were often absent because they were mainly working down the mines. There were even quite a few ladies in big hats and gauzy dresses who interested Ragwasi very much; so much so that he collided with a cheeky boy on a bicycle who cursed him for a country bumpkin and then made off before he could be served out with the cuff he so richly deserved. Out towards the west of the town lay the Native and Coolie Locations, which were not uncomfortable places to live in themselves, but made me very uncomfortable to see because I did not like this racial segregation; my children are half white and half black (actually one of them has a distinct yellowish tinge – I wonder if he's mine at all) and I was not sure what that would mean for them in the future. Everywhere we looked though, we could see and hear the reason for the prosperity of this great new city; piles of yellow spoil from the gold mines towered up over the south of the city while the deep *boom* of dynamite breaking up the rocks in the shafts came up from below, and in that sound I sensed a glimmer of hope.

Many traders and merchants shared my opinion that as war was bad for business and that the Stock Exchange would crash, cooler heads would prevail and a deal would be done to keep the gold coming out of the mines and into the pockets of the Rand Lords, the miners and the Transvaal treasury. Others held that as the Boers were only a very few in comparison to the full might of the British Empire, the hotheads among them would listen to reason, calm down and be bought off with a bigger share of the riches. There were others still who said that if the Boers did go to war then they would be writing their own death warrant because all the black people of Africa who they had mistreated and dispossessed would rise up as one and clear them off. Even though the trickle of English people leaving Johannesburg had turned into a flood during September, there were still those who thought something might turn up.

'Ragwasi, do you not think that a war would be so expensive that it would ruin everyone?' I said, nodding at a heavily laden wagon trundling past. 'Does not your business sense tell you that all profit will be swallowed up, commerce halted and industry ruined if war does come? Isn't it good business sense *not* to fight? Wouldn't it be better to do a deal – a *business* deal – like Rhodes used to do all the time?'

'We are past the time of business sense,' said Ragwasi, watching the wagon and then shifting his attention to a pedlar carrying all his wares in a big pack on his shoulders walking in the opposite direction. 'And when the *smousers* are leaving for the countryside in search of better business than can be had in the city, then war is definitely coming.'

'Why so?' I asked, watching the man, a Jewish man I thought, as so many of the smousers are.

'Because they meet people and know people from all aspects of business,' replied Ragwasi, clicking up the reins. 'And when business dries up in one place, they follow the scent of it to another, just like an elephant will move from water hole to water hole. So if the smousers are going, the business is going and the only thing that will drive out business is a war.'

I watched the smouser and thought on this. Many of the ones I had dealt with were Russian Jews who had been driven from their homes because of their religion and whenever I saw them I was minded to think of the legend of the wandering Jew who had insulted Jesus and been forced to wander about forever as a punishment. This always brought me to thinking of myself, who had been forced to wander as punishment for my own sins, and I now thought of my nephew Stamford, wandering somewhere for his own sins. I hoped that he would be forgiven them and that he would come into his own, as I had done. And then I hoped that the smouser would be just like the elephants that find their way across great distances of desert in their search for water, and find some good business somewhere which would give him enough profit to pay for a place where he could settle and not have to wander so much, for really business is the lifeblood of all people and no-one can live long without it.

'Here is the first of the shops we must go into and buy things from,' said Ragwasi, distracting me from these sombre thoughts. 'Where is the list?'

'But I thought you had it….'

*

Apart from all the long list of things we had to remember not to forget – a very long list, often revised and added to frequently, and only finally found at the bottom of the scoff box where Ragwasi had put it to save it from being eaten by mice or rats and then put the box underneath everything else - also, we needed to buy guns and if you wanted to buy guns, well, Johannesburg was the place to go. Even though in this war I hoped to keep the whole of the British Army between me and the Boers, I knew to my cost that war opens up all sorts of opportunities for scoundrels, freebooters and the unscrupulous. Robbers are just the least of it, believe you me, and the best way to keep them off your property and away from your family is by having lots of guns. Of course, being hunters and traders we already had many guns but there had been a lot of technical developments in military rifles since I had bought my first Martini-Henry back before the Zulu War and both Ragwasi and I agreed that we should buy the best and most modern rifles that we could for when the war came. They had changed from being single shot rifles that gave off a big plume of white smoke when you fired to bolt action, magazines rifles which used smokeless powder. This meant that a man could fire much faster than before and, because there was no smoke to give away your position, remain hidden for longer; this was important because to win, half the battle lies in concealing yourself from an enemy. Ragwasi favoured the German Mauser because he had heard that it was more accurate but I favoured the British Lee-Enfield because I thought that although the Mauser was more accurate at a long range, it would be no good if all we could get were British bullets. In the end, the argument was settled for us by Gert Van Schalk, a Johannesburg gunsmith who we respected as a man who knew all that anyone needed to know about rifles.

'This Mauser is a very fine hunting rifle,' he said, showing us how good the sights were. 'And if you want a rifle for target practice, then I would recommend the American Springfield, although it is a rather delicate piece. For war though, I would recommend the Lee-Enfield. It seems to me to be more solidly made and will probably be able to stand being knocked around more than either of the other two weapons.'

'You are *certain* there will be a war?' I asked.

'Do you know what the Boers say about the British Empire?' replied Van Schalk. 'They say that the sun never sets on this Empire because God would never trust an Englishman in the dark. The Boers will fight. Count on it.'

That settled it for us; we bought Lee-Enfields, for in a war it is always better to have something reliable and rugged than something more finely made in case a horse stands on it or some such thing. Actually, at the time, Van Schalk should not have sold any guns at all to Ragwasi because in theory for the past ten years black men had been forbidden to own guns by law, but this was a restriction that was easy to get round. We just ignored it along with all sorts of other things like Native Passes that were supposed to be strictly enforced and were not, and no-one with any sense in the Bechuanaland Protectorate ever bothered Ragwasi over his gun or his lack of a Pass. We took our new rifles, bought a box containing one thousand cartridges – because we did not know how long a war would last and experience had taught us that you can never have enough bullets in a war.

When all our other errands had been run, Ragwasi sold his diamond (and instantly traded the proceeds for a lot of paper shares, as far as I could see) and we decided that we would set out for Kuruman straight away. I did not like the city, to be honest; however new and neat the buildings, and some were as high as five or six storeys, they made me feel hemmed in and hunched, as though I was riding down a canyon, and the constant clatter of tongues wagging and wheels rattling irritated my brain so I could hardly hear myself think. As we left though, heading out by the wheels and cables of the mine workings, I could see Ragwasi thinking and calculating, his eyes flicking about him, taking everything in and rolling what he saw around inside his mind.

'How much gold is there in Johannesburg?' he asked, finally.

'Half of all the gold in the world comes from here,' I replied. 'Probably a million pounds Sterling comes out of these mines every year.'

Ragwasi said nothing. This was remarkable for he would usually make some exclamation when such large sums of money were mentioned. It appeared that I had stunned him into silence and it was only much later, when we had camped well clear of the Witwatersrand and I was wrapping myself up in a thick blanket against a bitter wind that cut like a knife that he said anything else.

'When this war comes uPelly, and the British drive Kruger off his lands,' he said, giving me his characteristic upside down grin. 'Where will Kruger bury his gold?'

Chapter 2

Magersfontein

Right up until the last minute, there were lots of people who thought there would not be a war. For myself, I knew that war was certain when, sitting back on my own stoep a few weeks after our return from Johannesburg, I saw the familiar smudge of dust rising off the red earth that a small troop of horsemen make and made out among them the glint of polished silver on khaki tunics and pith helmets. They came on at a clip that was purposeful rather than urgent and I saw also that they rode high in the saddle, shoulders back, reins held in the left hand, their right hands free to draw swords or pistols. On their saddles and slung about their persons were canteens, blankets, chop bags, saddlebags, bandoliers of ammunition and over their shoulders, Lee Enfields the colour of polished chestnut to match the black fringed bays on which they rode. It was only a minute or two more before I recognised their leader; and I knew what he wanted before he asked.

In those last few minutes of peace, I looked around at our lolwapa and for the first time in my life I understood what real happiness was. Ragwasi and I had built our homestead at the foot of a semi-circle of low olive green koppies which had enough brush, camel thorn and blond grass to support the goats we grazed there and still allow a share for the springbok, zebra, elephant, rhino and giraffes that came through and in which we delighted. He had built his hut and the separate huts that each of his wives demanded in the traditional shape of the horned buffalo, with his main house in the centre, Boitumela's in the place of honour due to a first wife on the right, with those of her relatives following on; on the left were the huts of his Left-hand wives, each in due precedence, while behind the centre were cooking and storage huts and huts for children. They were good huts, yellow ochre, gold and sienna sat under their silver thatch, each door a nose and each window an eye, like the face of some ancient, quiet person long gone. Our families would gather in the cleared area in front of Ragwasi's hut to gossip, put bright beads of turquoise and red and white in the braids of the women's hair, show off new dresses and hats, scold children and prepare mealies, while those whose job it was to look after the pumpkins and gem squash that day would be seen raking and hoeing in the gardens beyond the scrub thicket fence. The sound of squealing children playing chase, catch-me and tig fitted perfectly with the chitter and chatter of the bright weaver birds and iridescent, long beaked bee-eaters, while above the Ha-di-das cackled raucously at the crows.

My own house was more of a four square construction with walls and roof of green painted corrugated iron, surrounded by a wide veranda for summer and hosting a large sandstone chimney breast for when the winter nights demanded a roaring fire; the stoep was my favourite place and I had bought two strong wicker chairs and a table for the purpose of sitting and talking with Ragwasi while the moon rose and the million stars of the clear Karoo sky glittered out of the luminous sky. Down before us was a good river of sweet water that ran all year and which we had dammed into a small lake around which gathered willow, fir, bluegum and date palms like village elders come to discuss a weighty problem, while up above the cotton wool clouds in the azure blue of the sky proceeded one after the other like great flat bottomed barges under sail on the open sea. The dam I had stocked with trout and I had taught all the children of this desert both to fish in it and swim as each came to the age suitable to the learning. In the high summer of the Karoo when the heat hummed and whirred that water was a blessing I can tell you. We had even sunk a well and put a wind pump over it; Tepo was there now, supervising Joseph as he drew up water for cooking. I wondered when I would be free to enjoy it once more and savoured those last moments all the more. As soon as she saw the dust too, Tepo's eyes came up to meet mine and even at that distance I could see the frown; she was no stranger to war and she knew what the sound of drumming hooves meant.

Such excitement as flying horsemen is not a secret that can be kept from a small Kuruman lolwapa and before the men had crossed the final mile, already the whole population had turned out to see the spectacle, even though many of those gathering wore the frowns that gather on women's faces when war comes. The horsemen, a knot of four, came into the lolwapa scattering a troop of purple guinea fowl under their hooves, and drew up before my stoep.

'You are welcome, Tom Cole,' I said. 'Or *Colonel* Cole, as I see you have become.'

Tom G. Cole, the man who had rescued me from drowning off the Gambia River back in 1873 and who I had ridden and fought with on several occasions since, was as hale and hearty as a soldier's life could make him. He was a strong, broad-backed man with no hint of the boy left in him; he was completely bald now, but compensated with a large and full moustache that emphasised a bearing that had nothing but military in it; whipcord, leather, lyddite and ramrod; startling eyes of piercing blue; crows' feet, yes, but no sign of the decrepitude that I could feel creeping up on me.

'Cole uLootant! *War eng*?' cried Ragwasi, smiling. 'What is happening with the war? Will you drink beer with us?'

Calling Colonel Cole *uLootant* – Lieutenant – was one of Ragwasi's affectations; he knew full well what the difference between a Colonel and a Lieutenant was, just as he knew the difference between a Sergeant and a Private, but he chose to pretend that he did not simply to cover up the irksome facts that Tom Cole was younger than him and that he himself had never carried a rank higher than Trooper.

'Don't mind if I do,' said Cole, dismounting with a grin and handing his reins to one of the troopers. 'If you don't mind, I've a mind to billet down here for the night. Then we can discuss the proposition I have brought for you at our leisure.'

'And don't I just know what that will be?' I said, shaking his hand. 'We've been expecting you. You need scouts, I take it?'

He removed his pith helmet and brushed some of the dust from his tunic.

'That's about the size of it,' he said, tightly. 'And extra hands for Kimberley until the army gets here in strength – which won't be long, by all accounts.'

The sun had been sinking while Cole had approached and now there was a blue tinge on the eastern horizon and a silver one to the west. The wind was warm and flowers were beginning to carpet the red desert earth. Spring was coming.

'Very well, Tom,' I said. 'Get your horses watered, the men can put up in the barn yonder and we'll see what few bits of scraps, old bones and stale bread we can rustle up for you.'

*

Spring came with September and with October came the war. As British troops began to arrive at the Cape and in Natal in ever greater numbers, Kruger jumped the gun and invaded in the hope that some humiliating defeats could be inflicted on the British Army to make the government in London think again and withdraw. This tactic had worked back in 1881 when the Boers had risen up against British rule, defeated the army at Majuba Hill and persuaded that scoundrel of a Prime Minister Gladstone to go back on all the promises that he had already broken once, twice or a hundred times already; but things had changed now. The Prime Minister in London was Lord Salisbury who was a downy old bird and not one to be frightened by harum-scarum alarums into headlong flight from honour and abandoning the black man to his fate. He was more like Lord Hartington, who had stood by government promises to the Tswana back then and had sent soldiers to tell Kruger where to get off and allowed we Tswana to save at least some of what was left to us. So when Kruger sent his forces into Natal in 1899, he was met at Elandslaagte railway station and at Talana Hill and given a severe licking and sent back up the escarpment to await the inevitable counter-attack. The government in London roared and all Kruger could think to do in reply was besiege Ladysmith, Kimberley and Mafeking which was like trying to prevent your house being burned down in a bush fire by going indoors, locking the windows and hoping the flames will blow themselves out. To be honest, we were quite puzzled by these developments but also quite happy, because this was not the normal way that the Boers usually fought and if they had forgotten the secrets of their own success, this could only be good for us.

As he knew all along that we would, we had agreed to join Colonel Cole as Scouts but when the question of Kimberley came up, we absolutely refused to lend any help to that running sore of a place whatsoever.

'We know that Kimberley belongs to Rhodoss,' declared Ragwasi. 'And he has taken enough from the Tswana already. My sons will not go to Kimberley. I have spoken.'

'And I second him,' I said. 'We will fight the Boers but we will not die for Cecil Rhodes' pocket book.'

Cole had tried to persuade us that we couldn't really pick and choose what we would and would not do in a war but in this we were adamant. In the end he relented, and we sent our sons under Seretse's leadership to watch the border with the Germans in the Namib, who we did not trust not to join the Boers or grab some of our Tswana land on their own account while we were busy about the Boers. We ourselves rode a little way down towards the Cape with Tom Cole to meet up with the Highland Brigade in order to act as scouts for them on their march from De Aar towards Kimberley. It was November and already the heat in the Karoo was building.

Now you will say that scouts are not needed when the army only had to follow the railway line to march all the way up to Kimberley but that is not what scouts are really for in these days of maps and telegraphs and heliographs and Observation Balloons. Their job is really to look out for where the enemy has been by following their spoor and also to use their local knowledge to point out where the good water is and where grazing can be found and all the little bits and bats of things that you only learn when you have been in the country a while. In this part of the Karoo, the land is quite flat for long distances but then there are ranges of flat topped hills with concave slopes which are like the famous Table Mountain but usually smaller and at the bottom of them the thorn trees grow quite thickly on the sandy shillet ground. In front of them, there is usually a sort of fold of other, lower hills which look a lot smaller than they are really. As well as these hills there are others where the table top looks like it has pushed out of the top of the hill like the top of a bottle when the contents inside have gone off. These are usually impossible to climb but they provide a lot of good cover among the rocky krantzes and out crops that reach out along their sides and shoulders. The colours of the landscape here can be quite dull, often just a sort of olive green or myrtle above tawny grass which means that any glint off a silver buckle will be seen from a long distance, as will any bright flash of scarlet or white. The sky is really the only strong colour in this landscape and it is a big sky of a marvellous azure blue which is so strong and clear that even when it casts down shadows on the sides of the mountains, those shadows are tinted a soft blue. There is hardly any haze on a still day and when the wind drops the only thing that will raise a cloud is the movement of horses or men or wagons and then the dust comes up and hangs in the air for a long time. For the hunter this is a very good thing because he can see a long way in the crystal clear air and the flight of his bullet will go undisturbed for eight hundred yards or more. For the British Army this was important because a Boer soldier could lay concealed very well, would mark the dust cloud of an advancing force and when presented with a big target like an army, could start to shoot from a long way away indeed; and as everyone knows, the Boers are brought up to be marksmen from the moment they leave their mother's teat. It was this sort of thing that Tom Cole wanted us to talk to the officers of the Highland Brigade about, in order that they might pay attention and learn from our experience.

So we road into the camp before Magersfontein at the beginning of December to find an army that looked like it had shaken itself out of parade ground stiffness and knew what its real business was about. The tents were laid out in strict lines as far as the eye could see, the horse lines were well organised and abuzz with soldiers bringing up water and fodder and taking away the dung to appointed heaps while the field kitchens were wreathed in steam and giving off a homely smell of boiled beef and potatoes. Tarpaulins had been pitched over boxes of stores and ammunition, the farriers were busy beating out a tattoo on their anvils and purposeful NCOs were directing men in shirtsleeves about the thousand and one everyday tasks that an efficient army that intended to stay efficient needed to complete each day. I paused to take in a deep breath and allow my instincts to tell me what I already felt; the good smells of horseflesh, canvas and polish, the creak of supple leather, the jingle of harness and the crack of a *vorlooper's* whip over a big span of oxen, all spoke to me of one thing – a determined confidence in victory come what may.

'These are the Tortoise soldiers that fought the Xhosa, Cole uLootant,' said Ragwasi, nodding his head in acknowledgement of a pipe raised in greeting from a bearded sawney and recognising the Tartan that many Africans thought looked like tortoise shell. 'Or they are the sons of their fathers if I am not mistaken.'

'Not mistaken at all,' replied Cole, taking a salute from a subaltern in the characteristic blue tartan kilt of the Black Watch. 'I shall introduce you to their commander soon. He fought the Boers back in 1881; this is not his first war by a long chalk.'

'This is a good thing Cole uLootant,' replied Ragwasi, solemnly. 'Because it is not Kruger's first war by a long chalk even longer. He will know that you are coming.'

'He knows it for sure,' replied Cole, as we processed down the central road of the camp, through the artillery park and on towards HQ. 'This Division of the Army has already driven him off the Modder River and now that the Highlanders have reinforced it, the intention is to march straight up the railway line, over the last line of hills at Magersfontein and relieve Kimberley. Look, there are the Guards in the far distance and just by here are the King's Own Yorkshires. The Lancers we've already passed and we should come across Mike Rimington's Tigers if they're back in from scouting yet.'

'Mike Rimington is here?' I asked.

'You know him?' said Cole. 'He's recruited a Mounted Rifle outfit from down in the Cape. Volunteers the lot of 'em and know the country. He should be out looking for the Boers right now.'

In fact we came across Mike Rimington a few minutes later when we arrived at Brigade HQ and we dismounted, shook hands all round and I greeted him as a fellow hunter and hard rider. About my age, he was thinning a little on top, with kind eyes always ready to smile over a sharp nose, a big moustache, with his wiry frame wrapped up in buckskin like an old leather suitcase. He was fluent in Afrikaans, Zulu, Tswana and Xhosa and insisted that any man who rode with him could speak enough to get by in at least one other language.

'*War eng,* Mike?' I said, speaking Tswana. 'How are you? What's happening?'

'*Sawubona* Ragwasi,' replied Mike in Zulu, flicking a bit of dust from the leopard skin band of his slouch hat. 'And hello to you too, Pelly, you old bugger. Lord above, the Army must be desperate if they intend to rely on you. Come on in. You can help me make my report to the Big Jock *induna,* Wauchope. '

'Anything I need to know?' I said. There was something in his tone, something weary under the joviality that I had never known in him before.

'You heard about Modder?' he asked, his voice low and speaking Tswana.

I shook my head.

'Hell,' he said. 'We won there. We got across the river all right. But the *price....*'

I waited, for I knew there was more.

'I've never seen anything like it,' he continued. 'Mausers, Pelly, from concealed positions. They cut us down from twelve hundred yards. *Twelve hundred*, Pelly. That is better shooting than I've ever seen, anywhere. The troops went to ground and just got pinned down in the open. Anything showing taller than a snake's head got picked off. It wasn't until we found a flank that the Boers pulled out. Four hundred and fifty men lost, Pelly. *In one morning....*'

There was not time to digest this information before Tom Cole interrupted and ushered us into the presence of Major-General Andrew Gilbert Wauchope, commander of the Highland Brigade, but the horror Rimington's tone was enough to send a thrill of alarm through me. Under the canvas though, the mood could not have been more different. The light was soft, calm, perfect almost and bathed the general in an almost saintly glow. Indeed the diffusion of the light through the canvas walls added that same ethereal glow to each of our countenances as though we had just arrived for muster before an Archangel, albeit a Gabriel with a Claymore and tartan rather than a long robe and flaming sword. With his pale drumhead-taut skin, Wauchope looked every inch the pinched, wiry Scottish aristocrat and his piercing hazel eyes and rusty brown hair kept short had just about the right amount of grey at the temples to convince you of wisdom. I knew him for a veteran soldier straight away because he had that air of cool, quiet competence that would win over even the most sceptical to his point of view; I did not think him charismatic though; he was to my mind rather a cold fish, who would always prefer a small whisky and water to a bottle of champagne. There was a brusqueness to him as well and when we came in, he did not bother greeting us but impatiently waved away any attempt at salutes while he pored over the reports and returns that lay on the table before him.

'I'll be with ye in a moment, gentlemen,' he said. 'And then I'll be most interested in your intelligence. What damn fool thought that a map scale of five miles to the inch would be of any use to an army on the march? Aye, that I would well like to know.'

When he had finished writing, he laid down his gold pen and then fixed Mike Rimington with a gaze that would not have shamed an eagle for fierce intelligence.

'Do ye have anything to add to what we already know?' he said.

Mike Rimington pulled at his nose a little and crimpled his mouth up.

'They're up there, General; but exactly where, I can't tell you. Any time we get up within twelve hundred yards we're met with a hail of bullets from the berg. The land in front is flat as a pancake so I would suggest that you find another way forward.'

Wauchope took this in and then nodded his understanding.

'Ay weel, we canne hope to cross that broad plain in daylight unless we want to be pinned down,' he said, sniffing. 'So we'll have to go by night in the old Tel-El-Kebir way. March up navigating by the stars, and then fix bayonets and at 'em with the first of the light. You know the land. Any objections? Speak plain, please. Dinnae stand on ceremony.'

'Well, General,' said Rimington, looking at his feet. 'Like I say, I can't tell you exactly where they are except that they are there. What I will say is that you'll need to have crossed the plain and be ready before the sun comes up. If your men are at the foot of the hills at dawn, you'll have the advantage of surprise and any Boers at the top will be silhouetted against the sky when they come to shoot back. Have your best men told off as sharpshooters ready to pick them off, would be my advice.'

'Colonel Cole?' said the General, shifting his gaze.

'Night navigation by compass is not to be relied upon, Sir,' he said. 'There seems to be a great deal of magnetic material in the hills about here and so a true North is not to be had from anything.'

'We'll be guided on our left by the road,' replied Wauchope. 'And we'll advance in column of companies until we get to the foot of the hill. Only then will we deploy into line. After that the artillery and Maxims will blast the hills and hopefully the Boers will show us a clean pair of heels as we go up the slope.'

The General turned to Ragwasi next. Like me, Wauchope had no racial hesitation towards black men because he had learned that skin colour has no bearing on soldierly conduct when he had commanded Hausas in West Africa. His disapproving gaze was bestowed on everyone alike.

'Big Jock Induna,' said Ragwasi, using an appellation that made Cole, Rimington and I wince but which the General didn't seem to mind. 'This is a different sort of war to the one that I am used to and I do not understand it. In the wars that I have fought against the Boers, they have always ridden hard, shot fast and then galloped away from danger to come back again when they have avoided that danger. They have fought in the way that uBuller taught us at the Devil's Pass and I have never seen them fight on foot from mountains.'

'And?' said the General, knowing instinctively there was more.

'The Boers are hunters, induna,' said Ragwasi. 'And they have armed themselves with the Mauser which is a hunter's rifle so I would expect them to fight in the way that they would hunt for game.'

'Explain yourself,' said the General, his eyes full of interest.

'Induna; a Mauser fires its bullet very straight and very flat and so to make the best shot, you must shoot it from a flat position,' continued Ragwasi, as I nodded in agreement. 'It is a very difficult shot to make if your quarry is at the bottom of the hill and you are at the top of the hill.'

'Aye,' said the General. 'That is true, but if the top of the hill offers you a clear shot and a longer range would you accept the difficulty? I understand that the field of fire at the bottom of the hill is obstructed by bush and thorn trees.'

This was a technical question to which every single huntsman and soldier had a different answer and each answer would be right in some circumstances and wrong in another and each one of us turned the question over in our minds before the General asked us each to speak.

'Top for me,' said Tom Cole. 'Or at least under the crest to avoid being sky-lined.'

'Same for me,' said Mike Rimington. 'You have a big army and that makes a big target. I'd take my chances on hitting *something* as far out as fifteen hundred yards and just about everything at half a mile.'

'I would hide myself in the bush at the bottom,' said Ragwasi. 'That plain is wide and will be lit up by the sun.'

The General turned to me and I felt a rush of terror at the thought that my advice might be wrong or stupid or not based on anything else but my hunches that might just be a lot of nonsense. His eyes were fierce indeed and they reminded me of the eyes of a leopard that had once come at me unexpectedly in the night and almost killed me. Back then I had felt a wave of peace come over me as I thought I was about to die in its jaws and now I felt something like it, although it was not *exactly* the same obviously. But then I realised that Wauchope was experienced enough to make his own mind up whatever I said. I took a deep breath and made my judgement.

'General,' I said. 'If I was you I would get across that open plain as fast as I could, as quietly as I could and in the deepest darkness I could find. And then go up that hill as fast as I could, firing all the way so as not to give the Boers time to rest, because I would not wish to be caught anywhere in the open when a Boer marksman can have time to put his foresight on my head, for he will not miss twice. I would agree with Tom and Mike, Sir. They are marksmen enough to take the downhill shot.'

Later in the day, during the last of a close afternoon, Ragwasi and I rode out with Mike Rimington to make a final reconnaissance and found everything that we had all said to be true. There was a very long, very flat exposed plain broken only by thorn trees in front of us and then a rugged line of steep koppies that went straight up out of this plain - which at this moment was being given a good battering by the artillery.

'That spur in front is Magersfontein Kop,' said Mike pointing, as we galloped away from the *crack* and *zeep* of a spatter of angry Boer bullets. 'It's full of krantzes and wait-a-bit thorn but if Wauchope and his Jocks can take it, they'll win the day and the road to Kimberley will be open.'

I looked up at the sky. There was a blurry haze out towards the West and it was beginning to drizzle.

'It will rain tonight,' I said. 'Wauchope will have the benefit of its cover.'

*

And now I must pause a moment because I have stamped on my second best hat and Tepo is shouting at me and telling me I am a stupid, bad tempered old man who should know better than to scare the grandchildren by leaping about and stamping and making a lot of huffing and puffing noises like a train that has gone off the tracks and that I should take this journal and put it in the compost heap or use it for kindling. She is right too; I did not ever want to be an angry old man and I try my best to be dignified and quiet and just stick to my cheroots and Cape Smoke. She is wrong also; it is not like I have been making mampoer again in that still I keep in that shady spot away from the prying eyes of her relatives –some hope! Anyway, I must take some deep breaths and light up another cheroot and remember that I am in good company; in that famous play *Cyrano de Bergerac* the baker's wife uses his poems to wrap pastries in and did not Don Quixote have all his books thrown about and burned? Yes, he did. So, as I say, Tepo is wrong because in this case I am right to be angry.

So, now I have calmed down a bit, I will tell you about Magersfontein because I was there; on that day the British Army suffered the loss of a thousand men killed, captured or wounded, out of a total of three thousand five hundred, and three quarters of them came from Wauchope's Highland Brigade. It was a long carnage that went on from just after first light at five in the morning until five in the afternoon. I will tell you it was like a springbok shoot. And I never saw a single Boer *all day*. Pass me my Cape Smoke for I need another little pull just to get the memory of that day out of my dry throat.

Now, it is an awesome sight to see an army on the march; the vast columns of thousands and tens of thousands of trudging infantrymen carrying packs, knapsacks and rifles, heads down, brows furrowed, doggedly eating up mile after mile, step by single step in clouds of dust that cover their uniforms and cake their faces so that they become white, or brown or red depending on the colour of the earth; guns rattling along at the back of the teams of gasping horses, bits in, harness straining, urged on by cursing riders and followed by more teams towing the Armstrongs; lancers and Mounted Infantry jogging by on bays and whalers and greys, leather creaking, spurs jingling, horse tails flicking at the flies, men rubbing raw hands, saddle stiff and sore; supply trains of hundreds and hundreds of wagons towed by herds of oxen, mules and horses spread out across square miles of open veldt so that their white covers look like clouds crossing a tan sky; the sound of squeaking wheels and rumbling tumbrils trembling across the earth; above all a smell of steel, oil, horseflesh and the cumin smell of sweat; and the iron hard murmur and mutter of determined men overcoming heat, exertion and exhaustion to move closer and closer to a day when they must face fear, bullets and the Boers head on, while each day the smell of enteric hangs over them like a miasma. As I say, it is an awesome sight to see the reality of that nebulous thing called power: the ability to make a whole nation bend to your bidding whether they want to or not and however much they demur or resist. The biggest thing I had seen before was the Zulu impi that attacked us at Khambula in 1879 and at 20,000 strong, that was only half the size of this army and only about a tenth as deadly. We were so many that I truly believed the Boers would take one look at the approaching dust and retire before us; the army looked like one of those terrible pillars of cloud that the Lord himself wrapped himself in when he led the Jews in the Exodus; at night the camp fires were not so much a pillar of fire but a galaxy of red, flickering stars to match the white diamonds above. All we had to do was to take Magersfontein and then Johannesburg and Pretoria would fall and we could all go home to our lolwapas.

The troops fell in just after last light – Northamptons on the left, Highlanders in the centre and Guards on the right - ready to make the march across those last three miles of open plain and as I had predicted, it came on to rain. Visibility was down to nothing but this was all to the good because in the pitch black of the night the army could advance slowly and deliberately without getting mixed up or separated or getting into all sorts of confusion when men had to stop to detach themselves from the wait-a-bit thorns. These thorns are very hard and sharp – I nearly lost an eye to one once – and strong enough to scratch paint off tin boxes; they catch on your clothes and will tear them to shreds if you just try to force your way through. The only thing that is worse than them is the English firethorn like the one my father grew up a drainpipe to stop me climbing in through the window. Anyway, everything was done slowly and deliberately; we had the best part of eight hours to cover those three miles and when the army went forward it did so sensibly, making sure that no-one got lost by laying out guide ropes, letting the hiss of the bucketing rain mask any little rattle of a buckle or a sporran, and making sure that everyone was ready to leap out of that dawn with a hell of a shout and storm that Magersfontein Kop before the Boers were out of their miserable wet blankets.

And everything went to plan until four hundred yards out when someone or something woke Johannes up and tripped the alarm and there was an immediate crackle of flashes, just like those strings of Chinese fire-crackers, and then the whole of the Boer line opened up. This was just about the only thing that I saw of the battle because Rawgwasi and I had joined up with Rimington's Tigers on the left, but we saw the flash of those muzzles and we knew then that the Boers were not *on* the hill but at the foot of it, in trenches, where the flat trajectory of the Mausers could be used to best effect. There was a hell of shout from the Jocks of course and some confused cheering and we followed the sound of rifle fire, shouting and the flash of muzzles as they went on forward and onto the kop. Or that's what we saw; what we didn't see as the sun came up, the rain ceased and the bush closed in was that most of the Jocks had been caught while they were deploying out of column and into their fighting line and pretty much scythed down. Wauchope was killed along with most of his officers and those who were not killed or wounded outright went to ground in the bush and scrub a couple of hundred yards from the Boer trenches and stayed there. The Boers now had the advantage of shooting out of the shadows at the Jocks who were now lit up by the rising sun; anyone who moved got shot; that was it; and the rest of the day was all about trying to get what was left of the Highland Brigade out of that killing ground before the sun baked what was left of them to death. The guns were brought up and a couple of Maxims went into action, but all they could do was blaze away and keep the Boers' heads down.

And before all the armchair Generals start up about what *should, could* and *would* have been done if they had been in charge, I will say that it was the same for the Boers. Every time they tried to move, they got shot flat too. There was a whole gang of Norwegian volunteers fighting on the Boer side – Norwegians! For crying out loud! What were they doing in Africa? Why weren't they sitting sensibly and quietly at home in their igloos? Well, they went forward under a sky so hot the whole lot of them probably would have melted if they had not got slaughtered in their turn first by the Jocks. So for the rest of the day, everybody stayed put as soon as they came under any sort of fire, until late in the afternoon when the Jocks, who had lain out in the terrible sun all day finally threw the towel in and ran for it; I can't blame them; they'd had bad luck and paid for it; even those who survived had such terrible sunburns on the back of their knees that the medical orderlies were popping blisters bigger than a man's fist. The rest of the army waited for nightfall and then came back too, in not much better state.

Yes! We all know what happened that day! It was a disaster! Ragwasi was right and me and Rimington and Wauchope and the rest of the British Army was wrong! But this does not mean that all those newspaper Clever Dicks were right with all their maps and bird's eye views and coloured pencils and arrows pointing in this direction and that direction and saying that *if* we had done this then *that* would have happened and *if only* those stupid Generals had listened to those same Clever Dicks sitting in their armchairs bumping their gums in London and Cape Town then the disaster would not have happened. Fiddlesticks! I say to them: Fiddlesticks to all of them! They think that modern war is the same as Waterloo and the Crimea where Generals eyed each other with telescopes across a mile of green grass and the soldiers stood up straight in bright uniforms of scarlet and blue so that they could be easily seen and muskets could not hit a barn door at more than forty paces. They say *why did the General not go another* way? Because there wasn't another way! It was a miracle they got that far as it was because an army that big needs a lot of water and where are you going to get it Clever Dick? There are no Corporation water taps in the Karoo! The Generals had less choice in this matter than Clever Dick has between choosing tea or coffee at breakfast! Fiddlesticks to all of them!

Bad luck.

That's all it was. No one was to blame. Not me, not the General, not anybody; not bad planning or incompetence or stupidity or whatever else those fools claim. It was just plain old bad luck which is what war is mostly composed of.

My own part in the battle was very limited. When the light came up Mike Rimington tried to find a flank that we could ride around and we headed off on the left of some Fusiliers hoping to reach Merton station on the railway line which was well in the Boer rear. He was hoping to bounce their laager and run off their livestock and supplies but each time we tried, the Boers saw us coming from a mile away and we would run into an uncomfortably accurate fire, first from the Mausers and then from some guns and we just could not get anywhere near either the station or the line of hills. I didn't fire a shot all day; you can't shoot at what you can't see and hope to hit it.

Not that we didn't try. At one point Ragwasi and I and one other fellow handed over our reins to a fourth man and tried to sneak in through the bush and got pinned down for more than an hour for our pains. We tried to build a little sanger out of the sandstone rocks that lay like flakes about the place but that only seemed to attract bullets like bees and we were reduced to wriggling backwards on our bellies all the way. Once back at the relative safety of our horses and feeling pretty winded, we decided that whatever happened that day we were not going to advance one further step in the direction of Kimberley and we made our opinions clear to Mike, who agreed.

'This advance has stalled,' he said. 'And nothing we do is going to get it going again.'

It was at that moment that I caught sight of a trooper who looked a bit young to have signed up for Rimington's Tigers. His kit was too new for him to have been in the country long and he was wearing a neckerchief that looked out of place somehow; no-one I knew ever wore a neckerchief; but there was something oddly familiar in the way he ran his tongue under his top lip before mounting up. It was a curious mannerism and nothing that anyone would really remark upon if they had not got used to seeing it before – a long time before.

'Who's the boy?' I asked, jerking my head in his direction.

'Oh him,' said Mike. 'Picked him up in Cape Town a couple of weeks ago. No use to man or beast of course but he can ride and he speaks Portuguese so I thought he might come in handy.'

I was about to ask his name but we were interrupted by the arrival of a large Boer shell and by the time we had mounted, scattered, re-grouped and then taken up a position several hundred yards to the left rear, the boy was nowhere to be seen and Mike was racing off to see if he could find another position to attack from. At the time, I was too busy to give the boy any more thought and it was only much later when we were back in camp licking our wounds and wondering what was going to happen next that the matter of that little mannerism came back to me. Mind you, there was so much confusion after that battle, what with the Jocks cursing, a panic that the guns might be lost and the Guards coming back in and cursing the Highlanders for running and everybody shouting at everybody else and the wounded crying out and the ambulances bringing the men in. It was hardly any surprise that I did not catch another sight of the lad, I was so busy binding up wounds and shooting the poor horses that had been wounded that by the time it came to sleep, I threw myself on the ground under a single blanket in the open and slept for ten hours straight. When I came to, Mike Rimington was away on another errand, Tom Cole was nowhere to be found, General Wauchope was dead and it seemed that Ragwasi and I were now on detached service, so to speak. The boy, I presumed and hoped, had gone with Rimington – if he was still alive.

But it was then that I remembered that mannerism; my sister used to run her tongue inside her top lip just like that before she mounted up and in that moment it struck me like a blow on the back of the head that I might just have met my nephew for the first time.

Chapter 3

Marching to Pretoria

'We are not interested in the possibilities of defeat. They do not exist.' *Ag*, sometimes you do need a woman to put you straight and Queen Victoria certainly put all those headless chickens and doom-mongers in the newspapers straight alright when she came out with that bold statement. They called it 'Black Week' because the British Army lost three battles in the space of a few days, being repulsed at Stormberg and Colenso as well as Magersfontein and because the Clever Dicks did not know anything about the realities of war, they thought the sky had fallen in. Ragwasi knew better though and so did I; we had seen a lot of war and we knew that wars were not won like the quick victories of the gambler but by the exhaustion of his wallet through the realities of probabilities. The Zulus had won quick victories and had then been worn down by the dogged advance of a British Army that did not give up. We Tswana had been worn down by the Boers who came on relentlessly over not days or weeks but years and we were perfectly certain that these defeats at the hands of the Boers that we had witnessed and suffered were not the end of the story by a very long chalk. Like poker, victory would always go to the player with the biggest pile of chips and Britain had more chips than Kruger could ever have imagined.

For one thing, the Boers themselves knew almost immediately that their gamble on quick victories to make the government surrender - like Gladstone had done after Majuba – had failed. They had hoped that the Afrikaaners in the Cape would rise up, but they did not, and Kruger realised that to advance over the Karoo and down the escarpment to stir up trouble would end in disaster, for the difficulties of distance were the same for the Boers as they were for the British. The Karoo desert is like a series of giant steps up from the beautiful temperate lands of the Cape, with each successive plateau being drier and flatter than the next. It is hot and arid in the summer, cold, bleak and full of sleet during the winter and never able to support a person in one place for very long. The grass is sparse and able only to support one or two sheep an acre, along with the odd ostrich, and the springboks that migrate through in the spring strip wide areas clean of the young shoots leaving little for those sheep that do survive the winter; the grazing is nothing like an English downland at all and so crossing it with only a few animals is a challenge. Taking an army across it was almost impossible and with the grass withering and the water holes drying out as the Karoo summer came on, the Boers did the only thing that they could sensibly do. They holed up in siege lines and laagers and hoped for a miracle; like I have said already, Generals have less choice over their strategy than you have over what to eat for breakfast. The result was that when the British advanced again in February, within two months of Black Week, Kimberley and Ladysmith had been relieved and the main Boer army forced to surrender at the Battle of Paardeburg. By the end of May 1900, the Orange Free State had been taken and we had begun making preparations for the advance on Pretoria and it was then that events took an unexpected turn for Ragwasi and I.

We were sitting in a water mill that had been converted into a canteen in a railway town called Colesburg, just on the Cape side of the Orange River at the time, slaking our thirst with pale ale and eating bully beef sandwiches with Colman's mustard and enjoying them both very much. Colonel Cole had sent us down here to help with the advance on Bloemfontein and while the town filled up with guns and stores and wagons and animals and troops, we were kicking our heels, eating the plentiful rations and staying clear of the enteric fever which had broken out among the army after Paardeburg. All this time, my thoughts were much occupied by the boy I had seen among Mike Rimington's Tigers and I was tormented by thoughts that he might have been killed at Magersfontein. This was a thought that gave me much discomfort for so far the only thing of any use that I had been so far able to do to find my errant nephew was to send an enquiry off to Mijnheer Cronjie down in Cape Town, because the other letters were now being besieged in Kimberley with my bank manager and solicitor who were also being besieged there. Mijnheer Cronjie was a lawyer and man of business who my father had appointed to keep an eye on me when I had first been exiled and I had learned both to trust and like the old fellow. And old fellow he was now, though still hale and hearty and given to trusting his sons and daughters with more and more of his business. The letter I had dispatched had asked him to keep his ear to the ground for any mention of a Stamford John Holtzhausen, with a very broad hint that this name might crop up in connection with the sale of diamond jewellery in a discrete manner. He had, of course, agreed but in the only letter I had received from him had declared that his researches had as yet proved unfruitful because there were so many young men, adventurers and so forth, flooding in to the Cape in the hope of gaining for themselves some of the fame, fortune and sometimes illicit opportunities that present themselves in a war. I did so want to bring some good news to my family; in the past I had all too often been the bringer of bad news and I did not want to be the one who told my sister that her wayward son had gone down to a Boer bullet at Magersfontein.

Ragwasi, of course, had his own concerns.

'Why do we not ride for Pretoria and Johannesburg now and quickly, uPelly? We know the way to cross the Karoo for have we not done it many times before?'

He was slavering at the thought of getting his hands on Kruger's buried gold, of course, and he was increasingly impatient with the new General 'Bobs' Roberts' deliberate approach to things. There is old saying that you should be very careful what you wish for in case God grants you your wishes in full and I did try to explain the wisdom of this to him but, Ragwasi being Ragwasi, he would not listen when his eyes were blinded by dreams of gold and his ears stuffed with the rattle of silver shillings and he lost no time and spared no-one else's blushes in making his feeling on the tardiness of the General known.

'Ragwasi, you know we must wait for the Army to move forward together,' I said, finishing my meal and heading out into the warm sunshine. Colesberg was as pretty a Karoo town as you could ask for; a town full of aloes and cactus and the odd dusty palm tree with plenty of squat, square, one storey houses, tidily whitewashed or painted that pink or yellow like you see on Battenberg cakes. Along the main street, there were plenty of big, deep houses with stoeps and pleasant back gardens whose owners had compromised with the billeting officers to open them as paying hotels and restaurants for the officers and other staff who came and went about and I intended to spend the rest of the afternoon drinking beer in one that had become my favourite. It was only a short walk but I reckoned that the cool shade and the dappled sun provided by the trellis roses out the back would be worth the effort on a day like this. 'Besides,' I said, stepping out into the street. 'If Kruger has as much gold as you suspect, you will need to get a wagon to shift it all. It would be a poor thing for us to turn up a mountain of riches and only be able to carry away what we could stuff into our saddlebags and pockets.'

Ragwasi pursed his lips and rolled his shoulders as if to admit the wisdom of this observation but without wishing it to get in the way of his plans.

'We could steal a wagon in Johannesburg,' he suggested, hopefully.

'Steal?' I said, facetiously nodding towards the tall chapel portico at the top of the high street. 'But that would make us sinners.'

'uPelly,' he rebuked. 'If we are to steal all of Kruger's gold then it is only a very small extra sin to steal a wagon to carry it away in. And stealing from Kruger who has stolen so much from us is not what I would count a sin at all. Besides,' he said, dodging a mule cart and indicating the fancy ironwork over the balustrades and windows of the bank. 'Once it is in *their* vaults, it will not be *stolen* gold anymore but will belong to us as legitimately as necessary.'

It was often difficult to fault Ragwasi's logic and I was forced to ponder on it as we walked down the hot street in the dusty afternoon towards the restaurant. Sometimes, for him, *right* and *wrong* meant *good for Ragwasi* and *bad for Ragwasi* rather than the stricter rules that I had learned from the Vicar at Dines Hall and those that Reverend Mackenzie tried to instil in my children in the Kuruman Mission school. Sometimes I think he and that pirate Rhodes had more in common than either of them would admit. A lot of the time I thought he was right though, even if his logic was not strictly what you might expect, but on his point that stolen money once entered into a deposit box in a bank suddenly gained moral and legal absolution, I could not agree and I took him up on it as we went into the bar, ordered drinks and found a shady spot at a rough table in the garden.

We were not really *arguing* but as you can imagine we were attracting a bit of attention, not least because the house was not really used to having black men who were not servants making free with the facilities – and certainly, Ragwasi was making free with the beer – and I soon noticed that one person in particular was eyeing us up with some interest. He was a British officer, very well turned out in smart khaki, a polished Sam Browne belt and boots like glass at the end of the longest pair of legs I have ever seen on a man. When he stood up, I saw the reason for those legs because on top of them was a huge torso, wide shoulders and a head so square I was immediately reminded of General Buller, who also had a head like an ammunition box. Neither Ragwasi or I were short men, but this man stood head, shoulders and a bit more taller than us and I reckoned that if either of us stood behind him, we would not be seen, so broad was he.

'*Hau!*' declared Ragwasi, looking up when he saw the giant coming towards us. 'That man is a warrior to be feared!'

The man came closer and then, stooping down a little, held out his hand for us to shake. His face was yellowish, as though only just touched by the sun, and he was very closely, clean shaven, which was very unusual because troops on campaign shaved rarely if at all when water was so precious a commodity. Thirty-five or nearer forty, I thought him, though indeterminate, with hair so black it was almost blue and carrying the sheen of some expensive Macassar oil on it, and he wore the open, friendly sort of expression which only the true aristocratic officer, secure in his superiority, could wear with equanimity in the face of a pair of scruffy country-boy colonials like us. Ragwasi fell for his charm straight away: sometimes he could be a terrible snob: I blame myself for awarding him the title of *Prince* back during the Zulu war.

'Beg pardon, Gents,' said the giant, his manner pleasant, his voice enquiring. 'But I couldn't help but overhear some snippets of your conversation and I wonder if I might presume upon you for a moment or two? Allow me to introduce myself: Harry Willoughby, Major, of the Leicestershire Willoughbys, Special Service, presently attached to the Staff.'

'Pleased to meet you,' I replied, introducing myself and Ragwasi. His handshake was firm but somehow greasy, a little clammy, like it had been kept under water too long and wrinkled up. 'How may we be of service?'

'*Prince* Ragwasi, is it?' said Willoughby. 'Not related to the Prince Ragwasi of Stellaland fame, by any chance?'

'That is I,' answered Ragwasi, gravely and hopelessly flattered.

'Then you must know my good friend Tom Cole?' said Willoughby, beaming. 'I say, what smashing luck to run into you two. This calls for champagne, I'd say! Dammit, will you join me? I insist on it.'

Now Ragwasi was not used to champagne nor to the charms of the English aristocracy and he could hardly contain himself when Major Willoughby asked him for a blow-by-blow account of the battles we had fought against the Boers and against the Zulus and then insisted on a track by track, hill by hill account of our travels in the Namib desert and then followed this up by requesting a spoor by spoor account of our hunting trips. To be honest, this seemed to be a bit more enthusiasm for a story than politeness or curiosity required and I began to wonder what Willoughby was after – because my instinct told me that he *was* after *something*. It wasn't that he didn't really try to bring me into the conversation, because he did, but after about half an hour of distributing his charm equally between us, it was as though he had made up his mind as to which of us was the easiest, well, *mark*, I think would be the right way to describe it, and had then concentrated his attempts to delight on the one most likely to revel in the attention. In a way, he reminded me of some of those ladies in Johannesburg who were adept at fluttering their eyelashes at a chap and then leading him swooning through a series of doors, each opening onto a room more sumptuously adorned with frilly things and dimmed lamps than the last, until finally, he hands over his wallet and she shows him through just one more door – and he finds himself out in the street, with only the sound of the bolt slamming home behind him to keep him company. So, by the time three bottles of champagne had come and gone, Ragwasi was eating out of his hand and despite my subtle and not so subtle signalling, ready to sign up to whatever Major Willoughby was priming him for. He was like a young fag thinking he was being picked for First XI cricket on his first day at the Big School when in fact he was being gently persuaded into cleaning the kit and mowing the grass in the outfield, and counting it a privilege.

'Well,' Willoughby said, after Ragwasi had finished a rather long (and almost entirely fictitious) account of how he had saved me from being eaten by a leopard. 'You chaps seem like just the sort of men I could use for a bit of a wheeze I've got in mind.'

'Count us in Will-uby,' said Ragwasi, before I could kick him under the table.

'Wheeze?' I said, warily.

Willoughby leaned back in his chair, kicked out his long legs and put his head back, talking as though he was really thinking out loud.

'Thing is,' he said. 'We'll be in Pretoria in a week or two and Johannesburg shortly after that and that presents the General with one or two googlies to field.'

He paused, opened and closed his mouth again, as though waiting to catch the right words.

'Ever seen what an army does when it gets into a conquered city?'

I waited.

'Not a pretty sight,' he said. 'Doesn't matter how well the troops behave on the march or in battle, as soon as they get into a town discipline goes to pot and all order goes out the window.'

He paused again, struggling to find a diplomatic way to say what he was going to say.

'Sad to say, the British Army is no different in this respect to anyone else, that's the Devil of it: Badajoz, Delhi, Peking. None of it very edifying, I can tell you.'

There was another long pause, which I thought best to leave uninterrupted and shot Ragwasi – a rather bleary eyed Ragwasi at this point – a look to tell him to do likewise.

'This time, we're going to keep them well clear,' said Willoughby. 'Heaven knows what these damn scribblers from the newspapers would say if they saw the imperial soldiery breaking into the gin store and going for the ladies. Not good for the prospects of reconciling the Boers to their future servitude either, I dare say.'

We were coming to it now. He shifted in his chair once more and turned to address us directly.

'What I'm after is a sort of Flying Column to go into the city after the Boer authorities have departed to hold the fort until the proper authorities – our authorities - get there. The General would really like to avoid the anarchy that always – *always* – prevails when a city is left to its own mercies; bad hats settling scores, looting, moneylenders being bumped off by their creditors, servants settling the hash of their masters; that sort of thing.'

'You want a police force?' I asked.

'Sort of,' replied Willoughby. 'Chaps who can secure the Town Hall, the Land Office, banks and the Telegraphs, that sort of thing.'

'And the Treasury,' said Ragwasi. I gave him a special, narrow-eyed look.

'Exactly, old man. Do you know your way around Johannesburg and Pretoria, by any chance?'

Willoughby had dug the trap. He had told Ragwasi that he was digging a trap and as far as I could see, he had put up a big sign saying 'Here is a Trap'. He had then invited Ragwasi to inspect the trap and agree that it was a jolly good trap which any sensible man should avoid. And then Ragwasi thought hard about what a trap was for – actually it is for trapping people – closed his eyes, held his nose between thumb and forefinger, counted to three and jumped head first into it.

'I know it like my wife's hut,' said Ragwasi. 'When do we ride?

Jah. He knew it like his wife's hut. And like the sound of her door being slammed shut and the bolt sliding closed when he had been at the mampoer and fallen over in the pumpkin patch again.

And what must a sensible man do when his old friend is drunk and blundering about but go with him and see he comes to no harm and doesn't break too many bones?

*

In our little Troop, Major Willoughby had collected a dozen or so rough riders, all of a similar stamp. There were a couple of hunters from down in the Transkei, a couple of Zulus from John Dunn's people in Natal, some Australians and a Canadian and two or three fellows from England; one of them was from my old stamping ground around Newmarket and, as one might expect, knew just about everything there was to know about horseflesh. I would guess that all of them had been soldiers at some stage because they all knew how to wear a uniform but chose to wear it in their own way, in the way that experience rather than the Field Regulations had taught them; useless bits of kit had been discarded; some carried two canteens; one of the hunters carried a Mauser rather than the regulation Lee Enfield. Ragwasi and I had been offered uniforms but the truth was that we had grown a little thicker round the mid-rift than the imperial tailors had allowed for, they being more used to ploughboys than stout yeomen if you take my meaning, and so we had taken a pick and mix approach like the others in the Troop. We dispensed with the puggarees, putties, and spine protectors and though we were tempted by the ammunition boots on offer, we decided in the end to stick with our own tried and trusted veldtschoen. Extra socks, flannel shirts and cotton drawers we pounced on, for a change into dry clothing is a real comfort after a wet night in the field and though we turned down the cork helmets, we did take a length of red cloth each to tie around our hat bands so that a sentry might more easily distinguish us from the Boers. Also, we drew a couple of the new Webley Mk IV revolvers, which looked sturdy and serviceable. Looking around at my fellow riders, I wondered if by any chance Stamford was among them; I had started to see his face everywhere now and whenever I saw a troop of horse or a platoon of infantry, I tried to see beneath the dust and beards, looking for that little twitch of a tongue running under a top lip that had first excited my curiosity.

If my thoughts were concerned with Stamford John Holzhausen though, Ragwasi's were fixed firmly on Kruger's gold and as we rode across the thin streams and by the willow shaded dams and abandoned farms of the Free State, there was nothing that Major Willoughby told us that did not whet his appetite for stealing it.

'We know from some of our chaps and from some chaps who we keep in touch with in Pretoria,' he said, giving us a knowing wink. 'That just before the outbreak of war, Kruger confiscated all the gold that was due to be shipped to Europe from the gold merchants – about a million's worth…'

'Rands or Pound Sterling?' asked Ragwasi.

'Rand,' replied Willoughby, brushing away a fly and spurring up into a canter. We followed. 'At roughly two gold Rand to the Pound Sterling. He also firked another half million out of the British banks there and confiscated whatever gold was held by the natives.'

'*Hau*,' said Ragwasi, barely able to contain himself.

'And then, of course, the mines have been running full tilt for the last eight months,' continued Willoughby, drawing up behind a column of Light Horse. 'So there's another million there - plus the silver, of course.'

'Of course,' said Ragwasi, trying to hide his interest by raising a salute to the commander of the column and receiving a certain amount of ribaldry in return. 'How much?'

'Probably another million there too,' said Willoughby, as though dismissing it as a trifling sum. 'And there was a tidy sum in the Treasury already. We guess it would be about, oh… er, say thirty million, thereabouts?'

I swear, Ragwasi almost fell off his horse.

'And, I need not mention the paper money – probably, the same amount again.'

At that, Ragwasi almost *swallowed* his horse.

'So you want us to secure all this money for the government, Major?' I asked. 'Is that the idea?'

'Not far off, old boy,' replied the Major, batting away at a flurry of dust thrown up by the riders we were now passing. 'But we'll discuss things in more detail when we're all gathered together.'

'When *we're* gathered together?' I said, warily.

'Certainly, old boy. Tom Cole and Mike Rimington are in on this wheeze too. I dare say we'll need all our combined wits if we are to seize the Transvaal's cash register before any enterprising young jewel thief is tempted to make off with the proceeds.'

It was now my turn to start.

'Jewel thief?'

'I confess I'm a fan of crime stories,' said Willoughby, seeing my discomfiture. 'Have you read *The Amateur Cracksman*? Very entertaining. Better than that dreadful *Rue Morgue* stuff. Bit more on the Kipling side.'

I breathed a little easier, but the significance of the book reference eluded me. It was hardly my fault that I had not read any of the *Raffles* stories at that time.

It was not that I distrusted the Major; I did not know him well enough to either trust or distrust him and nor was it the case that I found his flattery of Ragwasi and Ragwasi's lapping up of it anything but mildly irritating; as I say, I had been flattered by School Captains as a boy and had learned to dismiss this kind of charm as a pleasant sort of mild treachery – but I did have a certain curiosity about him. As I thought back to our first meeting, it struck me that there was just something wrong about the way he introduced himself as one of the *Leicestershire* Willoughbys, as though he could not conceive of the idea that a couple of colonial boys like Ragwasi and I would never have heard of the Willoughbys, *Leicestershire* or not. Somehow, it just seemed a little *too* presumptuous, a little *too* far, a little too much application of the regal charm, even for a man looking for a thing as rare and in demand as a pair of guides with special knowledge of the country. Above all though, as the days went by on the ride up to Pretoria, I often felt that there was another man watching me from behind Willoughby's eyes and that man was as wary of me as I was of him.

I wasn't the only one who had doubts about the Major either. One of the Australians, who went by the name of Cunningham, and was always hanging around on the outskirts of any conversation that Willoughby was having, also seemed to be keeping a close eye on our leader. I had paid little attention to this man before, but now, as the time for action came closer and his behaviour marked him in my hunter's eyes as an odd kind of animal, I began to watch Trooper Cunningham as carefully as opportunity allowed. He was rough cut and cool, and though he never raised his voice, I could sense a menace and a determination in it when he did speak; his face was lined with years in the sun and his hands had the leather segs of years in the saddle too; a broken nose was testimony to a life lived close to the bone and probably the bottle too and I concluded that this was no character to cross. I had once known an opium eater back in Newmarket, and this Cunningham fellow had the same dark, dilated eyes with the glitter of the snake in them. Among his own fellows, I saw several times that whenever Willoughby checked on them over a billy-can or a plate of mealies, he was polite enough but then shared a crooked smile and a sly joke with them once the Major's back was turned.

Ragwasi would have none of my misgivings about Willoughby though.

'You are just jealous, uPelly, that this great lord should find a kindred spirit in a fellow prince like me,' he said. 'And what is an Australian but a very low type of man? Put away your fears. Does this man Will-uBy not know where Kruger has buried his gold?'

Later that day when Major Willoughby took Ragwasi off on some errand that he chose not to share the details of with me, I thought back again to the first time I had shaken hands with him; then I had thought his hand to be clammy, but now the thought came to me that this was not enough of a description for it; *repulsively moist* was a better way of describing it.

*

I think it was outside Kroonstad in the last days of May or thereabouts that Colonel Tom Cole rode up with his troop and then drew us aside to tell us the lie of the land. It was after he had given formal orders to the troop commanders, which included Major Willoughby and Mike Rimington, who had also joined, that he came to sit at our small fire and share a cup of Camp Coffee.

'It's like this,' he said, handing round a bottle of navy rum which Ragwasi and I sloshed into our coffee. It was cold out on the veldt and nothing warms a soldier's heart more than a shot of rum on a dark night. We poured big ones. 'We are to ride as fast as we can for Johannesburg. We'll be well in advance of the rest of the army, so there's a chance we'll hit some resistance but not much because the Boers are pretty much on the run. What we want to avoid is the possibility of someone taking it into his head to do for Johannesburg what the Russians did to Moscow when Napoleon took it and neither do we want the city to go up in flames just because someone breaks into a gin shop and drops his cheroot, if you understand – there have been food riots already. There is a lot of private property there too, all left behind by British people, and there'll be hell to pay if it's lost, burned or looted.'

We nodded in agreement. It was much the same as Major Willoughby had already told us.

'So Rimington's Tigers are going to race in and secure the gold mines along the south of the city,' continued Tom. 'We think the mine guards will probably prevent anyone doing wilful damage to the shafts and machinery and such like but it's best to be sure.'

We nodded again. To be honest I had those butterflies in my stomach that come on when something momentous and exciting is going to happen. We were going to capture a city! A whole city! This was something that we had never done before and represented the forward motion that Ragwasi and I had always said was the most important thing in life. This was living life *audaciously* and I was fidgeting with excitement.

'I've got some fellows from the Australian Light Horse who are going to secure the Native and Coolie Locations to the west of the city,' he continued. 'We aren't expecting trouble – they'll be keeping their heads down until they work out what our arrival means for *them*. Wise men, I'd say.'

'They will not mourn the passing of the Boers,' said Ragwasi, cupping his hands around the warm coffee.

'Let's hope so,' answered Cole, taking the bottle back. 'My troop are going to get right down into the centre and take control of the British Consulate, the banks and exchanges around Commissioner Street.'

I felt, rather than saw, Ragwasi stiffen like a gun dog at the mention of *banks and exchanges*.

'You lot are going to get into Government House,' continued Cole. 'It's vital that we get control of the administration and tax records intact or there'll be chaos what with people demanding a rebate, claiming they've paid up, arguing that they *don't* own this or that and *do* own this *and* that. We'll need a new Doomsday Book to sort out the mess if the records are burnt up.'

'And of course there'll be absolutely oodles of gold, eh Ragwasi?' said Willoughby, appearing out of the darkness wrapped in a cloak, smiling like the devil and rubbing his hands gleefully.

'Kruger's millions!' agreed Ragwasi, taking the bottle from Cole and handing it up. '*Hau!* I would like to see them rounded up like cattle and put very safely in my own kraal for safe-keeping!'

We all laughed at this and sent the bottle around again, but later, when I had wrapped myself in my blankets and put my head on my saddle, I felt that niggle of uncertainty once more. It seemed to me that Willoughby was telling a joke within a joke, if you see my meaning; joking to conceal a truth that lay below and was only known to those who were in on it. And I was uncomfortable because I had an inkling that Ragwasi was in on that joke and I was not. He had laughed just a little too quickly and a little too long and in a pitch that was a little too high. I tried to put the thought out of my head but I could not, so I drowned it with a cup full of Navy Rum and fell asleep.

*

Major Willoughby gave us lowly Troopers our orders more formally the next morning. We were to ride for Johannesburg as soon as night fell and we were to ride hard, laying up during the day if need be, but pushing on at the best pace we could manage.

'Mark this well, gentlemen,' he said, in a voice that had a harder edge to it than I had heard before. 'Anyone who can't keep up will be left behind. There's water in the Vaal River and some little before that, but fill your horses to bursting point before we set out and carry an extra bag of oats. Make sure they're in tip top shape too because there'll be no remounts and it's a ride of two hundred miles and I want to do it in four days.'

We whistled at this. The horses would be good for nothing after a ride like that but Willoughby was adamant.

'The city depends on us,' he said, jabbing his hand down for emphasis. 'We cannot risk anarchy.'

So that was that. We spent the day grooming the horses, preparing our kit, double checking everything that had already been double checked and then double checking once more.

Cunningham and his mates were paying very close attention to their pistols, I noticed, and seemed a little false when I went over to ask if I could borrow a little rifle oil from them.

'You want me to clean it for you too?' said one of them in that sarcastic accent that Australians have. I was about to answer him with a little Tswana wisdom which involved several references to different types of dung and particular forms of truncated genitalia when Cunningham broke in.

'Give him what he needs,' he said quietly, and was instantly obeyed.

'Just joking, mate,' said the Trooper, flushing and looking damned uncomfortable.

'Anything else you need?' said Cunningham, turning to me. His manner was accommodating, but the tone of his voice carried a quiet unwelcome in it. He didn't want me speaking to his mates, that was clear, and it was clearer that he didn't want to speak to me either. I took the oil, backed off and ten minutes later, returned the tin without a word being said on either side beyond 'Thanks'.

Ragwasi was gorging himself on bread and tinned beef, stocking up for the days of hardship ahead and I was tempted to raise the matter of Willoughby once more, but something told me it would be futile. Ragwasi only ever learned from experience and it is a fact of life that people will only hear what they want to hear when their ears have been stopped up by the silver words that slip off the golden tongue of a charismatic man and so I got on with filling up our saddle bags with tea, army biscuit and biltong. About an hour before we were ready to leave, Willoughby called Ragwasi away once more on yet another errand that he did not need to share the details of with me and it occurred to me that these errands had been more frequent over the past few days than I had first noticed. You will say that I should have noticed, being his friend and a hunter, and I will say to you that it was precisely for these reasons that I did not notice; I trusted Ragwasi and had no reason to keep him on a leash. This time, they were only away a short time and when Ragwasi returned twenty minutes later, he carried a small satchel which he handed up to me.

'It is dynamite, uPelly,' he said, avoiding my eye. 'Will-uBy wishes you to carry one satchel and for I to carry the other.'

'Dynamite?' I said, noticing that Cunningham had suddenly appeared and was pretending to inspect the girth of a nearby horse. 'What do we need dynamite for?'

'Will-uBy says "Just in case",' replied Ragwasi, and I saw Cunningham's ears prick up.

At that moment the bugle called, ending my speculation about what both Ragwasi and Cunningham were about, and we mounted up and fell in behind Willoughby, Mike Rimington, an Australian Lieutenant whose name I did not know, and Colonel Cole.

We were a fine sight, I have to say. A hundred experienced, kitted-out and togged-up, battle-hardened mounted men, all khaki, bullets, boots and grit, ready to leave with the falling night on a mission to seize a city and win a war. Every man Jack looked fit and eager and bloody-minded and I dare say it would be hard to find such a collection of officially licenced toughs anywhere else in the world without scouring every mining town, barracks or hunting lodge between Sydney and Tipperary first - although one among them was beginning to suspect that not all was right with this little expedition.

It wasn't just Willoughby, Cunningham and Ragwasi who were troubling me though. We had been joined at the last by a fit, well-built young chap all wide shoulders and slim hips, wearing a new beard on a strong jaw and a slouch hat pulled well down over grey eyes and blonde hair. He was the chap that I had first noticed at Magersfontein and as he mounted a good bay horse towards the rear of the column, he made that curious motion of running his tongue under his top lip so familiar to me. He was also, or so it seemed, making a conspicuous effort not to be noticed by me, which was perhaps not so surprising because he answered to the name of Stamford John Holzhausen.

*

What a ride that was! I was broken to the saddle many years ago and I have spent most of my life since in and out of it but that crossing of the veldt from Kroonstad to Johannesburg almost finished me. To cover fifty miles in a day meant sixteen hours of travelling and at the end of that another hour of rubbing down, tending hooves and managing sore backs; then there was sentry duty on top. If an infantryman gets a twenty minute break, he lies down on the grass and takes it easy, but the mounted soldier must water his horse, adjust that rubbing bit or put a bit more oil on the girth. In the infantry, two hours rest are two hours rest but we needed an hour and a quarter for the horse, what with unsaddling, saddling up again, fetching water for the animal and persuading it to eat the grass we had to cut for it. I never put a bottle or a bite to my lips in those four days without having the reins in my other hand and when I lay down to grab what sleep I could, I had to tie the hobbled horse to my saddle and my saddle to me in case I woke up on the veldt with the horse gone. Covering that vast distance also meant that we could only really ride *half* of it if we wanted the horses to arrive in Johannesburg in any condition that would keep them out of the knacker's yard. That meant leading the fractious horse the other half of the way and I can tell you that that is no mean feat – how Willoughby's cob stood his weight I will never fathom.

Now the infantryman might complain about his sore feet and shaking off his sock show you a bright red blister full of yellow fluid waiting to be popped but this is nothing to what we endured for we had to walk those other *twenty five miles* each day in boots that were made for riding and not marching. I can tell you, I rued the day that I did not take up the offer of those ammunition boots because my light though sturdy veldtschoen were never made for such work. By half way through the second day, my feet were on fire and I felt every single stone that I stood on as though it was a boulder or a needle. On top of that my shoulders and hips felt like raw steak from the constant bashing of the rifle over my shoulder and my buttocks felt as though they were in shreds. Ragwasi suffered this too, even though he has always been more naturally padded than me in that department, and by the end of the third day neither of us felt as though there was a single bone left in our bodies. By this time too, the horses had had enough and it was no longer a case of leading them but rather pulling them until they were stumbling and biting your shoulder out of sheer exhaustion.

Neither did we have the comradeship of close companionship to help us, for the light on the veldt in the winter is so pure and clear that a marksman can easily hit a close packed body of troops at a mile or more. We had seen what the Boers had done at Magersfontein and had no desire to repeat the experience so we walked or rode separated from our nearest comrade by ten yards to the right and left and twenty between those in front and behind. There was no drum to stir us or band to sing to, just the sound of our own exertions gradually grinding us down, all to the accompaniment of a plague of ticks and horseflies that came up out of the veldt like a miasma. The fires that we lit before evening were small and just functional enough to raise a billy full of water to a tepid brew and were extinguished before darkness so as not to alert a passing patrol, for though the Boers were retreating, we did not know just how far in front of us they were or whether they were at that moment dug in and waiting for us in ambush. At night, the light of the moon was silver and strong enough to cast shadows which meant the temperature plummeted before dawn to put frost on the ground and lift us cursing from our blankets but the sun was still strong and by ten in the morning, we were riding in shirtsleeves; by noon we were wishing that blasted frost was back with us and by three in the afternoon dreading the cold of the coming night. If I am ever condemned to hell for my sins, I will count myself well prepared by that ride for whatever the Old Gentleman has in store for me, I can tell you.

When finally we reached Viljoensdrift on the Vaal River and were allowed to pause to properly rest and water the horses, we could see the beginnings of Johannesburg in the coal mines and brickworks of Vereeniging, just a few miles ahead, and we knew that the next day's ride would take us on to our objective and possibly into battle for we could not believe that the Boers would give up the city without a fight. Indeed, when Mike Rimington rode out a little way, he reported that there were fires burning in the city; Willoughby was equally burning to go on, but Tom Cole over-ruled him on account of the horses being so done up. Tomorrow would be soon enough, he decided: fresh men on rested horses would be needed when we swept in with the morning, and on this I agreed with him wholeheartedly.

'Well, Ragwasi, old friend,' I said, as we put our heads on our saddles, eyes weary, red-rimmed and full of grit. 'Tomorrow we will see the Boer humbled and his cities taken. How does that make you feel?'

Ragwasi looked more tired than I had ever seen him before. It was as though each movement he made was weighed down with stiffness and fatigue and I could see that he was limping on blistered feet. He tried to stretch but could not and his head went back in a painful grimace as he tried to shift the gnarled up knots in his shoulders and neck, but I could also see that this question had been on his mind throughout the pain of our odyssey.

'For all my life the Boers have brought war to me and my kin,' he began, his voice cracked and tired and full of dust. 'And though I cannot be sorry that they will now experience what we Tswana, Basuto, Xhosa and Zulu have experienced in these past years, still I cannot find pleasure in their defeat.'

I had not expected this answer but it was clear to me that something had been at work in his mind, digging away, scratching like a honey badger at a termite mound until it had broken open some new wisdom. He tried to stretch again, then dug his fist into the small of his back and screwed it around, massaging and kneading at his iron-bound muscles.

'I am told old for revenge uPelly,' he said, his voice as dry as the veldt we had crossed. I handed him my canteen and he took a sparing sip before continuing. 'And anyway, it will not be Kruger who will suffer but the children of Kruger and who are they if they are not Africans too, now?'

He took another small sip and handed the canteen back.

'They have been born and have been brought up to be men in Africa and there are many among them like you too, uPelly, who have come from other places and become Africans too. We must stop all this fighting and moving people on from one place to another.' He paused and stretched out his fingers. 'But I do not know how this can come about.'

'Does anyone?' I replied and then, seizing the moment, I decided to open my heart about the things about Willoughby that were worrying me.

'Ragwasi,' I began, but he cut me off before I could say more.

'But I will be happy to take Kruger's gold from him though,' he said, with a wink that had more tiredness than humour in it. 'That will make up something of what we have lost. *That* will make me *very* happy.'

*

We were up and in the saddle well before dawn heading for *iGoli*, Johannesburg, City of Gold, and as we cantered forward through the crisp air of the highveldt night, my mind was full of excitement and anxiety in equal measure; excitement, because a man cannot but feel excitement when venturing out into danger with a gun on his back and in the company of hard and capable men; anxiety, because Stamford John Holzhausen was somewhere off to my left and though I had not been able to talk to him or approach him in any way over the past days because of the extreme activity and what I was convinced was a reluctance in him to be approached, I was now convinced in my bones rather than my mind that he was indeed my nephew and I did not want to see him get a bullet; anxiety too, because I feared that Ragwasi had given in to avarice and that this failing would lead us into some terrible mischief or fate because no-one can steal gold without expecting a whole hat shop full of trouble in return. So when Mike Rimington peeled off into the yellow hills of spoil to take control of the mines which lay to the south of the city proper, I watched for Stamford, intending to give him a wave of encouragement, however seemingly anonymous. I watched in vain though; he wasn't there, and for a moment I thought that perhaps his horse had gone lame or some other misfortune had befallen him and Rimington had been obliged to leave him behind. In this I was mistaken too because then I saw him at the back of our Troop and I caught sight of the merest nod of acknowledgement between him and Major Willoughby and my anxiety increased, but for different reasons now. There was a connection between Stamford and the Major, but what it was lay concealed and added another big doubt to add to all the others that were piling up around me like storm clouds in a hot veldt sky.

It was with these things in my mind that we entered the eerie remains of what had once been the flourishing, buzzing hive of Johannesburg, Tom Cole leading his Troop one way and Major Willoughby leading ours another, and saw immediately that the war had not been kind to it. What a change had come over it! Of the hundred thousand souls who had been working, striving, digging, drinking, *hoping* here a scant year ago, full forty thousand of them had left for the Cape, the coast or the home kraals of Bechuanaland, Zululand and the Transkei; the last of the British who had chosen to stay for family or business reasons or just out of destitution had been expelled a month ago; the Boers were on Kommando service or captured and being shipped off to camps on St.Helena or Ceylon; the Africans who were left were there under martial law. The city, once full of boisterous, joyous life, had become sullen, deserted, gloomy, its lovely suburban villas boarded up, the windows of its commercial quarter blank eyed and empty, while corrugated iron fences and roofs creaked and banged in the cold wind; gardens had become overgrown; grass grew on the main thoroughfares; everywhere, the streets were quiet, nervous, fearing massacre and murder by louts, black rising or the British; in one window a skeletal dog lay stretched out, abandoned by its owner but still faithful to its guard duty. One or two buildings had been burned out and there were obvious signs of break-in on many of the grocery shops and bakeries, while here and there a door swung drunkenly on its wrenched hinges; on one famous department store, a sheet of frosted plate glass hung in front of the storefront display like a picture frame cracked and broken in a fit of temper. Turning one corner into a street like a canyon, I was haunted by the shrill wail of hungry cats which cut through the silence of the new morning like a finger nail dragged down a chalkboard and then in the distance a shot, then two more rang out like pointless defiance; the city had been abandoned and the British Army would soon be in possession.

Ragwasi and I had been recruited by Major Willoughby on the strength of Ragwasi's intimate knowledge of Johannesburg – which in reality was sketchy at best – but as we trotted through the streets, I got the distinct impression that the Major already knew the layout, for he led without stopping to consult either guides or a map. Through the grid we went, from Marshall Square up Sauer Street and onto Jeppe; crossing Fraser, Simmond, Harrison and Loveday, then left up past the railway station to Krugers Park and on up to the Hillbrow and Berea districts. Each time heading North and East; at first I was bemused and a little confused by the way the city towered over me, but then after a little while I began to get my bearings and recognising a couple of familiar landmarks, I realised that contrary to my first impression, the Major was hopelessly lost.

'Major Willoughby,' I called out. 'We need to turn about, for Government House is back the other way. We can just go straight down Banket Street to take us to Commissioner Street and it is just round the corner from there.'

At first Willoughby did not respond, so I thought he was preoccupied with something and had not heard me well so I spurred my horse forward, only to find Ragwasi taking a hold of my bit and motioning me to be quiet.

'What the devil?' says I, drawing in just behind the Major. 'We must seize Government House. Those are our orders. Tom Cole told us directly.'

'Change of plan,' said Willoughby, matter-of-factly. 'We ride for Pretoria.'

'What?' I said, pulling up short.

'Pretoria is where we're heading for, Mr. Pelly,' answered the Major without stopping. 'You are welcome to come along or you may stay here and miss out on stealing the greatest treasure trove the world has ever seen. Your choice.'

I thought I had misheard. *Treasure trove? Stealing?* I was stunned speechless and my mouth opened and closed like a fish rising. All that talk about gold I had thought was just hot air. My full understanding was that we were to secure the banks and the Treasury for the Imperial government. I never for a single moment thought anything else and never did I think that Ragwasi's lusting after Kruger's millions could be anything more serious than wishful thinking or a humorous affectation, but when I saw him ride on without a rearward glance, all my fears that he had been tempted beyond his capability to resist came to the fore.

With a rush of comprehension, I realised that the thought of stealing Kruger's gold had been fed to him little by little by the Major until that thought was all he could think of; all those little errands, the private jokes had been small stepping stones to tempt him across the river and now he had stepped off the last one and would drown in its flood. Poor, stupid, greedy Ragwasi; it was written across his shoulders and I never saw a more guilty back in all my life. My heart suddenly emptied. Then, when I realised that when Ragwasi had become aware of the Major's intention he had decided to keep this knowledge to himself, it was as though I had stepped into a mine shaft elevator without the elevator cage being present and I was in free fall in the darkness. Never before had Ragwasi lied to me; oh, of course, he had told the odd stretcher or tried to fob me off with excuses, but these were little white lies that he never expected me to believe in the first place. But now this was deception pure and simple and I felt sullied by it and sad that Ragwasi would lower himself to such base dishonour.

Looking along the line of troopers now passing me and taking in their winks and sly smiles, I realised that I was the only one among them who was not in on the plan and I felt my heart sink deeper, for only Ragwasi would have known that I would be no party to theft. It was he who had advised the Major to keep me in the dark; that was plain. Only he would have known that I would warn honest Tom Cole of this treachery the moment I heard of it.

'You coming or what?' said Cunningham, riding by with a sly smile beneath obsidian eyes.

'You damned cad, Ragwasi,' I cursed under my breath. 'And after all these years.'

Now I faced a terrible choice. Should I turn about and ride like the wind for Tom Cole to warn him of this freebooting raid or should I follow on? He would be in the city somewhere, but I was not used to these streets and could easily get lost and end up running into a Mauser bullet at any time. Even if I did find him, what could be done? Willoughby would have a long head start and Tom's hands would be full securing not only his own objectives but now the ones that had not been secured by our Troop.

To say I was torn would be like saying that a rag pulled through a mile of camel thorn was torn. I had known Ragwasi almost from the time I first came to Africa. We had worked and lived and fought and trekked and hunted together for twenty five years. We were business partners; more than that, he was my Chief and he was *ma bru*, my brother, closer even; our wives and families were so tumbled up together it was hard to tell where one started and the other ended. For a moment I thought that perhaps some brain fever had come over me and this was all a terrible dream brought on by sweating malaria but I knew that I would welcome malaria if only it could change this terrible truth (*Ja;* I should be careful what I wish for). Some madness must have come over him, for we were already rich! We still had a pile of the diamonds we had found in the Namib Desert all those years ago. We had land and cattle and owned shares in shipping companies and mines and all sorts of profitable enterprises. People will say that you cannot have too much money and although this is an attractive thing for people who do not have money to think, I will tell you that when you have enough, extra is not extra at all, but a burden because it makes you the target of flatterers, robbers and false friends. Sometimes, too much money is very dangerous to have; this was why we concealed our wealth and did not do extravagant things with it; what we wanted, we had and none of our respective families who needed, went without; we needed little, for neither of us desired castles. No, something had come over him; this was not characteristic of him and it was then I decided that I must rescue him from his own foolishness. People also say that you cannot rescue a man from his chosen folly but I say that an effort must be made for an old and treasured friend.

All this went through my mind in the time it took the Troop to trot by and so when I came face to face with Stamford John Holtzhausen, I faced a further dilemma. Should I quickly warn him of the dangers he was running by attaching himself to this piratical expedition? Should I exhort him to ride for Tom Cole or Mike Rimington while I went with Ragwasi? But then, why would he believe me? I would need to call him by his given name of Edgar Smithfield to gain his attention and then what would follow from that? He might not want to be found by an uncle he had never met; he might think I had come to arrest him and bolt; he might *not* be Edgar Smithfield even; who knew *who* he was? And, of course, I remembered the nod and becks he had exchanged with Major Willoughby and knew then that he was part of this conspiracy too. No, it was pointless. All I could do, out of respect for my family, was to go along and keep an eye on the boy until I could get to know him and perhaps redeem him at some later time. So it seemed to me that my choices were made for me. I dug in my spurs and became a freebooter.

Chapter 4

iGoli

Pretoria was another day's ride ahead of us and it was lucky that we came across a stud and livery stable that still had horses because ours were just about done up. One of the bays was on the verge of going lame while two others had split hooves bound together with lengths of rein as a temporary measure that would not last much longer; most of the others looked like bags of bones and my horse was so hungry it ate the thatch straight off the stable roof. Their riders were not in much better condition either and I swear that there wasn't a man Jack among us who wasn't wishing himself at home in bed; I was so stiff that I could hardly dismount and when I landed on the sand of the yard floor, my knees almost buckled. Only Willoughby seemed unaffected and while we off-saddled and transferred our kit to our remounts, he arranged for fried bread and bacon to be cooked for us, and then haggled a pretty fair price with a nervous owner for re-mounts and supplies. The smell that filled that yard was heaven itself and when the rich aroma of fresh coffee came along with it, I thought I might now understand what paradise was all about.

I chose a big, deep-chested roan to carry me on to Pretoria because I had an inkling that we would be travelling much further than that and I wanted a horse with more stamina than potential for speed; the Australians and Newmarket boys also chose the stockier, sturdier animals, but the Natal Zulus showed less experience, I thought, in choosing more of the thoroughbred. Ragwasi wisely chose a bay cob and Willoughby necessarily went for the biggest animal in the stud, a grey that looked more like it was used to towing guns than carrying a rider. When I looked around to see what Stamford was choosing, I finally saw an opportunity to get up close to him without arousing suspicion and so went over, the old hand assisting the inexperienced new boy. As a young man might, he had chosen a tan mare that was all fire and speed but before he could get the bit between her teeth, I intervened and recommended a sturdier, though less racy beast.

'Trust me,' I said, looking closely at him. 'You will need a horse that can really travel, man. This one will only win you guineas at the races.'

'Really?' he replied. He had a very honest, sensitive face, I noticed, and his accent was definitely English but even though I looked hard, I could see no strong trace of a familial resemblance. 'I don't know these African horses, I'm afraid. More used to Criollos. Rode them in Argentina.'

'I don't know that breed,' I said, making conversation. 'Tell me about them.'

We talked horseflesh and ate that glorious bacon while I tried to get the measure of this young man. He had the family fair hair and a sprinkle of freckles visible even under the dust, sweat and grime of our journey, but he was shorter than I and more stocky and even up close I had to strain to see any real resemblance to my sister who anyway was not much of a memory to me. He seemed pleasant enough in his manner and he had an easy way of talking which was unusual in a young man; he seemed to carry himself in a confident way that suggested he was older than his eighteen years allowed and this increased my uncertainty as to whether he was an actual relative because whatever faults my family had, a lack of respect for elders was not one of them; I was always main terrified of my father. Neither could I see much in him that might tempt a Countess, but I confess that I am not a very good judge of what is appealing to such grand people, having spent very little time with the aristocracy though I have heard stories. Countesses are few and far between in Bechuanaland, I can tell you - if you discount Boitumela in a bad mood, that is; then she is perhaps as haughty as any Countess you may care to name. Anyway, by the time an hour had passed and all the arrangements for our onward ride had been made, I was still no closer to a conviction that Stamford was my sister's boy – he did have that same little mannerism of running his tongue inside his top lip though, which I had now convinced myself in my own mind that it was unmistakeably one of Hattie's traits - and as we mounted up my thoughts turned more to enduring the journey ahead; every step that horse took and every time it tugged at the bridle in a way that I found irritating from the outset reminded me that I was not eighteen any more. Still, I was grateful for the way its broad back eased the pressure on my posterior; even so, the sorest thing was my heart.

Ragwasi had *lied* and I was all at sea because of this.

We reached Pretoria with the last of the light fading over the blue Magaliesberg to the west and the wide streets, shaded by purple feathery jacarandas and wide enough to turn a full span of eighteen oxen in, as empty as those of Johannesburg. I had not been to Pretoria before and so I could not but be amazed at its magnificent architecture; the Raadsaall built to house the Boer parliament was good enough to compete with anything that London or Paris could show and the deep red sandstone of its construction now blazed like fire in the setting sun. On the opposite side of the vast Church Square stood the Palais de Justice, not quite completed but rising up from its scaffolding like a veldt Neptune, its mansard roof shining like the scales of a mermaid's tail between the towering horns of tritons while just by was a stout stone gothic church that was so English you would have been forgiven for thinking it had been lifted up from East Anglia and plonked down straight here had it not been for the corrugated iron roof. None of these fine buildings of stone and brick held any interest for Willoughby though as he threaded his way through the wreckage of abandoned wagons and mournfully lowing stray oxen, for his full attention was fixed on the fourth building dominating that square; a fine building made in the Dutch style, with ornamental gables and window garrets set high in the steep roof and a long gothic arched arcade along the front; the *Nederlandsche Bank en Credietvereeniging voor Zuid Afrika* which to you and me means the Transvaal State Bank but in that light might have been a vampire's lair.

'Very well, gentleman,' called out Willoughby, as we drew up in front of its arcades. 'This is where Kruger keeps his millions, so let's get on with our business and be away as soon as we can.'

His manner was crisp and brooked no dissent – not that anyone apart from I seemed to have any misgivings whatsoever about robbing a bank. The Natal Zulus quickly commandeered a wagon and began inspanning oxen to pull it; three other men rode off to stand guard about the square and warn of trouble or unwelcome visitors. Ragwasi and I were beckoned forward.

'Dynamite, please,' said Willoughby, eyeing up the stout wooden door and massive ornamental ironwork which stood in a stone portico firmly anchored by great quoins of solid masonry. 'We'll have to blow this.'

I looked at Willoughby and then at Ragwasi, who was still avoiding my eye, and thought that perhaps I should say something, even if it was only to register a protest at this thievery, but when Willoughby turned his eye on me I could see a gleam there that told me anything I did or said would be to no avail.

What could I do? I shrugged and handed him the dynamite.

It took him no more than a minute to arrange the charges expertly and then put a match to the fuse. There was an orange flash, a crack like lightning and a hell of a bang and the splintered door blew off its hinges and Willoughby was through it with a cry of excited triumph before the smoke had cleared. Ragwasi and I followed, with Stamford and a couple of the Australians coming closely behind as we went straight through the lobby, pushed through the counter doors and into the strong room behind, where we were confronted by the formidable six feet high battleship steel door of the biggest safe in the African continent.

Willoughby looked at it and raised his eyebrows as though this was something unexpected, then gave a perfunctory twist at the great dial standing proud of the centre of the door like the boss of some fantastic shield.

'Dynamite won't open up that old possum,' ventured one of the Australians, knowledgeably. 'That's an Old Kent Road special. Chubb's best combination lock, Major. And Chubb's best is bloody good.'

'Indeed it is,' replied Willoughby, with an equally knowledgeable wink. 'And where brute force won't suffice, one must use a certain *finesse*. What do you say to that Mr. Holtzhausen?'

'I'd say you might be right, Major,' replied Stamford, taking off his hat and coming forward to kneel at the dial. 'It looks like a six drop pawl model, but we'll soon find out, if someone would be good enough to light a candle.' From inside his pocket he pulled out a stethoscope, fitted it into his ears and then pressed it against the door and began to twirl the dial clockwise with a rapid turning motion of his hand.

Stamford was a *cracksman*? This boy was a master criminal? This possible nephew of mine knew how to crack safes? For the second time that day my stomach gave a lurch and the dizziness of shock made me reel. The penny dropped: *Stamford*; as in Stamford Raffles, the famous explorer; as in *Raffles*, the gentleman thief of fiction that Willoughby so admired. What a fool I was.

I had considered myself to be a fair judge of men and their characters but in that moment I knew that I would have to revise this grand opinion of myself. First, Ragwasi, a man that I had known for so long I had forgotten how long it was, had lied and deceived me and I had fallen for it. Then Willoughby had conned me – me! – who thought he could spot a chancer at a thousand paces. Yes, it is true that I was doubtful of his character, but I did not know why I was distrustful of him and so I could not be redeemed by such slim virtue. And now this slip of a boy who might just be family was now revealed as an expert cracksman! And I had suspected nothing more than that the boy had a guilty conscience and a police record to slip! God knew how many others I had been wrong about! Was Tom Cole a living deception too? My world was turning upside down and all that was seemed fair had turned foul. I looked around and seeing Cunningham's black eyes wondered if I was wrong about him too. No doubt he was a rogue but alongside these fellows, I was willing to regard him as an absolute paladin, a knight in shining armour!

Ragwasi caught my eye and then dropped his like a guilty man going through the scaffold trapdoor.

Willoughby sniffed.

'Sorry not to let you in on the secret, old man,' said the Major, nodding almost an apology to me. 'Operational security, what? Need to know and all that?'

'Quiet now, please. Absolute quiet,' said Stamford curtly, and then, mouth open and stethoscope in, he began to turn the dial very slowly anti-clockwise until at some stage, he nodded to himself, repeated the process and then several nods later, put his ear right up to the steel door and gently shifted the dial back and forwards, listening intently. Presently, he sat back on his heels and removing the stethoscope from his ears blew out a short breath. 'Six pawls, as I thought,' he said. 'How much time do we have?'

'Not as long as you need,' replied Willoughby.

'Very well,' said Stamford, as decisive as a doctor with a patient. 'Then I'll ask you gentlemen to wait outside while I concentrate. I will need absolute silence.'

'Good man,' said Willoughby. 'Go to it.'

'I'm staying,' I said. Not only was I amazed at this turn of events but I could not find it in myself to sit outside in the lobby with Ragwasi so close. His betrayal of me was hurtful and I could not find it in myself to hide this hurt. I found his presence distasteful, to be honest, and as I did not really know how to go about redeeming him, I felt it better to keep a little distance.

Willoughby looked at the boy for agreement. Stamford nodded and we were left alone.

'Here,' he said, handing me a notebook. 'You can write I take it?'

This did not need an answer.

'Good,' he said. 'Turn to the squared off page and write down what I tell you. Write it down *exactly*. It must be *exact*.'

It felt strange to be spoken to like this by someone so young; even stranger, that he might be my nephew; even stranger still than that was the thought that my young nephew was an expert safe-cracker. Wonders will never cease, hey? I found the page and saw that there were numbers written neatly and precisely along the top and bottom of the squared page.

'Ready?' he asked.

I nodded and he put on his stethoscope and began listening earnestly, moving the instrument around the lock as a doctor would explore a man's chest, while at the same time carefully, gingerly, turning the combination dial. From time to time, he called out a number and directed me to mark an X in a place that corresponded to two co-ordinates, rather in the same way that one would find a place on a map by reading off the grid. To my mind, it was a very slow process and although I have learned patience in my profession as a huntsmen, it seemed that a different kind of patience was required for this kind of job and I soon found my mind wandering back to those times at school as a boy when all I could think of was the stable and the football field and would always try to choose a desk by the window so I could look out of it when the Latin became more pointless than usual. Of course, this is why I am ignorant. Anyway, I found the slowness hard to bear, especially as I earned a very sharp look of rebuke each time I made to fidget, and was always taken by surprise when a number was called out and then made to feel very stupid when I had to be instructed over and over again as to where I must make the mark on that grid. I gathered that he was listening for some sound which betrayed the inner workings of the lock but I could hear nothing except the slight click whenever he moved the dial and although I tried to concentrate, I found this task to be very tedious. As I have said, I am not used to this kind of stillness and the heaviness of the atmosphere unrelieved by even a breath of wind, I found to be oppressive. Nor did I care for the cold smell of the steel, which reminded me too much of swords and bayonets and I longed for a green scent on a breeze in a sunny day.

By my reckoning, it was taking much longer than Stamford expected and this in turn caused Major Willoughby some anxiety, judging by the number of times he looked in at me with his eyebrows raised in a question. Each time, I could only shrug; this process might have been witchcraft for all I understood.

Sometime before midnight though, Stamford gave a little grunt and, declaring himself satisfied, took back the notebook and began to inspect it closely. Then, taking back the pencil, he made some calculations, wrote down a series of numbers and then read them off.

'2, 12, 16, 27, 38, 82,' he said, finally.

'You have the combination?' said Major Willoughby, appearing on the instant.

Stamford shook his head. 'I have the numbers, but I don't know which order they follow.'

'What next then?' I asked. To be truthful, it was very fascinating to see the concentration on this young man and I had a sudden wish that Ragwasi might see him at work so that I could boast about how clever my nephew was.

'Trial and error,' he replied.

'How long will that take?' said Willoughby. 'Time is rather shorter than it was when it was in short supply, old chap.'

Stamford shrugged. 'There's no telling; five minutes, four hours. Getting the numbers is the easy bit - if the numbers are correct; putting them in the right order is the hard bit.' He turned to me. 'Each time I try an unsuccessful combination, you must cross it out and then give me another. Choose as you will; it makes no difference as long as you don't waste time by repeating.'

'Quick as you can, then,' said Willougby, turning on his heel. The impatience was bleeding out of him and made my own seem trifling by comparison. As he left, I could see that he was rattling clicks off his fingers as though that might advance matters.

'Any order?' I said.

'Like I say,' replied Stamford, his hand poised over the dial. 'Just keep a record.'

'2, 12, 16, 27, 38, 82,' I said.

He raised his eyebrows in despair.

'Don't you think I would have tried that one already?'

He knew how to make his uncle feel stupid, I will say that.

'12, 16, 27, 38, 82, 2,' I said.

He spun the dial and then tried the lock but without success.

'Next,' he ordered. 'And cross that one out.'

I gave them to him in reverse order.

'There's method in your madness, I see.' He spun the dial. No go.

'Next.'

'16, 27, 38, 82, 2, 12.'

The lock spun and whirred to no avail.

'Next.'

I put the sixteen at the end and read them out again. Nothing.

'Next.'

'How many possible combinations are there?' I asked.

'About seven hundred,' replied Stamford. 'Make sure that candle doesn't go out.'

'*Ag.*'

At some time in the night, we were disturbed by a crackle of gun fire and Major Willoughby appeared a couple of minutes later with questioning arched eyebrows.

'Boers,' he mouthed. 'Towards the railway station, I think.'

I shrugged. Stamford shook his head.

'Next,' he called out, and I read out a new set of numbers.

Nil.

'More.' The candle flickered and guttered as a waft came in from outside.

No.

'Again.'

'Next.'

'This could take all night,' I said, lighting a second candle.

'No,' said Stamford, coolly. 'Three or four hours at the most. Next.'

I gave him more numbers picked at random.

Zero.

'Where did you learn to do these mathematical things?' I asked, still searching this unfamiliar face for signs of my sister Hattie.

'At Newmarket School,' he said. 'And then at a school run by Portuguese Jesuits in Buenos Aires. Next.'

'They must be very proud of you,' I said.

'Huh?' he replied, his face a picture of concentration. There wasn't a muscle in his body that wasn't fixed on getting that door open.

As the candle flickered, I read out an ever lengthening series of number sequences, rolling through them, arranging them by system and then by guesswork, until by midnight we had made more than two hundred failed attempts and it seemed that as I wrote and recorded, the numbers were simply dancing around and mocking me like sprites or tokoloshes. I thought that we would never get the right combination but Stamford was confident and never gave up; at one in the morning, I read out a stumbling list of numbers that I was sure I had already repeated at least once and Stamford span the dial, paused, then gave a wide, satisfied smile.

'Open sesame,' he said.

The door refused to move.

'Damn,' he said, scratching his nose. 'Thought I had it. Back to the drawing board, I suppose.'

'Eh?'

'I must have made a mistake,' said Stamford, running his tongue under his top lip. 'We'll have to start again from scratch. These aren't the right numbers.'

'What?' I said, in disbelief. Now I was glad that I had not invited Ragwasi to witness how clever this man pretending to be my nephew was.

'No time old boy,' said Willoughby, appearing once more. 'There's activity down towards the railway station. Boers – lots of them.'

'It's the only way,' replied Stamford, still cool. 'You can't pick, blow or drill these safes. You have to work out the combination.'

'No other way, you say?' Willoughby was impatient, but trying not to show it. 'Well, think of one, old boy. There is rather a lot at stake here, I say.'

Stamford shrugged. 'I suppose if you could get hold of the man who set the combination we could put a gun to his head?'

At first I thought Stamford was joking, but the look on his face in the candlelight told me he wasn't.

'I dare say Mr. Kruger will be long gone by now,' replied Willoughby, lighting a cheroot. 'Word is that he's set up a new HQ further north. Any other ideas?'

The preposterous image of Kruger with his big goblin nose and oyster eyes fiddling with the lock, tutting, cursing and then rooting through his waistcoat pockets in search of the piece of paper he wrote the combination of the State Bank on came in to my mind just then, and then…I remembered how my father remembered the combination to the wall safe in his study; it was a three figure number; the day of his wedding.

'No, wait, though,' I said, before thinking properly what the consequences of my words would be. 'Kruger is a man like any other and he would choose numbers that he could remember easily. If you owned this bank, what numbers would you use?'

I looked at the numbers on the notebook before me.

2, 12, 16, 27, 38, 82.

'What if the numbers are dates?' I said.

Willoughby raised his eyebrows and tilted his head.

'Dates?'

'Dates,' I said, looking at the numbers. 'People choose numbers that they can remember – like birthdays.'

'You might be right,' said Stamford, peering at the paper. 'Four of these numbers are under 31, which means they could be days, two of them are under 12, which means they could be months, and two of these numbers are over 31, which means they could refer to years. Does Kruger have any children?'

'About seventeen,' replied Willoughby. 'Try again.'

'Anything big happen to him in '38?' asked Stamford, still staring at the numbers. 'Or '81?'

A thrill of understanding ran through me: '16, 12, 38. The Day of the Vow.'

Both Willoughby and Stamford looked at me without comprehension.

'Back in 1838 when the Boers trekked away from the Cape Colony they were attacked by the Zulus at Blood River. On 16th December 1838, they made a vow that if God would save

54

them from the wrath of the Zulu, then they would keep the day holy from then on. Kruger was at that battle.'

'Jolly good,' said Willoughby, blowing out a stream of smoke from his cheroot. 'And 27, 2, 82?'

I shook my head.

'But the combination is wrong,' said Stamford. 'So one of those numbers is wrong.'

Willoughby looked at the numbers once more.

'Wrong by a lot or a little?'

Stamford pursed his lips: 'I'm good at this game,' he said, his pride a little injured but his confidence still strong. 'It's wrong by a little. But which one is wrong, I couldn't say without starting again.'

Willoughby drew in another lungful of smoke, opened his mouth, put his head back and stared at the ceiling, as though he was looking right through it, and began to think. This went on for quite a long moment, the smoke gradually gathering in his mouth like a fog and I thought he might choke if he did not blow it out soon, but then I noticed that he was drawing in air through his nose at the same time as allowing the air from his lungs out through his mouth. It is a trick that is used by Sangomas to convince the unwary that they can die, go to the spirit world and then come back and I could not but be secretly impressed at this further display of Willoughby's talent for deception. Before I had finished thinking this thought though, he suddenly expelled the smoke from his mouth like he was spitting out a genie. Then, tapping off the ash from his cheroot and talking as though he was addressing the genie hanging in the air above him, declared with a finality that was impossible to question: 'The date is 27th February '81.'

Stamford looked blank once more, but I knew the date.

'Battle of Majuba,' I said.

'My father was there with the 58th when Kruger beat us and regained independence for the Transvaal,' said Willoughby. His look was momentarily stern, but then it broke into a great, wide grin. 'Looks like I might avenge the old man. He'd like that. 27, 2, *81*: try it.'

Stamford put in the sequence 16, 12, 38, 27, 2, 81.

There was a very heavy, very satisfying *clunk* and the door swung slowly open.

'Bulls-eye,' said Willoughby.

The sound of that door opening must have been heard on the other side of the square outside because suddenly our whole troop were trying to crowd into that room.

'Wait,' commanded Willoughby, taking the candle and stepping into the room. He peered around slowly for a moment and then, most unexpectedly, a frown came across his brow. 'This isn't right,' he said.

There did not seem to me to be very much wrong. The room was a good twelve yards by six and along the length of one wall the shelves were piled high with blue banknotes in pristine paper wrappers, while on the lower shelves were rolls of silver coins wrapped in cardboard tubes, their ends open and glinting in the candle light. In the centre of the room was a large wooden crate without its lid and split down one side allowing a cascade of loose gold coins to fall out like a rupture in a dragon's hoard. There was a fortune there just in the stuff lying loose all over the floor. More striking still though, was the pile of thirty gold bars stacked up in one corner like the bricks of Croesus' palace.

'Stone the crows,' drawled Cunningham from the corner of his mouth.

'Strewth,' said his mate.

'*iGolide*,' said Dunn's Zulus in unison.

'Golly,' echoed the Newmarket boys.

'*Hau*!' exclaimed Ragwasi.

'Wait outside,' ordered Willoughby, frowning. Even with all this wealth strewn around, the room still had all the air of a bare cupboard; it was strangely cold, and smelt of stale paper, oil and iron filings. 'There's something wrong here, I tell you.'

'You think it's been booby-trapped?' asked Cunningham. There was a note of disbelief in his tone, but he stayed out of the room as directed anyway.

'Mr Pelly, come forward please,' said Willoughby, and when I obeyed – his manner was pleasant but his tone would admit of no opposition – he directed my attention first to the banknotes and then to the sheaves and sheaves of paper dockets that lay on the shelves opposite. 'Are these notes genuine?' he asked. I picked up a couple of packets, felt the embossed paper and gave an affirmative nod. 'How about *those*?' Moving across to the other side of the room I picked out a couple of dockets and glanced through them. 'Land Registry Deeds,' I said. 'Genuine, as far as I can make out.'

'Mr Holtzhausen, come forward please,' said Willoughby. Again, his manner was pleasant but his tone was very insistent. 'Please ascertain if there is another vault connected to this one. Perhaps concealed?'

Stamford came into the room rubbing his hands together for all that metal had sucked any warmth out of the room and into itself. He was puzzled, I could see, but did as he was told; he knocked on each of the three walls, three times in different places and shook his head.

'Try your stethoscope, please.'

Stamford looked even more puzzled but again did as he was told, ranging along each of the walls, both high and low.

'Sorry, Major,' he said, with a quizzical shrug. 'This is it.'

Willoughby picked up a coin from the floor, inspected it and then flipped it to me. I caught it as it span and saw the orange gold image of Kruger land face up in my palm, a small '9', stamped at the bottom.

'It's a gold pound,' I said, and then, looking around at this pirate's trove. 'And there's a lot of them.'

Willoughby shook his head, dismissively.

'We've been bilked,' he said. 'And…'

Before he could finish his sentence, Cunningham pushed his way into the room and my stomach gave that flip that it gives when I am in danger and I cursed inwardly, as I have cursed so many times in my life, that I was too stupid to see this situation coming. There really is no honour among thieves and I found that my instincts and good judgement of men had deserted me once again. I should have listened to my own warnings and realised that a man with opium eater's eyes like Cunningham's was as untrustworthy as a snake; they were plain enough now his fangs were bared.

'Major Willoughby,' said Cunningham, his service revolver in his hand and an iron-hard determination etched across his face. 'Thanks for your help in getting us here but I think it's about time that I let you into a little secret, mate. This stuff is marked down for me and my lads and so we'll just take the lot and go, if you don't mind. That's *if* you don't mind.' There was a rasp of threat in his voice now. 'But if you do….'

Willoughby's face flushed brick red with anger and for once he seemed to have lost his composure; he did not look to me to be the sort of man to give up on his prize now that he had gone to such lengths to win it. But then, neither did Cunningham and I only hoped that that gun would not be used and thought that it must be – Willoughby was a giant who could so easily pick up the bushranger and snap his neck with not so much as a small shake. I could not hope to avoid being injured in such a desperate fight because in an enclosed space between walls so thick, a bullet fired would ricochet around that room like a ball on a bagatelle table until it lodged in someone's – anyone's – body. Stamford backed into the corner and appeared to shrink. I braced myself as best I could and waited for the worst; but then Willoughby did something incredible.

'Oh, do help yourself old boy,' he said, standing back and inviting Cunningham into the room. 'In fact, why don't you bring your saddle bags and fill 'em up. Indeed, why don't you fill your boots too and ride back barefoot?'

These brave words, I took to be a bluff, and I looked to Ragwasi, now standing behind Cunningham, for help in the coming melee, but he was not looking at me at all. Rather, he was ignoring the gun, the gold and the Australian but concentrating on Willoughby and trying not to look puzzled. This, I found doubly unnerving for it seemed obvious to me that Ragwasi would read Willoughby's unconcern as a stratagem preparatory to his strike.

'Well, that's right gentlemanly of you Major,' said the Australian, politely but without a smile. 'But I'll need you to wait outside while me and the lads get the wagon loaded.'

'You are robbing us?' said Ragwasi.

'That's about the size of it, mate,' replied the Australian as his compatriot came behind Ragwasi and cocked his own revolver.

'As you wish, old chap,' said Willoughby, striding past Cunningham, Ragwasi, the second Australian and out of the vault. 'But don't expect me to help carry the loot for you, eh? Got better things to do.'

This time Ragwasi did catch my eye and for a moment I forgot his transgression towards me, stunned as I was by this strange pantomime. Willoughby's demeanour was completely at odds with what I would expect from any man, reasonable or not and I wondered what method was at work in his madness at dismissing this robbery within a robbery.

'Fair Dinkum,' said the Australian. 'But only those who help, get a share.'

'Mr. Holtzhausen, come with me please,' called Willoughby, from outside, his boots clearly audible as they marched out into the lobby of the bank. Stamford looked from me to the Australian and then, his face a picture of confusion, did as he was told.

The gun followed Stamford as he left and then swung back to point at me. Well, this was not the first time that I had been bilked or robbed; as a young rake in the gambling hells round Newmarket it had been a common enough experience and so I had learned to read a highwayman's face and recognise if it belonged to a man who was bad, mad or just dangerous to know. The bad took pleasure in cruelty and usually showed it in a crocodile smile, the mad had glittering snake's eyes, while the dangerous to know treated the whole affair as a business transaction; Cunningham, despite his eyes, I took as the latter; the mad and the bad would never have held themselves together for long enough without betraying their nature considering the conditions we had endured. This was a relief because businessmen understand that a deal is always preferable to violence; give a little, never take the lot, and the victim goes away grateful for his deliverance and disinclined to go to the law or seek revenge.

'Do you mind if I take a souvenir?' I said.

'You don't want in?'

'No thanks,' I replied.

'Here,' said the Australian, tossing a heavy roll of gold coins to me and indicating the door with his pistol. 'The Major said you were an odd one. I guess he was right.' He tossed another roll towards me and I had to catch it with both hands because it was so heavy. 'Take that for the cracksman. I presume he's family of yours?'

I caught the coins and put them in my pockets. 'Family? Why do you say that?'

'No reason,' replied Cunningham, with a shrug. 'I just thought.' He waved the pistol at my pockets. 'This buys your silence, you understand?'

I nodded. 'Give me a roll for Ragwasi too. He's coming with us.'

Another roll of coins came my way and I turned for the door, intending to give Ragwasi his consolation prize of Kruger's gold. Ragwasi had already gone though.

I touched my hat to the Australian and went out of the vault, through the lobby and out of the blown-in door into the cold night air where a mule wagon had been found to complement the ox-wagon, animals yoked up to it and the Troop were busy readying for their getaway.

'You in Pelly?' called one of the Newmarket men, going in to start clearing the vault.

'Too risky for me,' I said, raising my hat to them and giving them a smile. 'Unlike you, I've got to live in this country after the war.'

'You could live anywhere you like with a fair share,' came the reply, but I did not answer and kept walking over to the Palais de Justice, where I could see Willoughby sitting on the steps smoking a cheroot by the light of a lantern. Ragwasi and Stamford were with him, cupping their hands around their cheroots to keep off the cold, and I was relieved to see that they had thought to bring my horse as well as their own.

'Not tempted?' said Willoughby, brightly, all trace of his anger brought under control and dismissed. His face seemed to me to be as yellow as a full moon and just about as readable. Stamford's face was blank too, while Ragwasi kept still, his eyes down as though he was a little boy who had been denied pudding. Well, I could understand that look at least; he had come within touching distance of achieving a lifelong ambition to rob Kruger of his gold and then been robbed in turn before he could get his hands on it; he must have felt like Moses glimpsing the Promised Land and then being denied entry to it by a mean-spirited God.

'Major,' I said. 'You must be a very rich man and a very influential one to be able to disobey orders to go off on a treasure hunt and then act like nothing has happened when it all goes belly up.'

Willoughby laughed. 'Cunningham's a fool, old boy. He's missed the main chance.'

'Is that what you meant when you said that we've been bilked?' I answered.

'It's the oldest trick in the book,' he replied, nodding and blowing smoke in the direction of the bank. 'Mr Holtzhausen here knows it, don't you?'

Stamford pursed his lips and nodded. Although he appeared to be taking a very philosophical stance at missing out on the sort of wealth that young men are wont to dream of, I could tell he was disappointed at all his efforts going to waste.

'Well, Major,' I replied. 'It is one that I am unaware of so I would be grateful if you might enlighten me.'

Willoughby gave a short laugh, looked up at the stars that spangled across the dark heavens as though the secret of fate was written there and then proceeded, like a schoolmaster, to teach me a lesson that I seemed to have missed.

'Well I suppose you do deserve an explanation, seeing as we have been less than honest with you so far,' he said, drawing out a silver cheroot case and offering me one. I confess that I needed a smoke and so took one. 'If you wish to be successful in relieving a great house of its valuables without attracting a hue and cry, it is essential to ensure that the owner of the house remains unaware that his valuables have been lifted for as long a time as is possible. Get my drift? Good. Well, the simplest way to achieve this is to switch the jewels or whatnot with items that *look* the same but which are really copies cheap enough to deceive at first instance.'

'Are you telling me that all that metal in there is just gold painted lead.' I was aghast.

'Not at all,' replied Willoughby, holding up his cheroot like a conductor of an orchestra holds his baton for silence. 'Now, stay with me here, Pelly, for I can see your education is all ahoo in these matters. The other way to keep the Peelers off the scent is to leave the diamonds where they are and go for the cash but – and this is the trick – never steal all of it. Always leave enough behind in the chap's wallet to convince him that he might just have mislaid the rest, or spent too much of it. That way, if he does send an express for the village Bobby, the first thing he will have to do is convince Constable Jones that the money has indeed been stolen and not just been lost down the back of the sofa, handed over the at the saloon bar or diddled away at the races.'

'I'm sorry, but you have indeed lost me.' I turned to see a couple of bags being manhandled heavily onto the mule cart by the Newmarket boys. Beside them, the Natal Zulus had drawn up a second cart, this time spanned with oxen, ready for their share.

'What I'm telling you, Mr Pelly,' said Willoughby. 'Is that *that* vault has already been raided and that what is left is just enough to cause a distraction.'

'There must be a million pounds in gold there!' I protested.

'Precisely,' replied Willoughby, stabbing his cheroot at me. 'So where's the rest of it?'

'I beg your pardon?'

'Pay attention, Mr Pelly, please,' said Willoughby, mockingly insistent; but I could see that he was really very irritated under his insouciance. 'There should be *thirty millions and more at the very minimum.*'

He was right and I had forgotten how he had tempted Ragwasi with such sums.

'So now,' continued Willoughby. 'I intend to go after the real prize, and not be *distracted* by the paltry leftovers that mark the limits of the imaginations of those chaps presently under the leadership of Mr. Cunningham and simultaneously under the impression that they have robbed me of a fortune. Are you interested?'

I could barely believe my ears. Having risked a hanging for desertion, then lost a fortune to men less scrupulous than even he, Willoughby was now attempting to go double or quits on his wager against fate.

'Not on your life, Major,' I replied. 'Whoever managed to move that amount of money from a vault like that is not likely to take kindly to being relieved of it by me – or you. And that's if you can find them. And if you can outgun them.'

'Well, that is a shame because, Mr Pelly, I have the highest regard for your bushcraft and horsemanship and I will certainly have need of it.' Willoughby puffed on his cheroot a little and then, coming to some decision, changed his tack. 'A chap like you will no doubt know the rules of *vingt et un*.' I did: I had lost my money, my father's money and my reputation playing cards before being punished with exile to Africa. 'So, let me ask you – let me ask all present,' he nodded at Ragwasi and Stamford. 'You have sixteen in your hand, do you *stick* or *twist*?'

'Stick at sixteen, every time,' I replied. 'And a man who doubles up on a lost wager is a fool.'

'The safest course is always the best, some say,' said Willoughby. There was a light of amusement growing in his eyes as he said this; dangerous amusement, like a stupid boy holding on to a lit firecracker for as long as he dares. He turned to Stamford.

'*Twist*,' said Stamford, throwing his hat in the air and catching it. 'Fortune favours the brave and to hell with the consequences.'

He *was* family, I decided. He was as reckless as I had been at his age and had the mad grin to match; bad blood will out, they say.

Willoughby turned to Ragwasi. He was not a regular card player, but I had taught him the game on condition that we only played for bottle tops and beer; he eschewed even the slightest risk, which made fleecing him very easy indeed; he *always* stuck on fifteen.

'*Twist*,' said Ragwasi. My heart sank.

'Congratulations, Ragwasi! You are, as I supposed, a man of superior instincts,' said Willoughby. '*Twist*. Every day of the week. If the stakes are high enough. And *these* stakes are worth the risk, old chap. *Any* risk.'

Willoughby came closer to me and I saw in his eyes the look of the true gambler; for him, the stakes were nothing and the risk was all; it was hardly even the winning that mattered; everything was the thrill of the game, the thrill of the chase, and I could see that he was already thrumming with excitement. He was fired up, excited beyond measure, and when he lit up another cheroot the sulphurous flicker of the match on his blue-black hair was like a quicksilver shiver of gold and devilment. Oh, I had seen that gleam many times before, by gaslight and candle light, under the sun and the moon, in every gambling hell, genteel card room and bookmaker's booth of my youth. It had the sharpness of concentration in it, the wildfire of madness, the abandon of lust unleashed. It was the look of the gambler poised on the edge of the wager, the moment when the cards are about to turn, the horse about to leap at the starting pistol, the dice about to roll and the devil about to dance and Willoughby had it in Spades. He was in it for the game, for the adventure, for the sheer *risk* of it and I knew all too well that a gambler cannot be held back from the table when he believes his luck is in.

'Come on, man! Join us! For fellowship and the greatest adventure ever!'

He was persuasive, I will tell you that. In fact, his enthusiasm was as infectious as enteric fever and just as lethal and my whole being screamed *No! No! No!* But then I had to think of Stamford and my promise to Hattie; and I still owed Ragwasi at least one attempt to rescue him from his folly.

'So where is the rest of this gold now?' I asked, deflating as I gave in.

From the direction of the railway station, the piercing whistle of a steam engine split the night.

Chapter 5

Pilgrims Rest

A few years ago, I saw my first automobile. It was a 1903 Model A Ford automobile and it was a very plush and fine thing with proper chesterfield sofas to sit on, a brass horn polished brightly, a carriage that any two horses would be proud to pull and was painted that lovely colour of red that you find on pillar boxes. I was most impressed, even though it rattled a bit and kept firing off like a rifle which is a result of some problems with the paraffin or motor spirit or whatever it is that you have to put in it to make the engine run. It is not coal, at any rate, which would make more sense because we have a lot of coal up at Dundee and on the Rand, but no paraffin which we must bring from America, which seems a long way to bring anything just to make an automobile do what a horse can do much more easily.

At first, I did not think that automobile to be so good because I wondered how far it could go and what would you do if it ran out of paraffin in the middle of the Karoo desert? But then, I answered myself, there will probably be a day when there will be a store selling paraffin even in the Karoo and the riders of an automobile would plan their journeys about the country in the same way that a man on a horse does so that he does not run out of the necessary things. I was also impressed by the way people spoke of bigger and better automobiles that would be made and that they might be used not just to transport people but also goods and that would be the end of wagons and transport riding. This would be a shame, I thought, because Ragwasi and I had started out all those years ago as transport riders and it would be a shame to see an old way of life go out of fashion. Again though, I answered myself, probably the transport rider would just become the rider of the automobile wagon and probably the blacksmith and the farrier would become mechanics and sellers of paraffin.

Watching the men gather round the machine to talk about it, inspect it and for some curious reason they all kicked the tyres, I realised that the horses' days were numbered because if men can tinker with and talk about things that can go faster and further, then they will become enthusiastic about them and they will all stop being horsemen and become automobile riders which is not much of a revolution; and so although things will have changed a bit, they will really have stayed the same. This is wisdom: really, I think that the only time I hear wisdom spoken these days is if I talk to myself. Anyway, I saw that automobile in Cape Town and I was impressed because I thought it represented the future because this is an age of invention and progress.

Now I am telling you these things because whenever I think of that automobile I think of that night we robbed the bank in Pretoria for two reasons. The first reason was that Pretoria had been built for the convenience of the Boers who like to have big wagons pulled by long strings of oxen, sometimes eighteen animals at a time, and so the roads needed to be very wide in order for them to be able to turn around and go back to where they had come from in the Groot Marico or somewhere wild like that. Also, I do not think the automobile was invented when the Boers built Pretoria's wide streets because if it had been they could have squeezed more streets into the same area and made more from the rent of the shops and banks and what-have-you that would be built there and so I wonder if they were kicking themselves when the first automobile was displayed there before the war and wishing that their wallets were fatter. Certainly I think that this was why Kruger would not get into it when he was invited because he was too mean to stump up the two shillings that the showman wanted to charge people for a ride in it and was thinking of all that lost rent money. Anyway, the real point is that Pretoria had really been built looking backwards to the past rather than looking forward to the future like Johannesburg whose narrow streets were laid out in a scientific (but very confusing, if you were not used to it) and rent-friendly grid. I do not blame them for this because the past is a very comfortable place where you know what is what and where everything is, even if it has been difficult and downright dangerous at times, unlike the future which is always uncertain.

The second reason why I think about that night in Pretoria is that I cannot help thinking that my fellow Troopers would have given several bars of gold for a motor-wagon to help them move that haul because the mules they had got hold of turned out to be very forward beasts. Every time they got a big heavy bag of gold ready to heave up onto the tail gate, the mules took a step forward, braying like they were laughing, and the Troopers stumbled and dropped the load and had to pick everything up and start again, cursing. Even when one of the Newmarket men went to hold the mules' heads, he fared not much better because these were Boer mules and so did not speak English. This meant that it took the Troopers much longer to do the job than they had allowed for and much longer than that because they had no carrots to tempt the animals to behave. Now there is a lesson for life: if you are going to rob a bank, don't use mules or if you do, bring extra carrots! (I think I should stop now as Tepo has taken away my Cape Smoke and is looking a bit like a storm threatening).

*

Ja, the storm has passed. Some of the grandchildren have been at Ragwasi's mampoer and have made themselves sick. Why is that my fault? I do not know but it seems it is. Never mind. I am used to squalls and anyway, I blame the parents. They should bring up their children properly. Did not Ragwasi and I set them a good example, hey?

Ja, so there we were shivering in the cold on the steps of the Pretoria Palais de Justice and watching all that gold being loaded onto the mule cart and watching Major Willoughby smoke cheroot after cheroot as he worked out our next move, when it occurred to me that I should somehow try to get a message to Tom Cole, if only to let him know that I was not a deserter to be shot on sight, which I feared I had become. I wondered if the telegraph office would still be working but then remembered seeing all the wires off the poles as we rode up from Johannesburg and so had to abandon this idea. Leaving a note was a possibility but then I thought that the Australian leader of this gang would not take very kindly to me breaking our contract so soon and so dismissed this idea too. In the end, I came up with the idea of looking out for a Trooper who might be willing to hedge his bets against the possibility of being caught in possession of a pile of gold that the British Army would undoubtedly consider to be the rightful property of the Queen and end up dangling from the end of a rope. To this end, I took the opportunity of sidling up to one of the Newmarket men to make what I would call an *oblique* approach by scrounging some more cheroots.

'You are going to be a rich man,' I said, nodding towards the waggon. 'Any chance you can spare me a few smokes?'

He did not reply but simply cradled his rifle in his arms and looked gruff.

'Look, mate,' I said. 'I got a family back in the Bechuanaland Protectorate.'

Again, no reply; just a narrowing of his eyes, but at least he handed me a pouch of baccy.

'We're going on, as I take it you know,' I continued, talking low. 'But between you and me, I'm not sure the Major is all *there*, if you take my meaning.'

'He's fucking barking,' said the Newmarket man. 'Mad as a wasp.'

'*Ja*, so,' I said. 'Just in case I don't come out of this with a full hide, will you take a message for me?'

'Depends what it is,' he replied, fixing me with a stare.

'Just give my regards to my family and tell them that what I have done I have done for them, hey? Man to man, hey? You'll do it?'

'And how would I get this message to them?' he replied. There was no change in his expression but I knew he had taken my bait. 'If I was to agree. *If* I was to agree.'

'Just pass a note to Colonel Tom Cole,' I said and seeing him wince, continued. '*Ag* man, you can do it anonymously. I've known him for years and he will know what to do.'

'No promises.'

'You a prince,' I said, walking away satisfied. I was sure Tom Cole would hear *something* now and perhaps soon.

By the time I had returned to the steps, Major Willoughby had come to some decision about how to proceed and was now urging us to mount up and follow him in the direction of the railway station. He led, followed by Stamford and I, with Ragwasi bringing up the rear, and we quickly trotted across the Church Square to get the horses warmed up.

'It stands to reason,' said Willoughby, pointing to several parallel piles of cow dung that lay across the open space like mole hills on a bowling green. 'At first I thought the gold had been moved by ox wagon but that would be far too slow. That amount of metal would need to be shifted fast and the best way to shift anything bulky at speed and over a reasonably long distance is by rail. And that's what the thieves were doing while Stamford was fiddling with that blasted knob. That's what all the activity by the railway station was. They were loading the gold there.'

As we trotted down Paul Kruger Street towards the railway station in the silver pre-dawn light, he expounded further the theory that he had worked on through all those cheroots.

'So we need to follow the railway,' he said, brightly. 'And that means going North and Eastwards because everywhere else is in the hands of Her Imperial Majesty's armed forces. I'd even go further and hazard a guess, chaps, that whoever has stolen the pelf is going to find somewhere to stow it; a barn or conceivably a cave in some remote location and hope to keep it under his hat until the ballyhoo has died down; damned difficult that; no honour among thieves, eh? Apt to get jumpy and start making demands for a quick dividend and a disappearing act to rival the Indian Rope Trick.' He flicked a hand backwards towards the bank to emphasise his point. 'Nevertheless, if that's what they intend to do, they'll need to get transport to take it *away* from the railway to the barn, cave or whatever, and so they'll leave spoor, which shouldn't be too difficult to follow, I dare say – not with trackers like Ragwasi and Mr. Pelly here.'

He beamed a smile at me that was only just this side of manic.

'The alternative would be to make a run straight for the coast and put it aboard a ship bound for the Wide Blue Yonder; that way, any faint hearts can be paid off along the way, with the balance still intact and ready to be entered on a Bill of Lading as something inconspicuous – can't just write 'swag' on it, eh? – then loaded aboard a convenient vessel while the Customs Officers are enjoying a siesta.'

I swear, the ideas popped out of this man's head like rabbits from a warren.

'Which means Portugoosers dozing in the mid-day sun, what? Which means *Mozambique*. A ship and all the paperwork? That will take time, I dare say, and so allow an enterprising body of men like ourselves to have a damn good chance of relieving the blighters of their ill-gotten, eh? Good job we brought you along, eh, Mr Holtzhausen? Knowledge of the Portugooser lingo and all that.'

This exposition, which I have to admit made *some* sense to me at the time – provided you discounted the hanging that it was going to earn us - brought us to the railway station which though deserted, still had the smell of smoke, coal smuts and axle grease about the place. Willoughby dismounted, went inside and then came out five minutes later with a prettily coloured postcard map of the Transvaal in pale blue and yellow, complete with some flattering portraits of Kruger and his old pal General Joubert, and a basic layout of the railway network showing the northern loop that went up to Pietersburg before heading for the coast and the southern loop which went the more direct route through Middelburg to Lourenco Marques and the sea in the Portuguese colony of Mozambique.

'Perfect,' he said. 'Now, do we need anything else, gentlemen? No? Tickety-boo. Let's be off then.'

Well, if he was as mad as a wasp, at least he was good-natured in his madness; but this did not lessen my resolve to avoid the sting when it came.

*

We did not hurry on our way as there was no possibility of us outrunning a train, but instead we went along steadily and carefully for even though the cities of Pretoria and Johannesburg were about to fall, this was still a country full of Boers who might as yet be unreconciled to the reality of their defeat. As the dawn came up, we left the city behind us and let the horses take us through blue grass still wet with a silver dew and a mist that hung between the land

and the stars like albumen and which swirled in vortices as we parted it. It was going to be a bright, high day on the veldt with air as crisp and clean as champagne and linen sheets on a laundry line and despite my misgivings about this whole escapade, I could not help but feel my heart rise on such a brilliant prospect. Nor was I disappointed when the morning came full strong; it was a fine day indeed, with a view to the horizon in every direction and the sky pale blue a hands breadth above it, a few whipped cream clouds in the far distance and then, ever bluer, ever more perfect the higher it went. It was a day for Angels with a capital 'A'.

Sometime in the mid-morning, Major Willoughby signalled a halt and we took shelter under a stand of willows by a clean dam that reminded me of home. In the soft blue-green light of that dappled oasis, we off-saddled and took turns bathing in the refreshing water, sluicing off the dirt and grime of these past days' travel, enjoying the fresh air and warm sunlight on our limbs and, finally, preparing a decent meal which we need not wolf, from the provisions that we had picked up (and left payment for too: Major Willoughby was insistent on this) from the looted grocery stores in Pretoria. There was excellent coffee with sugar and bacon and tinned meat, which Willoughby complimented by making Indian chapatis from a bag of flour, baking them quickly on an old frying pan that he had picked up for the purpose. This was the first time I had eaten bread made quickly like this, for usually we would make pot-bread when out on the veldt, and I resolved to remember this for the future for pot bread usually takes hours to bake in the embers.

Once the horses were seen to and our bellies were full, we took turns to wash our small clothes and lay them out on the bushes to dry. Stamford did not seem to be used to this female domestic chore so while Ragwasi stood sentry and Willoughby took a nap, I took it upon myself to show him how to do it best.

'You must get a good lather up first,' I said, taking the shirt from him. 'And then you must rub the cloth together to remove the dirt.'

'Thanks, Uncle,' he replied, and for a moment I thought he meant it literally instead of just in the friendly, jibing way that a young man might address an old hand.

'It's nothing,' I said, winking at the joke and then handing him back the shirt. 'Now you try it.'

He rubbed the collar a little and then put more soap on it.

'You went to Newmarket School?' I asked. I was trying to be casual because I had to maintain the fiction that I did not know anything about Stamford John Holtzhausen even if he knew who I was. 'I know that place. I'm from that area myself, originally.'

He grunted a little and rubbed the shirt harder, concentrating *too* hard, I thought.

'I suppose it must have changed though,' I continued. 'It's more than twenty five years since I was at school.'

'You went to Newmarket School?' he asked.

I shook my head: 'I went to school in Sudbury. Just some fellows I used to know attended the Newmarket School.'

'It was pretty expensive,' said Stamford, holding his shirt up to the light. 'My parents had to ask my grandfather to pay the fees – until we moved out to South America at any rate.'

'You got a big family?' I asked.

'I'm the eldest of three,' he said, leaning forward to dip the shirt in the pond. 'Father is an engineer.'

'Any family still back in England?'

'An aunt and some cousins,' he replied, holding up the shirt once more. 'But I haven't seen them since we went to Argentina. My mother writes, of course.'

'*Ja*, now wring it out,' I said. 'Then rinse it again and again. You have to get all the soap out or it will chafe you. Can I ask you a *personal* question?'

'Depends what it is, Uncle,' he said, teasing.

'Where did you learn to open safes?'

'Oh, *that*,' he replied, as if being a cracksman was as ordinary as learning to lay bricks. 'I had a position with a locksmith when I left the Jesuit school in Buenos Aires – until the police took him away. He taught me the trick of listening for the sounds of the lock and then working out the numbers of the combination.'

'Was it difficult to learn how to do this thing?' I confess, I was impressed by just how cool young Stamford was. He really did not betray any sign that he knew who I was.

'It's a knack,' he replied, wringing out the shirt and scattering water like diamonds in the sun. 'Easy when you know how – if you have a head for the mathematics, that is.'

Later on, as we rode eastwards towards Middleburg in the late afternoon, I went over what he had told me of his circumstances that fitted with my family. He had one aunt; correct, but he did not mention an uncle (me). He had two younger brothers or sisters; correct, if Hattie was his mother. His father was an engineer; again correct, if Hattie was his mother. The only thing that did not fit was Stamford's attendance at the Newmarket School, because my father had been sent to that school as a boy and his experience there had made him determined never to inflict it on any of his own subsequently. That was why I was sent to school at Sudbury – not that it did me much good, admittedly. Still, my father was an unbending fellow and I found it hard to believe that he would either sanction or pay for a grandson of his to go to school there. I think he would rather have attended a penal colony than Newmarket School.

And yet, Stamford had called me *Uncle*; and this made me more certain that he knew who I was because this was a reckless thing to do for a person with a secret to keep; and I knew all about the streak of recklessness than ran through my family bloodline.

*

Middleburg wasn't much of a town and probably would never have existed if someone hadn't decided that it would be a good place to bunker coal and water for the railway. There wasn't much to see and what was there had been put there for no frivolous reason; a church, some warehouses, a station yard and a few red corrugated iron roofed stores on a board walk lining a dusty street. The grass was winter yellow here, like straw, growing in tufts on a soil that was sandy, shale and pretty much like the Karoo; in fact, it was hard to tell any difference from the railway town of Colesberg where we first met Major Willoughby, right down to the flat topped koppies away in the distance and right down to the number of armed men milling around in it - only the armed men were Boers, not British and that made a very important difference to me.

'In you go, then, Mr. Pelly,' said Willoughby, snapping shut a small brass telescope that he carried with him. 'No time like the present.'

I wrinkled up my nose at the borrowed homespun clothes I was wearing, cursed my lot at being the only plausible candidate for this reconnaissance and gathering up my courage, spurred up the horse. Willoughby was too English to pass for a Boer, Ragwasi was too black and Stamford was too young for this sort of caper.

'Just concentrate on listening and you'll find out what we want to know in a jiffy, I'm sure,' said Willoughby. 'Every person in that town will be talking about that train and nothing gets tongues wagging like the arrival of a mysterious train at a time of uncertainty. Start with the pub. Can't go wrong there.'

'You look like a Boer, uPelly,' said Ragwasi. 'You will be fine.'

I wasn't sure. The jacket and the trousers which we had taken from a deserted homestead (and paid for by leaving a single Kruger gold pound in the bedside chest) were fine and a man with a good horse, a bandolier and a rifle – Lee Enfield or Mauser didn't matter – looking tired and disheartened was not likely to be an object of much remark as we had seen many riders and small troops of riders like this in the past day or so. They were all headed in the same direction, away from the British Army. The hat, however, was not to my liking, being shapeless and in reality a little too large, so that it sat on my ears and weighed on them. This was no small thing because of course it is always the small things that give a person away; tell a big lie and no-one will believe it is a lie because it is so big; tell a small lie and people will be alerted because they are used to being lied to in a small way all the time. So the hat worried me because I did not think that a man could keep wearing a hat that irritated him by weighing on his ears for so long, which would mean to a sharp eyed observer that he had not had that hat very long; and if he had not had such an old and battered hat so very long then he must have stolen it or taken it from a dead man, or he did not belong to that hat at all, and that would be suspicious. And believe me, the Boers have sharp eyes.

So, feeling nervous but trying to look just tired enough to not need help and be left alone, I walked the horse into the town just as the sky was turning a very beautiful and striking copper and blue with the waning of the sun, when I knew that many people would be indoors cooking, and looked for a saloon. There were a few children in bare feet and dungarees playing hopscotch on the boardwalk outside a chandlery and I was very tempted to stop and watch them for in that little moment of innocence, I saw a great hope. Kids, I remembered, were not so touched by the great events of the world as we adults and so are able to live through them perhaps better than we ourselves can. They do not seem to need very much more than a regular supply of sweets, plenty of chops, a rugger ball and their mothers to tuck them in at night to be quite content. This is something that we should learn from; getting on with your neighbours, being polite, respecting each other's property and treasuring the living day seem to me to be simple and not very difficult things to do – or would be if the world was only made up of people like you and me. Unfortunately, there are people like Cecil Rhodes and Paul Kruger in it too and so we shall never have peace. This is what I was thinking when the sun began to set behind me, sending my long shadow ahead of me and making me realise that I had indeed stopped to stare and should now move on before I attracted attention to myself.

Continuing down the emptying street, threading my way through the stationary carts and the odd pedestrian, I passed a tailor's store, now empty; it had a Jewish name on it so I presume the family had packed up - or *been* packed up - and shipped off to the coast with the other foreigners; all that was left was a dummy with a tape measure round its neck, standing behind a dusty window, without a head. Underneath the stoep in front, two rats were contending for some rubbish, while a shrike kept hopping and darting down to see if it could steal the prize from under their noses. Ahead, another rider was coming up the street; he was stiff, chin on chest, and by the way he carried his left arm, I guessed he was wounded.

The temperature was dropping quickly as the sun disappeared and I realised that I was getting cold. I had lost weight these past months in the saddle and though my belt was tighter, the leanness came with the price of feeling the cold more. My thumb ached with the beginnings of arthritis, making me feel older each time it throbbed or gave a twinge, and in that moment I felt another great hope, or rather a great longing, that I would somehow come through all this war and upset and disturbance to enjoy the simple pleasures of a good fire in my own hearth with a glass of my own mampoer and damn the rest of the world. *Ja*, I knew then that I was definitely on the verge of almost becoming an old man. One day, I shall succumb to the temptation and become one.

Past a couple of side streets and then I spotted the unmistakeable spoor of a pub. There was a big stoep, with a voorkammer behind it, several horses tied up to the rail outside and the warm glow of lights and a fire clearly visible through the windows and the welcoming door. A few men were standing outside, smoking, idling and, I thought, eyeing me up with perfect suspicion, but then I remembered that this is how everybody in a small town looks at any newcomer and with the war going so badly for the Boers, suspicions and rumours of spies and traitors made everything doubly worse in this respect. I walked the horse up, nodded to the men on the stoep and dismounted.

'*Kan ek hier kos kry?*' I asked, speaking my English accented Afrikaans.

'There is food here, yes, and welcome,' replied one of the men. 'Where do you come from and what news is there of the English?'

'Johannesburg by way of Pretoria,' I replied. 'The English will be there in a day or two.'

'What Kommando are you?' asked the second man.

'Free State,' I replied, tying up the horse. 'What is left of it.'

The two men looked closely at me as if sniffing me to see if I was a spy. I took off my hat so as not to give myself away.

'You don't sound like one of the *volk*,' said one.

'I've been here since before the last war,' I replied, truculently enough, though my stomach was a-flutter. 'I paid my dues and made my loyalties clear then and I'll not answer to you, Kruger or anyone else who doubts it. I am a free man and a free citizen of the Free State.'

'*Ag*, man,' said the first man, giving way. 'Just asking. Can't be too careful, hey? No hard feelings, hey? Come inside. Welcome, friend.'

The room was busy and I could see that the rooms towards the back of the pub were busy too as the waiters bustled through bringing big plates of food, steaming hot and hot from the kitchen. There were families here, many of them from the city, devouring the food ravenously, glad to be in a farming area and away from the shortages that had plagued Johannesburg, and the conversation was loud, brisk and for a little while overwhelming. My Afrikaans was good enough but I needed to concentrate before I got my ear in and could properly understand what was going on around me. I had not long to wait before one of the waiters showed me to a small table in the corner which, with its single chair, suited me very well and I ordered whatever the kitchen could produce as long as it came with beer and was shortly rewarded with a big pile of lamb chops, a plate of mealies and a baked potato. It was good food too; solid, simple and tasty and I ate slowly and deliberately, determined to get through it all even though my nervousness had taken away my appetite, because a tired soldier who does not make the most of a good cooked meal would make himself very conspicuous indeed.

Under the thatched roof and bare beams of that pleasant house I watched and listened as families talked of all the big events that were coming, or had recently happened, in between mopping at mouths and spooning pap into babies' mouths. It was an unusual scene really because the Boers are very much a home loving people and although it is not unknown for the men to gather on a stoep together to pass the time and tell the news, it is unusual for them to bring their women and children with them. But this was war and I soon realised that these were people on the move, trying to get away from the British Army and many of them were very afraid; there was a young woman, blonde and so white she was almost translucent, pushing away a wisp of hair from her face as she held a baby on her lap; next to her was another woman, stronger, I thought, with that tawny red complexion that lionesses have and green eyes to match, and next to her a leathery old woman with a round face and rheumy eyes. They were all marked by the signs of toil; young hands grown old, knuckles like roots, forearms marked more by the yoke and milking pail than by embroidery or counterpoint; sheep's milk, not asses milk. One man in worn out boots was reading from a newspaper to those huddled around him and the story he was telling was not making anyone feel better because the newspaper was one of those penny dreadful scandal sheets that make their money by writing the very worst things that they can write and this particular edition was filled with blood curdling tales of British cruelty and barbarism. I wanted to tell him to shut up because not only was he relating a pack of lies – according to their reporter, the town of Colesberg had been raised to the ground and the whole Boer population put to the sword which accorded with no truth I was aware of – but because he was clearly upsetting those who listened to him. For a moment I wished that some Angel of Mercy would swoop down from above and silence him but then I realised that there was good reason for these anxious faces and weary brows because those older folk among them remembered the times of the trek and the battle of Blood River and also the terrible massacres of defenceless families and children that the Zulus had carried out among them.

At that moment I felt a sympathy flood though me like an infusion of hot tea in a cold night, for these people were afraid for their lives, for their families, for their missing menfolk, for their friends about the country and for their futures. Looking around I could see that many of them had already born loss and that others would bear more; the Boer prisoners were being sent to Ceylon and I knew that was not a healthy climate because many people came *from* there to recover in the gentler Cape; and there was enteric abroad, a pestilence that marched with the army. For a moment, I had a premonition that all these people were doomed to separation, exile, sickness, dispossession, impoverishment and death soon and I felt a wave of sadness engulf me, for though these people were my enemies and had brought much suffering to my people among the Tswana, they were still recognisably *people*, people who with better leaders and a little less religion could really make a claim to be among the best of God's children. Again I wished for that Angel of Mercy to come down, but this time to put a wreath of victory around the heads of the victorious generals and then bang some political heads together and get them to agree a peace that would allow all these people to go back to their farms and reflect on how to make a South Africa that everyone can fit into and make a decent living; and again I was overwhelmed by sadness for all the funerals that will need to be held, for all the sad little ceremonies above those small mounds of earth once watered by rain but now by tears, for all those widows and orphans spread across Africa and England and Australia and Canada and everywhere else that the war would touch. It made me think about how all of humanity is connected by grief if nothing else and if I had not been startled back to the reality of my immediate task by a voice on the table behind me, I am sure I would have broken down in tears there and then and been discovered and shot for the spy I was.

'Pilgrim's Rest, you say?' The language was English though the accent was Irish and the man he was talking to was Russian. They were part of the international volunteers - anarchists and Fenians and all sorts of adventurers that had come here to fight against British imperialism on the side of the Boers.

'Train carrying treasury has gone to meet with government there,' said the Russian, rolling his 'r's like rolling stock. 'Kruger will fight on from there.'

'And the war is to continue even after the damned British have taken the capital?' asked the Irishman. 'Well, I'll be damned there's hope for us all yet.'

'*Da*,' said the Russian. 'Kruger will fight Cossack kind of war. Guerrilla war.'

That was all I needed to know. The train had gone on from Middelburg and the gold aboard it had not been stolen as Willoughby assumed, but had been taken by Kruger himself and was going to finance even more war and so bring down a greater wrath on all the people sitting in this room, for I knew for certain that the Imperial government had spent too much in blood and treasure to be denied victory and that the Boers were too few to avoid defeat.

Cursing Kruger's stupidity, I finished my meal, left payment and then went out into the chill night to my horse as in a flash of conversion like St. Paul must have had on the road to Damascus, all doubts about the rightness of this robbery fled from my head. For in that moment I remembered a Latin tag that had been beaten so deep into my thick skull all those years ago at school that it was still there: *sinus bellum pecuniam est*, which means literally *money is the sinew of war* without which it can't be waged and those sinews were all piled up in the sacks that had been taken from the *Nederlandsche Bank en Credietvereeniging voor Zuid Afrika* and piled up on that train. If Willoughby had got there a few hours earlier, we might have ended the war there and then by stopping Kruger taking his money away with him but we hadn't and so there would be war and more war until all that money ran out. That was a lot of war, I can tell you. So now, it seemed to me, that if I could rob Kruger of his millions, he would not be able to continue the war and so there would be peace and no more funerals. It would also mean that I would save the Boers themselves from a terrible and certain destruction. Now *that* would be a strange twist of fate, indeed. So now, I realised, I was as committed to this enterprise as Willoughby, Stamford and Ragwasi, which was another strange twist of fate too. Honestly, I felt like I was spinning down a corkscrew.

*

Somewhat to my surprise, Willoughby was delighted by the intelligence I brought and poured me a shot from his hip flask, even before I had managed to get out of my disguise (it was itchy; I suspected fleas) and warm my bones at the camp fire.

'Why, that is absolutely marvellous!' he said, clapping a great hand on my back. 'So old Kruger has smuggled his millions up a spur of the railway to a secret lair in the mountains! I say, what jolly good luck!'

'What's lucky about it?' I asked. Some of my earlier enthusiasm had evaporated as I thought about the practicalities of relieving the Boer government of its treasure. 'Whatever's left of the Boer army will be guarding it and they will keep a very good watch over it, I can tell you.'

Willoughby flourished the map.

'Look, old boy,' he said. 'If Kruger has sent all that filthy lucre up a spur then all we have to do is blow up the rails behind him and bang goes his chance of getting it away to the coast. If, as you indicate, he wants to finance a war with it instead of enjoying a jolly comfortable retirement, he'll have to move all or part of it by ox wagon or mule cart convoy once the railway is turned into scrap iron, and that presents us with all sorts of opportunities for startling the beasts into a stampede and rounding up the cargoes.'

'You cannot stampede oxen yoked to a wagon,' said Ragwasi, rather sourly. 'Believe me, I have tried.'

He had too; it was back during the war over Stellaland and it was a spectacular failure. He had come back bruised to buggery with his arse hanging out of his breeches.

'Never mind, never mind,' continued Willoughby, wafting away the objection and raising a cloud of sparks from the fire. 'We'll come up with something. You tell me that this place 'Pilgrims Rest' is in mountainous country? Well, there must be plenty of places where we can mount a raid or lay an ambush. The key thing is to blow up that train.'

In this, I could not disagree. Pilgrims Rest is a small and not very important gold mining town which lies in a very rugged part of the Transvaal where the uplands can reach up to 7000ft and then drop away very suddenly into deep, sheer sided valleys with no way across. The ranges lie rank upon rank, the hills interlaced like fingers, with pleasant valleys full of jacaranda and bluegum and wide rolling grasslands rubbing shoulders with gritty koppies and canyons that seem to open out just under your feet without any proper warning. The bush here is very mixed too, with large stretches of thick acacia thorn that go on for miles and miles and miles and through which there are no roads to speak of and only winding animal tracks to follow. Buffalo, leopard and lion are common here, as well as the gentle giraffe and the populous springbok; up against the Mozambique border there is good hunting and good water if you know where to look for it and just to the east of Pilgrims Rest is the escarpment and I do not know of anywhere else in South Africa where the drop is so stark. It is not like going down across the Karoo, which is like descending steps. Here it just drops straight down thousands and thousands of feet to the Blyde River and it gives me a strange tingling and slightly sickening feeling to just think about the sheer state of those cliffs.

'Excellent,' said Willoughby, very satisfied after I had drawn him a little sketch map and told him what I knew of the country. 'How much dynamite have we got left?' And then, as an afterthought: 'Do you know I dare say we might even be in for a medal for a stunt like this. Thanks of Parliament, even. We'll have to hand over some of the proceeds to HM Government, I suppose. But not too much. Just enough to be convincing, eh? Be worth it to keep the Peelers off our tails, eh?'

Stamford arched his eyebrows as if considering whether to stick or twist but said nothing. Secretly, I hoped that he would agree to the plan because if he was my family then getting him out of trouble with the government would fit in well with my wishes. I also found myself borne up on Willoughby's enthusiasm. Ragwasi seemed more troubled though; he seemed not to greet this news with much welcome, but I did not feel it right to ask him what it was that was worrying him. I was still smarting from his betrayal and, to be truthful, I did want to punish him for it before I would try to forgive him. He was *ma bru* after all.

*

'It's rather like Switzerland,' said Willoughby, smiling. 'Without the mountains of course.'

We were sitting just under the brow of a high sandstone koppie on a long spine of a ridge looking at the railway line as it ran along the Sabie River down below, some way south of

Pilgrims Rest. Above the sky was a clear blue and although the air was still midwinter June fresh, there was a smell of green in it, as though spring was on its way already, which it was in reality, because up here the seasons are different than down in the Cape. The sun was bright too and it glinted off the rails like tin foil and made the water in the brook just by look exactly the same colour as the iron.

'Ever blown a train up anyone?' Willoughby asked this in the same tone that you or I might ask if a person has ever read a particular book or seen a particular show at the Musical Theatre. 'No?' He seemed surprised.

'I guess you just blow up the rails and de-rail the whole caboodle,' I ventured.

'Bit more complicated than that,' he replied. 'Though it's true that a stick of dynamite under the rails will do the trick, old boy. Problem is, of course that the driver is liable to spot that wheeze as soon as the bally bang goes off, throw out an anchor and put the engine into reverse *tout suite*. And if we just blow the rails, well, I'm sure they have spares and the means to make the necessary repairs.'

'Gallop up, climb aboard and then shoot the driver,' offered Stamford.

Willoughby sucked his teeth and raised his eyebrows in a question aimed at Ragwasi.

Ragwasi looked blank.

'Blow up the train then,' offered Stamford, once more.

'Yes,' drawled Willoughby, in a long drawn out sort of sigh like you might get from a Professor of something or other. 'Bit tricky getting the fuse timing right though if the train is moving. Plus, as I'm sure you have noticed, the blighters are sending that little trolley down to inspect the track before the engine comes down, eh? Wouldn't you? In course you would.'

'What about the guards?' said Ragwasi.

'Indeed,' said Willoughby. 'What about the guards indeed.'

We all sat for a moment on that hill pondering the unlikely probabilities of success. There were four of us, with eight sticks of dynamite and four rifles against a big Boer Kommando; we knew there was a big Boer Kommando because we had been watching that train chunter up and down the line several times a day for the past three days and it was positively bristling with guns.

'Trick is to bring the train to a halt,' said Willoughby, fiddling with his telescope, opening and closing it and then spinning it in his hand. '*Then* blow it up beyond repair, making sure to block the track so that no other engine can use the dratted thing. *And* kill the driver – I'm presuming that there is a finite supply of Boers capable of driving a train, eh? After we succeed in doing that, old Kruger will need to commit the loot to animal transport and that's when we can start to lift it.'

'What about the guards?' repeated Ragwasi.

'Indeed,' repeated Willoughby. 'What about the guards? Or indeed, the passengers.'

'Passengers?' I said. My mind's eye was suddenly full of all those people in the pub in Middelburg. 'What passengers?'

'Well, I dare say Kruger will be sending couriers and whatnot about the place,' replied Willoughby. 'And perhaps the train will be bringing them back up too.'

'We can't rule out civilians being aboard too,' I said. I did not want to be responsible for blowing up women and children.

'Hmm,' said Willoughby, looking doubtful. 'Hmm.'

That evening as the last of the light put hot fingers of rose pink across a steel blue and silver sky, the thought returned to perplex me. Blowing up a train so that Kruger could not get his millions out to pay for his war was obviously a good thing but killing innocent women and children was obviously a bad thing. I would like to be able to say that in general the men in this country of whatever nationality or colour did not take pleasure in waging war on women and children but if I was to say that, I would not be telling the whole truth. One of the big reasons why the Boers were so harsh on the black people was that the Zulus had massacred very many Boer women and children in Weenen county when Kruger was a boy. It is also the case that lots of Bushmen and Tswana and Xhosa children were taken as slaves by the Boers over a very long period of time and it is also true that the British blew up the caves in which a lot of Chief Langalibalele's people were hiding after he had revolted just at the time when I came to Africa. I would like to say that the men of this country would never *willingly* wage war on women and children and perhaps this is closer to the mark, but it shames me to say that this is as far as I would go because sometimes terrible things are necessary for the greater good. For when I thought about this agonising problem, I began to weigh up if I would be justified in killing *some* women and children, if I could save very many more from the death and misery that a guerrilla war would bring. Also, I had to wonder if the life of a woman was worth more than the life of a man or if the life of a child outweighed them both and my mind went round and round trying to square all these circles. I am not a philosopher or a priest, so I do not know if what I decided was right or wrong in the strictest of moral terms but in the end all I could think was that it was better to risk killing some women and children if it meant saving lots of others, but also that we must do everything we could to make the risk smaller. Whether this makes me a good man or a bad man, I do not know but what I do know is that being at war is not the same as being at peace and somehow the rules are different but it is difficult to know what those rules are because things happen in a war that the people who make the rules up have never had to experience or even think of. In the end, you must just do what you can in the best way that you can and hope that you can live with your conscience afterwards. *Ag* man, the things a war turns a man into.

'We must find a culvert or some such place,' said Willoughby, sipping coffee and allowing tendrils of smoke to drift upwards from his nostrils. Despite the days spent in the sun and saddle, his complexion was still yellowish, a little like cheese or a harvest moon and I wondered if he might have some oriental blood in him. 'Then allow the inspection trolley to pass before someone nips out of the bush and waits for the train to come along.'

'But the fuse timing…' interrupted Stamford.

'Yes, I have been pondering on that and I do believe I have a solution,' replied Willoughby, sounding like a professor once more. 'It would seem to me that whether we blow the train or the culvert, the material result will be the same, so therefore – following me? – we might plant the dynamite on a tolerably short fuse which will either – one - blow up the culvert and send the train into the ditch –two - blow up the train *and* the culvert, thus achieving the same result, *or…*' He held up his finger as though about to explain a difficult equation to an eager student. 'Three - bring the train to a halt just short. Whereupon, some intrepid soul leaps aboard, shoots the engineer, takes the brakes off and sends the train into the ditch and our noble aim is achieved. *QED.*'

'What about the guards?' said Ragwasi.

'Thought about those chaps too,' said Willoughby, in a tone that carried iron rails in it. 'You and I will keep them busy by pouring magazine after magazine into what is likely to be a very confused scene, what with all the drama and the steam.'

We pondered this idea, all four staring into the embers of the fire and seeing the firebox of the engine reflected in them.

'Who will lay the dynamite?' asked Stamford, finally. I could see he had taken note that it would not be Ragwasi or Willoughby.

'Well,' replied Willoughby, with a little tick in his cheek. 'Given that the calculations required to establish a practical bracket in which the firecracker can to do its worst, I rather thought that you would be the ideal candidate for the job.'

The fire gave a little flare and I could see by the orange light that Stamford was excited by the prospect.

'Jolly good show,' said Willoughby, approvingly. He too had seen the eager look on Stamford's face. 'Light the fuse and stand well back. Actually you should make yourself useful by coming back to join Ragwasi and myself. It won't be long before we'll be beating a retreat, I dare say.'

'And my part?' I asked.

'Your job is to be the intrepid soul who leaps aboard and makes sure the engineer puts the train into the ditch even if he manages to stop the engine in time.'

'I don't know how to drive a train,' I pointed out. Inexplicably, my mouth had suddenly gone dry.

'You don't have to,' replied Willoughby. 'On the off chance that Stamford does get his sums wrong and the engine pulls up short, you just climb up on the foot plate, stick a gun in the engineer's midrift and get him to pull up the anchor, or whatever the devil it is they do.'

'Then I'll be on a train about to run off the rails,' I said. 'And likely to explode when it does.'

'Then jump off.'

'Then the engineer will put the brakes on again.'

'Then kill the engineer *after* he has taken the brakes off and *before* you jump off.'

He had worked it all out, I could see.

*

The spot we chose was a little further northwards where the railway came around a long, slow, forested bend and crossed a wide shallow stream by way of a series of brick pillars at head height that were more substantial than a culvert but would probably not qualify in a railwayman's eyes as a viaduct. There was plenty of bush to hide in, long grass by the stream, a feathery line of acacias mixed in with some evergreen bluegums to provide a good position for the covering rifles and a convenient hollow to the west where the horses could be concealed. There was also a good track along a spur, through a concealed hanging valley and off into thicker bush beyond which we reconnoitred as a more than viable escape route before pronouncing ourselves happy with the plan. The date was set; on the morrow, we would wait for the train that tended to come through in the afternoon and then attack it.

I went to sleep that night in no good temper because if we were to succeed and make good our escape we needed to be able to depend on each absolutely and in our little band, trust was not exactly present in abundance. I did not trust Willoughby's gambling instinct, Ragwasi had lied to me about getting mixed up with the Major in the first place and Stamford was quite likely to be an imposter. What they thought of me was anyone's guess too so I was not in the best of tempers when I rolled myself into my blanket, not much improved by the time I awoke and damned hipped when later that day I finally took up my position with Stamford a little way from back from the brick pillars.

'What's the matter Uncle?' he said, as he unwrapped the fuse from around the dynamite. 'You look nervous.'

'I am nervous,' I replied, handing him another stick. It felt greasy and I was not happy at that thought either because when dynamite sweats it becomes unstable. 'This is not a thing that we should do lightly.'

He gave me a mischievous wink and then taking his stethoscope out from around his neck, led the way to the railway line.

'Useful things these,' he said, putting in the earpieces and then kneeling down to put the instrument on the rail. 'Bang on the money,' he said after a few moments. 'The two-thirty Express from Pilgrims Rest to Kingdom Come will be along shortly.'

In this he was correct as cocky young men always are, for within ten minutes a trolley appeared from the direction of Pilgrims Rest, being pumped along by two men in homespun and wide-brimmed hats while two others smoked pipes and cradled rifles in their arms. As they approached the stream, it slowed to a halt and while one of them stayed aboard, the other three hopped off and began inspecting the brick pillars, but only in a half-hearted way, as if they thought the whole job was a waste of time.

'Slovenly looking crew,' whispered Stamford.

In this I was tempted to agree, but at that moment a great swell of nervousness welled up in me, making my heart pound and my pulse race as that picture of dead women and children conjured itself up once more. We were hiding in a stand of elephant grass and I was reminded also of a field of corn being scythed down which was another picture in my mind's eye that I did not want to see. I looked up at the sky and saw that it was a perfect silver blue with a few billowing clouds piled up like cream cakes gliding through it. The sun was warm and the grass was green and the breeze moved the bark on the bluegums like the tresses of a golden girls' hair and I thought *what a perfect day it would be for a picnic* and then an anger came up in me once more at Kruger and his bloody millions.

'Can you tell how big the train is by listening to the rails?' I murmured. 'We must not blow up a passenger train, remember?'

'No,' he replied. 'Major Willoughby says we must just trust to luck.'

'Does he, indeed?' Once again, this piece of information had somehow managed to avoid me.

The Boers called out to each other after a quick look at the pillars of the culvert and then climbing back on the trolley, began to make their way southwards.

'Right,' said Stamford, darting forward eagerly. 'Here we go!'

Following after to the railway, I had to admire his nerve as well as his skill as I watched this confident young man alternate between chipping out bits of mortar from the brick piers, scrambling up the bank to put his stethoscope to the rails and then slipping back down to measure out the fuses according to some mathematical formula of his own invention. He seemed to have a knack for this sort of thing and I wondered how his mother would feel about him if she saw what he was up to – or how his father would feel about him blowing up things that his engineer colleagues had toiled so hard to build. I also wondered if she would be a little proud of him, like I was, even though I knew that I should perhaps be ashamed of this pride.

Meanwhile, I moved to my own position in a donga about twenty yards up the track from him and thirty yards back, hoping on hope that his calculations would prove correct and that I would be spared the necessity of becoming an assassin. It was a terrible enough thing that we were planning to do and I did not want to add to it the horror of killing a man up close; I had done it before in war and had been revolted by the necessary savagery of my actions; though it was a justified killing, I did not relish the thought of seeing the light go out of a man's eyes again. When, a little while later, I heard the sound of the approaching train I confess that I caught myself praying that Stamford would blow the train sky high and so spare me from that fate, whatever the cost. It was an ignoble thought but what with everything that had happened since riding for Pretoria, I was in a moral maze from which a college full of Greek philosophers would find it hard to escape.

It was not long until that old Puffing Billy came wheezing around the bend, blowing out steam and smoke and smuts and squealing and clanking like a cast-iron drum major in a rusty minehead band and Stamford waited until the it was in plain view before he lit his fuses. I saw him put away his stethoscope like a doctor coming to a decision, caught the spark of the match and then clearly saw the fizz and galvanising splutter of the fuse by which time I was pleased to say that he had made himself scarce by crossing beneath the brick pillars and racing through the bush to where Ragwasi and Willoughby were preparing to rake the train with gunfire. To my intense relief, I saw that there were no passenger carriages, just a black, sooty engine pulling a coal bunker and behind that an empty flatbed car and a guards van. What it was doing or where it was going, I have no idea but neither did I have much time to ponder further because the dynamite went off with a terrific *crack* just as the engine went over the first pier, tipping its whole weight sideways so that it fell into the water, demolishing the other piers as it went, scraping along with a terrible screaming groan of bared iron twisting and tearing on rock and a hiss of escaping steam. Coming on the heels of the first explosion came a second, infinitely greater, as the boiler blew sending up a billowing cloud of water vapour like a thunderhead building over the veldt during the rainy season, while a roiling wall of tumbling steam ran up the donga and spread left and right like a fog cooked up from a sorcerer's cauldron. An absolute hailstorm of screeching metal followed on the instant, stripping branches from the trees, clattering across the rocks like a stick rattled along park railings and sending up horrible whirling dust devils to add to the frothing steam. And through it all, I heard the high pitched scream of a man being cooked to death by the super-heated steam; then suddenly cut off, as though choked, and upon the instant I heard the heavy sound of wet flesh hitting the ground around me. I closed my eyes, put my hands over my head and waited for the madness to end. When it did, the partially cooked pink head of the engineer sat no more than three yards from me, grinning at me in an agonising rictus, which is a sight I wish I will never have to see again in life.

If I was relieved at not having to kill that poor man directly, I can also tell you that I wasted no time in making good my escape. Running down towards the track, I saw the wreckage of the engine, the pipes of its boiler tubes peeled up and out, shredded like flax while pieces of plate steel lay sticking out of the ground, twisted and discarded in pieces like Don Quixote's armour. There was a fire sputtering out of the smokestack, while pieces of burning coal scattered across the veldt as though a flaming meteorite shower had just struck the earth, setting light to the dry grass and starting several bush fires within the instant. The firebox itself, lay glowing and smouldering like the vomit of a dying dragon while the air was filled with the terrible smell of charred and roasting flesh. How many men had died in the explosion, I could not tell, but there was nothing left of the guards van and the flatbed carriage had disintegrated completely in a shower of splintered wood and metal.

I crossed the track, trying to keep away from the engine in case there should be more explosions and almost twisted an ankle as my foot slipped in some nameless eviscera before recovering and plunging on through the bush. Stamford was a little way in front of me and I caught up to him when he stopped to pick something out of his boot.

'Are you well?' I called, breathless from my own exertions, and for the first time saw a questioning doubt in those grey eyes.

'I…I…' he stuttered.

'Check yourself down man,' I commanded. This was a veteran's trick to discover if you have suffered a wound because sometimes a man can be so keyed up in a moment of violence that he does not notice if he has been hit. I patted myself all over to show him and he did so, but slowly as though he was stunned. Turning him around, I checked for blood but I could see none and so I simply assumed that he was overwhelmed by this introduction to the terrible, awesome violence of war.

'Did you hear…?' he said, a catch in his voice.

'Never mind that now,' I said, taking him firmly by the arm and thrusting him on ahead of me. 'We have to *trek*. That explosion will have woken every Boer in the Northern Transvaal by now.' There was a *crack* of rifle fire, followed by three or four more shots. 'That will be Willoughby taking on the trolley guards.'

'Do you think he is dead?' said Stamford. His voice was almost dreamlike and I realised that he had probably never killed anyone before and was now undergoing the awful realisation that actually killing someone is very different than talking about it or planning it. It is a bridge that once crossed disappears behind you.

'Later,' I ordered, thrusting him on. 'Later.'

We joined up with Willoughby and Ragwasi and then taking one look back at the scene of devastation, we untethered our horses and rode away. Behind us, the black engine lay upended amid a wreckage of buckled rails, shattered brickwork and broken rock, its belly torn open and glowing like a vision of hell and a pall of deathly smoke rising through the disappearing steam. Just by was the Guards van, from which two dead men hunched over the cracked window sills like broken manikins, while on the track sprawled two more. It was a terrible, sacrilegious thing that we had done in bringing war to that beautiful landscape and a no less terrible thing to have brought death to those men below; how Stamford would take it when the reality of his act had sunk in was beyond my power to fathom. Becoming a killer affected men in different ways; the bridge that he had crossed and which had then disappeared behind him would cut him off in a place that only he could go.

'Well done, men,' said Willoughby, grimly. 'Well done.'

I think of that day every time I get on a train now. And my hand always trembles when I hold it out for the collector to punch my ticket. And I cannot look him in the face because his face is always pink and partially cooked and grinning. And for this same reason I cannot eat tongue sandwiches either.

*

We lay up for a day or two in a shaded, dun hollow below a sandstone escarpment the colour of dried blood and waited for the immediate hue and cry to subside. After that we took turns – four hours on, four hours off – to spy on the crash site making sure that no proper effort was being made to repair the damage. Of course, some men came down - mining engineers probably, I thought, - walking up and down a bit with their hands in their pockets, shaking their heads and kicking at the stones, but it was as clear to them as it was to me that they did not have the equipment to clear the track and rebuild the carriageway. Willoughby added to their misery by taking a couple of pot shots at them, which I thought was risky because the Boers have some excellent trackers among them, but he was confident that we could shake them off in the event that they followed us – which they didn't. A couple of trains came up from Middelburg carrying more soldiers and quite a few women in their white bonnets, while another engine came down from Pilgrims Rest so that for a while there was something of a queue on that crowded line. In addition, there were still parties of soldiers coming up the valley on horseback, as often as not escorting wagons and carts full of families, their possessions piled high upon them. Ragwasi got down close enough to overhear one party confirming what we had already suspected; Johannesburg and Pretoria had fallen to the British Army but instead of being sensible and surrendering, Kruger had begun a guerrilla war by attacking the waterworks at Bloemfontein.

Stamford took a little while to regain his composure and I did my best to help my nephew – I could not help thinking of him as such by now – through this time by keeping him active and busy. Whenever he was tempted to stare at the horizon or into the embers of the fire, I would invent a job for him to do and so prevent him from becoming morose. I taught him to make pot bread by mixing up mealie flour with some water and a little tinned butter to make a dough and then seal it in a metal pot for it to rise. This takes quite a long time, so I was able to keep him busy checking on it, until it was time to bake it in the fire where he clucked over it like a mother hen. He seemed to know quite a lot about horses, so I asked him about these too in order to keep him talking. I was also very tempted to ask him about his identity, but I thought it would be ungentlemanly to take advantage of his shocked state to interrogate him; and to be quite honest, I was growing to like him for himself and was beginning to think that I should leave him to tell me his secrets in his own time and then only if he wished to. When it was my turn to reconnoitre the crash site, I took him with me and kept him close by; I could tell he was pained by the sight of the carnage but it was my view that a man cannot face up to the reality of his actions if he is kept from seeing their consequences.

'You have done your duty,' I reassured him. 'You need not be ashamed.'

'But I did it for the sake of the robbery,' he answered.

'You did it for many reasons,' I replied. 'For the gamble, for the adventure of it and to prove to yourself and to us that you *could* do it. In doing so, you have served your country anyway, so you can hold your head up.'

Ja, I know this is convoluted logic and perhaps not entirely the full truth, but sometimes it is necessary to say things like this to young men. The world would never run straight if everybody told the absolute truth all the time. No one could stand it even if they could work out what that absolute truth was actually.

Working out what Major Willoughby was up to was even worse though. He had given up a fortune in that bank in Pretoria because it was not a big enough fortune and instead had decided to go for broke and take all of Kruger's millions, but I could not see any way in which he could be successful now. The gold would be guarded, broken down into smaller loads and moved by animals on any number of routes. Even if we ambushed the convoys – the heavily guarded convoys – and survived the shoot out, we would only be able to secure a fraction of the gold that we could have taken before. Nor could we guess just when Kruger would be moving the gold. It was the beginning of June, the dry season in this part of the world, and so perfect for moving quickly; if Kruger intended to get his gold out then he would have until late September to move it because after that the rains would come down and turn every track into a quagmire and the horse sickness would take every animal that the rinderpest spared, so really he had plenty of time to do his planning. Did Willoughby have his own plan? Did he know something that I didn't? I had already come to the conclusion that it was the game rather than the prize that mainly drove him, but he would still want to take some reward for his pains or he was a bigger fool than all the fools of gamblers that I had come across in my life. Then one night as we sat around the fire, it came to me that Willoughby was trying that most dangerous of gambling tactics; he was going to play a weak hand as though he wanted to lose every trick and so force his opponents to make sure he won at least one of them; he was going *misere*; and the trick he was going to win was going to be the last one and the biggest trick of them all and so scoop the whole prize.

'The Army will be racing down the railway line to the coast any day now,' he said. 'They'll want to cut off Kruger from Mozambique at all costs first and then they'll come up to Pilgrims Rest to winkle him out of his lair. That means if the old *Nibelung* –' (*Ja*, I had to look that one up too. It is a greedy dwarf from a big, noisy German opera) '- wanted to get out the gold out that way, he'll have to bring his gold down here on his remaining train, cross-deck it to one on the other side of the break and then make a dash for Komatipoort on the border if he wants to shift it quickly and in bulk. It's a big gamble.'

Willoughby's eye fired up absolutely when he said the word 'gamble' as though someone had blown on an ember. I noticed with some satisfaction that there was no answering glint in Stamford's eye though. Ragwasi avoided my questioning glance, but I could see he was concentrating hard.

'You think he'll take it?' I asked.

'Well, *I* would,' replied Willoughby with a nonchalant smile. 'But I don't really have Kruger battened down in my mind as a gambler. Always thought of him as the plodding, methodical type to be honest. I think he might have made a run for it a week or so ago, but he's left it a bit on the late side now.'

'Why do you think he's going to Mozambique now? He could have gone straight for the border before.' I said.

'Good thinking, old man,' he replied, lighting a cheroot from the end of a stick. His shirt was unbuttoned and a smut had stuck to the hairs of his chest. He caught me looking and brushed it away. 'And, by the way, this pot bread is damned good.' He took another piece of Stamford's handiwork and continued, happily munching between sentences like a boy who had scrumped an apple. 'I think Kruger brought his filthy lucre up here so that it could be broken down into more manageable loads so that it could be sent off to his generals - perhaps squirrelling some away for later too.'

'Kruger is burying his gold in the mines at Pilgrims Rest?' asked Ragwasi.

'Possibly *some*,' confirmed Willoughby. 'But I think that now he will be shipping it in one or more convoys of carts or mules or whatever northwards to the Oliphants river, then eastwards along the Limpopo river, perhaps by boat.'

'That's deep bush,' I said. 'And the Limpopo is shallow at this time of year. Hardly ankle deep in some places.'

'I would count those things as advantages, if I knew the country,' answered Willoughby. 'Makes it easier to evade the pursuit. Added to which, the Limpopo comes out at Xai Xai rather than Lorenco Marques. That's a smaller port and less likely to attract the attentions of Customs. With the British Army drawing a noose around him, I should think that he would want most of his gold overseas and the very last thing he would want would be to see the loot seized by the Portugoosers.'

I pondered this for a moment for there was a lot to think about. All taken, though, it made good sense and I could see that Ragwasi was nodding in agreement too. There was no doubt that Major Willoughby had more ability to think clearly, weigh up the different factors and calculate the odds than in anyone I ever met before, saving Cecil Rhodes. He had an optimism about him too, which I suppose all gamblers must have if they are to believe they can beat the odds and become rich faster than ordinary folk, but this optimism took the form of taking contrary information and turning it into something useful somehow. I never had the impression that he believed in fate; he was more of a 'seize life by the throat' sort of chap; one who believed that whatever your circumstances, be they humble or high, you make your own luck. When I pointed out that taking a wagon over the Limpopo bush would be a very difficult thing indeed, he turned to me and said: 'Good. That means Kruger will have to use mules,' which just shows, because he was entirely right. I guessed he was educated beyond the turf too and I wondered if he had been to Cambridge, which set me wondering in turn about my old comrade Nathan Walker who was dead these fifteen years past and who had endowed a stipend for a Cambridge scholar. He was a man of many secrets too, but his secrets were different and not of his own making and so honest ones. Major Willoughby of the *Leicestershire* Willoughbys, I was not sure of; sometimes it seemed to me that he was wearing someone else's personality.

'So the plan is to go north and steal the gold when it is on the Limpopo?' I said.

'Or before,' said Willoughby.

*

We rode north, through a better Eden, drinking in the clean, sweet breezes that have travelled a hundred miles and have picked up only the scent of grass and clean earth and the heady smell of animals. Here the game was plentiful and drifts of springbok nibbled at the young shoots of the grass that is perpetually renewed by a mild climate and good rain. By the streams that fed the Sabie, Blyde and Oliphants Rivers, troops of zebra came down to drink, reflecting blue and silver against their black and buff stripes while warthog trotted here and there, busily going about their business like hurrying clerks among the stalking, bespectacled secretary birds, their tails held straight up importantly and followed by a squealing rambunctious scrabble of little porkers behind them. Ragwasi shot one and we absolutely feasted that night on the wonderful smoky flavour of the best pork the world can provide; Stamford needed some persuading to begin with, but then ate more than even Ragwasi. He was a very hungry young man and we had been eating rations for too long; I was on the last hole on my belt and like the rest of us, Ragwasi was looking like a scarecrow, an impression not helped by the wait-a-bit thorns that plucked at our clothing and tore long rents in them. There were hippos there too, their rumps looking like great, smooth, muddy, gleaming rocks in the water as they grunted and splashed and made their tails flicker very quickly to spread their dung. We considered shooting one for meat too, because there is good eating on a hippo but we decided against it for eating a whole hippo is a task that should not be attempted by only four men and we did not have time to make biltong either.

The presence of hippos also meant that we had to camp a good way away from the river and away from the tracks that they make too, for a hippo will come out of the water to graze on the land at night and only returns to the water to sleep through the day. It is never a good idea to get between a hippo and water as they are aggressive and surprisingly fast and light on their feet, like a fat eunuch in a wrestling match. Their jaws can snap a man in two as easily as you can break a biscuit. And, of course, where there are hippos, there are crocodiles. This is a bad thing because Ragwasi can never resist a crocodile and at the very mention of the word, he will start to slaver about new boots; his wallet is made from crocodile skin and is his most precious possession and rarely seen in public. You can eat the tail of a crocodile too, but it is not to my taste, I have to admit; it does not taste as bad as lion, which tastes like a tomcat has sprayed in your house, but it is the thought of its horrible grinning eye that puts me off a crocodile. I prefer to stick to chicken or good honest warthog.

However, it was not a hippo or a crocodile that paid us a visit that night, I can tell you. Nor was it the lioness that gave us the problem – Ragwasi chased her off with a burning branch from the fire with no hard feelings on either side. No; we had camped under a big, grey barked tree with a spreading crown, like an oak, that stood in a wide clearing and had hobbled and tethered the horses to a picket line. This open space we hoped would give us warning if a leopard or a lion drawn to us by the presence of the horses approached for we had no intention whatsoever of losing our precious mounts; a good decision, as it turned out. What was not such a good decision was allowing Stamford an extra chug on the last of the Cape Smoke flask and then accepting his offer to do the first watch while we rolled ourselves into our blankets. It was still cold late at night, though the evenings were pleasantly warm, and I suppose I should not be too harsh on him for consoling himself with one or two extra chugs while the last snaps of the embers flew up into the darkness; it was another reason for me thinking that he and I were related because a love of the bottle, moderately indulged (of course), is one of my peccadilloes and clearly one of his. I was tired and no sooner had I knotted my hands behind my head to look up at the clear sky and the river of stars flowing across it than I was deep, deeply asleep.

I came to with a start. There was a snuffling sound about me and although it first occurred to me that it might be Ragwasi snoring, I knew on the instant that it was not and I froze. It was as though some giant with a terrible head cold was standing by me, bubbling snot through his huge nose and rattling the phlegm in his throat. A moment later, I caught the strong smell of dung and animal sweat and opened one eye to see what was about me. I could see nothing at first; the stars were clear, blazing like fine white phosphorescence in a blue night so deep I might have dived into it and swam all the way to the Milky Way. Then something, an arm I thought, swung across my view, blotting out the stars with a broad sweep and then turned, twisted and coiled like a monstrous snake around one of the branches of the tree and shook it and I felt the patter of small fruit falling around me. The giant snuffled again and then, as I opened my other eye and turned a little, I saw a great gnarled trunk of a tree right by my head; only it was not a tree because there is no tree that I am aware of that has toe nails and those toe nails were glowing like crusty old pearls, nicked and marled with sand and lined with age and experience. Looking past that gnarled old foot, I saw another and then as my eyes adjusted, I saw a massive head above me swinging in the darkness and down came another shower of berries about me. It was then that I realised that what was blotting out the stars and snuffling like an ogre was really a big matriarch and when I listened harder, I knew that she was not alone.

She was quiet though, and I thought content, and so in that state I resolved to leave her. The very last thing I wanted to do was startle her, for that foot, that ever so delicate foot which creaked and swayed like a ponderous old barge rocking at anchor on a mud bank, that foot need only move a little way and it would crack my head like an egg. Indeed, though I was tense I was also relaxed for I was sure that she knew I was there beneath her feet and had no intention of disturbing me. She was so quiet that she had tip-toed up and into our camp without alarming the horses and had actually stepped over Ragwasi and Major Willoughby to come under the tree. My greatest fear was that something would startle them awake and though Ragwasi was experienced enough *not* to do anything alarming even on being startled, I was not sure that Stamford or Willoughby would have the good sense to lay still and silent.

The great elephant snuffled again, rattled the tree ever so gently and then, as the yellow fruit pattered around me again, I felt her trunk come down and saw how gently she picked up the berries with her nose; one, two, three at a time, and swept them up into her mouth as delicately as a man might eat peanuts in a bar. I could have kicked myself; I had thought the tree was a fig or a jackalberry when he had made our camp but in this I was very wrong for this was a marula tree and its fruit is the thing an elephant desires more than anything else in the world. How could I have been so stupid? *No-one* camps under a marula tree unless they are so very fond of elephants that they wish to tickle their tummies and this is not something that I would ever recommend that a person should try. I closed my eyes and prayed that she would soon eat her fill and move on.

This was not a prayer that was immediately answered for as soon as I had mentally called out for my guardian angel, I felt something wet and strong begin to lift up the blanket around my feet. Thereafter, a searching little hand came up between my boots and travelled along and up my trousers, sniffing and snuffling until it had reached my knees. I moved my head a fraction to see what this new thing was and saw the shape of a calf's head, its skin smooth and covered with hair like an old man's stubble, all outsize ears and curiosity, its trunk buried between my boots and wriggling about like a hose pipe. My belly was already full of butterflies, but this now made me want to giggle because I will tell you that little trunk was causing me no small disturbance in the tickling department; I pushed a hand down inside my blanket to try to keep it coming any further northwards and wondered if I should give it a little slap. Oh My Lord! It reminded me of Tepo when she was in a frisky mood although I do not think that she would be flattered by this comparison. What to do?

At that moment, Ragwasi did a fart. It was a big fart, a real postern blast and that little elephant's ears went right back and started flapping and so of course this gave me a good idea. I farted too, quite a big one, but not as big as Ragwasi's – no-one can do farts as big as Ragwasi – and I swear that little fellow's trunk froze and then shot out of my blankets like the bolt being pulled back on a rifle. On the face of that poor little chap was an expression of such amazement that I really wondered what he would do next. What he did do was sneeze and cover me in elephant snot, which I suppose was his way of paying me out. What his mother did was worse though. Her trunk came down quickly and felt for the calf, ran over its head and back, caressing it and then caught the smell of fart, then it wriggled, opening and closing almost like a hand, then sensing that something was not quite right, withdrew, disappearing upward into the shadow of the great matriarch. A moment later and she let out such a bellow that it was like the Last Trump and then, with a sound like a carpet being shook out from a balcony, let out a trump of her own.

Everything from that moment was chaos. Ragwasi leaped up. Major Willoughby came to with a hell of shout and fired a pistol into the darkness, which missed the elephants fortunately, because there is one thing worse than having a startled elephant standing in your camping place and that is having a wounded, startled elephant standing in your camping place. Stamford sat bolt upright in his blankets and let out a shriek, which I cannot blame him for shrieking because later he told me he thought the Devil had come for him in the darkness; *ja*, his conscience was guilty alright. The horses went crazy too and for one wild moment everything was upside down and back to front and all over the place too. When Willoughby fired a second time, I saw by the split second light of the flash that the matriarch was now up on her hind legs and it went right through my mind that Kruger's millions could all go hang if that big old girl would just refrain from bringing those massive feet down upon me. A third shot, and she spun around in a sort of slow motion, like a big battleship breaking away from her moorings and was away, making the veldt tremble and splitting the sky with her furious cries and leaving me frozen in a sort of ecstatic paralysis. Willoughby fired one more time into the air and I saw by that last crack that the calf was trumpeting along with Mama into the veldt and I was glad that both they and we had come away from this situation without a mutual disaster.

'What in God's name was that?' said Stamford, his voice incredulous as the silence returned to the night.

'That was what comes from sleeping under a marula tree,' I replied, in a voice that seemed to be coming from someone other than myself. 'Elephants. A mother and a calf.

'No,' said Stamford. 'I meant the smell.'

'That would be Ragwasi,' I replied.

*

We came across our prey the next day after we had left the sweet pineapple savour of the marula fruit and gone into an area where the scent of honey and spice in the air rose above it and told me that there was curry bush about. Ragwasi had scouted a mule train while out and about on his own and led us through the bush towards a promontory where we could observe without ourselves being observed.

'Nothing will be easier than lifting that gold,' said Ragwasi, pointing with satisfaction. 'They have only three men to look after more than forty mules.'

Willoughby gave a broad smile in reply. 'Kruger must be *very* short of men,' he said, looking at the line of mules, heavily laden with long wooden boxes, threading along on a dusty track through the valley below. There were new leaves of bright lime colour on the trees and the branches looked fire-blackened and ash-grey by contrast but they had not thickened up enough to provide real cover.

'How many do they need?' asked Stamford, who had little experience of mules.

'One man to three mules is about right,' answered Willoughby, peering through his neat brass telescope. 'That's what we worked on in India.'

'There are still only four of us.' I warned. 'And those men will be fully aware of the importance of what they are carrying.'

'And the value,' said Willoughby, snapping shut his telescope. 'Think of the temptation they must be resisting.'

To my surprise, we took few precautions as we rode down the hill and I could only imagine that Willoughby had some plan in his mind that was so simple and obvious that it would communicate itself to us though some mesmerist's trick. My skull was too thick for it to penetrate though and as we caught up with the mule train just as it was going into a patch of acacia thorn, we were discovered and the distinctive sound of Mausers being loaded came clear over the drumming of our hooves. We drew up sharply, Willoughby with his hands in the air, controlling his horse with his knees alone.

'*Wie is jy?*' shouted the leader, a dark, thin, olive skinned man with a hook nose and highly aggressive eyes. 'Who are you? What do you want? Be on your way.'

'Steady on, old chap,' called out Willoughby, in a voice that could not have been more fully English if it had come from the Prince Edward himself. 'No need for unpleasantness, what?'

He held up his hands to show they were empty. 'Parlez?'

'*Fok jou, khakie*!' came the response. 'We are armed and will fight.'

'Yes, of course, you will,' replied Willoughby. 'And no doubt you will have noticed that my forces now surround you and are ready to open fire on my command.'

'What?' said the Boer, looking around nervously. This was news to me too. And to Ragwasi, I could see. I couldn't make out what Stamford made of this because he was ahead of me and all I could see was his broad back, but I guessed that he was wearing his best poker face probably.

'Come, come, old chap,' continued Willoughby, confidently. 'Don't tell me that a man of your experience and bush craft hasn't picked out my troopers up ahead and on that knoll to your left.'

The Boer raised his rifle to cover Willoughby, but his eyes were peering left and right into the bush and I could see his companion scanning his surroundings frantically too. From somewhere ahead, I could hear the third man cursing at a mule, which seemed to have cast its load and was now rolling on the ground. I tell you, being a muleteer is not an easy job at the best of times and these were not the best of times. Still, it did not take the Boers long to grow very nervous indeed because they could not find any spoor of a big troop of Englishmen and the news that they had been overtaken by one was very big news to them. *Ja*, this was also very big news to me because I could not see them either.

'Parlez?' repeated Willoughby.

'You're bluffing,' answered the Boer, his eyes flitting around while the muzzle of his Mauser never strayed from pointing at Willoughby. I held my breath and wished that I already had my Lee Enfield in my hands instead of it being over my shoulder; instead, I loosened the Webley in its holster as surreptitiously as I could; this Boer was no fool.

'Last chance,' said Willoughby, still nice as pie but allowing a bit of steel into the cut glass. 'Come on, old chap. Won't hurt to hear the terms, eh? What have you got to lose?'

Still, the Boer kept scanning the bush, and I could see he was listening hard for the sounds of soldiers too, but the mule up ahead made enough noise for a whole army and when his eyes flitted back to Willoughby and his grip on the stock relaxed, I knew that Willoughby had won this contest of nerves.

'Good man,' said the Major, dismounting.

At that moment, I swear a sakabula bird actually came flapping out of a tree, waving its long tail and perched on his hat for a moment.

'Come, come, Sir,' he said. 'We are brothers in arms, comrades of a sort. Though we are on opposite sides, we are both honourable men who know how to serve our countries. I honour your bravery, Sir and I have no doubt that you accord me the respect that I accord to you. But there is a time when it makes no sense to fight. You know very well that the British Army is in Johannesburg and Pretoria and the war is all over bar the shouting. Where is the gain in fighting on? Both my country and yours will be poorer for the loss of either one of us. Do we not have families of our own to look after?'

I saw the Boer blink at this and knew he was lost.

'And will our politicians make the same sacrifices? I think not.'

This hit home. There isn't a Boer alive who wouldn't put more trust in the smile of a crocodile than the words of a politician.

'Come now, Sir,' said Willoughby, all open-handed and manly. 'Let us put an end to this senseless effusion of blood. For be certain, Sir, that you are covered, outgunned and cannot win.'

Well, I could tell that the Boers were demoralised by the news of the fall of their country and it is no shame to yield to overwhelming force if you can expect reasonable treatment.

'You'll grant us our parole?' said the Boer, finally.

'My word on it,' replied Willoughby. 'As an Officer and a Gentleman.'

Well this was laying it on not just a bit thickly but by the bucket load because I doubt if Willoughby could claim to be either of those things now he was a deserter. It did the trick though. The Boer, wrinkled up his nose, let his head drop a little in resignation and then lowered his gun.

'Weapons, please,' send Willoughby, and the Boers came forward and laid their rifles down before him. I could tell they hated this and I did not blame them, but secretly I felt a feeling of vengeful happiness come over me, for it is not often that the biter is bit hard like this. Like I have said, I did not want to feel bad things towards the Boers but at the same time I could not forget all the bad and mean things that they had done to us.

Willoughby nodded when the last gun went down and Ragwasi and I went forward and quickly took control of the reins of the leading mules; the animals were arranged in two long, completely unmanageable strings and I wondered what we were going to do with them ourselves. Then Stamford opened one of the crates just to make sure that they contained what we were after and when he gave a confirmatory nod, we actually got the mules started and on the way towards the knoll as if expecting help to come from that quarter.

Just as we were on our way though, Willoughby detached the hindmost mule and handed the reins to the Boer.

'Please accept this,' he said, in a voice full of consolation. The mule he was giving them was the one that had been rolling around on its back but its load was still made up of a lot of very valuable gold. 'To cover any expenses that you might incur in making your way back to Pilgrims Rest.'

I will tell you now that the Boer's eyebrows nearly shot off his head and through his hat at that suggestion but as Willoughby was now covering him with a pistol, there was little he could do but swear under his breath because he knew then that he had been sharped.

'Don't take it so hard,' said Willoughby, spinning the pistol in his hand and grinning like a showman. 'I mean, I shan't be telling Kruger about that load, eh? And there's no reason why you should either. What you do with it is up to you. Bury it sharpish, somewhere secret though, would be my advice. Then wait for the war to end and snap up a jolly little farm somewhere out of the way, if you get my drift.'

The Boer glowered.

'Do you know why the sun never sets on the British Empire?' he said, chewing his lips bitterly, his eyes flashing like flaming coals. 'Because God would never trust you *bladdy* people in the dark.'

*

This was only the first of our robberies and the four we did in the next five days followed a similar pattern of picking up the spoor by waiting on a high point, quickly observing the number of mules and guards, a sudden swoop, a big gambler's bluff, followed by the corruption of the guards so that they would not return to Pilgrims Rest and raise the alarm. It was so simple, Willoughby hardly needed to issue orders and the hardest part of it was keeping a straight face when he told one outrageous lie after another; the only refinement on the plan was to send Stamford off to a flank or knoll and have him drop a cup or a magazine at a given time, making the sort of military noise that would earn a young soldier a cuff round the ear from his Corporal, and so adding that significant little detail to give authenticity to Willoughby's charade. We did let one train go by though, because Willoughby thought that the guards were too young to be corrupted; it was his view that they would probably be full of patriotic pride and more willing to fight and die for the freedom of Kruger to eat beef and keep the Blacks down and so would be a bad bet. He also said that it would not hurt if Kruger's agents in Mozambique were able to report that the gold shipments *were* getting through. There was method in his madness, I'll readily admit. In fact, after we pulled off the third robbery, I was almost overwhelmed by his play acting genius; he should have been on the stage, I tell you.

He had also paid attention to the onward movement of the gold in a way that left me even more in awe of his ambition. We were now in possession of almost two hundred mules laden with unimaginable quantities of gold coin and thick, heavy bars and there was no possible way that we could manage a train that size between the four of us, but Willoughby had it all worked out. All along, he had been planning to move the gold out to Mozambique but when his plans had been upset by the events in Pretoria, he had simply adapted his original scheme to accommodate the new circumstances. Instead of using commandeered mule carts and wagons to shift the stuff, now he planned to recruit huge numbers of labourers from the local Maroti people; in the meantime, he farmed out the mules to each of several villages tucked away in the hollows and nooks of the land with instructions to care for the animals well in return for a promise of generous payment.

'Been here for donkey's years, the Maroti,' explained Willoughby, as though he was describing a set of tenant farmers on his estate in Leicestershire. 'They know all the routes through the bush between here and the coast. Don't like the Boers either. Been under

91

Pretoria's heel for the past ten years and don't care for Kruger one little bit. Don't care for the British government much either, come to think of it but, business is business, as they say.'

'You don't think they'll just rob us and take the gold for themselves?' asked Stamford. He was letting a string of gold coins cascade through his fingers at the time. 'There's no honour among thieves, I hear.'

'Too bally true!' agreed Willoughby. He was in a jovial mood as he had every right to be for he was now in possession, I estimated, of more than five times more gold than had been left in the Pretoria treasury. 'But then again, one must be very careful whom one robs.' He paused a moment as though making another calculation. 'And the Maroti know that a haul of this size would be very likely to bring an army down on them if they purloined it. No; they know it is better to take a cut off the sirloin than try to eat the whole cow.'

'But it *will* bring a whole army down, won't it?' I said. 'If not the Boers, then the British, hey?'

'Oh, I dare say Kruger will be busy enough dealing with the British Army for the next week or two and we'll be long gone by the time old Kitchener and Bobs Roberts decide to come looking for us,' said Willoughby.

Ragwasi had been silent for most of the past few days, making no comment on the proceedings except when it involved practical matters. 'Pass that rein,' or 'where are the matches,' or 'I'm just off to use the privy,' were just about the only words he addressed to anyone and this I found most uncharacteristic of him, for normally he would talk very much. I wondered if his conscience was troubling him or if he was worried about just where Willoughby and the gold were taking him. It had certainly been on my mind that this gold might take me all the way to the gallows if I was not hanged first for being a deserter and I am sure that the same thing was on his mind. We were different from Willoughby and Stamford in this respect; we were grown men with responsibilities; we had families and children to look after and though we had gone to war loyally, as any man who recognises his duty should, we were not born gamblers like they were. I had learned that gambling was a quick way to get nothing in return for a lot of my hard earned money and even Ragwasi's unsuccessful forays into the trading of shares were accompanied by at least a little thought about the worth of the shares he bought. What we did had consequences for people other than ourselves, but this is something that a gambler cannot afford to think about; he must just count the odds and hope that he can beat the cards. For myself, there was a growing feeling that the odds of coming out on the right side of this enormous wager against fate were growing ever more adverse by the day and that perhaps the time had come to fold and count the continued possession of a whole skin as a worthwhile profit. If it had not been for my responsibility to Stamford, I would have taken that deal too. I think Ragwasi was coming to feel this way too because something he did make me suspect that he was playing a different game to the one both Willoughby and I assumed he was playing.

My suspicions were aroused because when we took in the third lifted mule train to a dusty village at the end of a track of drifting grey sand, Ragwasi did something very odd. We had dismounted and Willoughby was as usual conducting negotiations with the headman translated into Portuguese by Stamford when I saw Ragwasi slip away towards the rear of the long column of bad tempered and braying mules. I thought nothing of it then, simply assuming that he had gone to check on some brute or other but later, when the negotiations had been concluded and we were about to leave, I did a last count of the animals and discovered that one was missing, though its load was not. About to bring this to the notice of Major Willoughby, two things then struck my eye; the first was the sight of a young Maroti man clearly unused to riding but making a brave attempt to do so, holding the reins of the missing beast high like he was on a hobby horse, bouncing along, up and down on the straw mat that protected the mule's back and I watched for a moment as he headed in a southerly direction; the second was that Ragwasi was seeing exactly the same thing that I was and not doing a thing about it. Neither did he look like he was about to alert Major Willoughby; so neither did I - even when the same thing happened again after the next successful robbery.

Chapter 6

Bourke's Luck

Some years ago I met a man called Tom Bourke who had tried to make a living as a gold prospector. He was a very miserable man because he had spent a lot of time and a lot of money digging around in a lot of places and had never once come across the thing that he most desired. All he had to show for his labours was broken fingernails and bitterness towards the prospectors who had found all that gold on the Rand and he had taken to drink as a result, which was understandable given the circumstances because he told me he had wandered all over that piece of the world panning and prospecting every day for months and never found a thing. For other prospectors, he became a bit of a legend. That is to say, they would ask where old Tom was digging and then go somewhere else to dig; or they would ask in which river he was panning and then go to another river. 'Bourke's Luck' became a bit of a saying among them – not that anyone ever said anything to his face, which got longer and longer as the years went by – and no-one who did not want a shovel around the back of the head ever mentioned Cecil Rhodes' name in his presence. After a while, people would avoid mentioning Bourke's name too, in the same way that actors have a superstition about saying the name of a certain play out loud, in case it brought them bad luck; the only time they did say his name was in a bitter or pitying sort of way; 'I wouldn't wish Bourke's Luck on him,' or 'Poor chap, he's got Bourke's Luck'. The stories of his luck spread far and wide and got taller in the telling the longer they went on; it was said that once, when he was very hungry, there had been an explosion in a soup factory but all he had with him to eat up all that free good soup that came down the street towards him was a colander and a fork; or that he had been the only person ever not to catch a fish during the sardine run off Durban when millions of them come into the shallows and almost jump into the pot of their own accord. Sometimes, people with poor taste and bad morals – gamblers, I mean - would pay him to stand next to one of their competitors, which was very cruel on both the competitors and Tom Bourke. And so poor old Tom passed into legend as a bit of a figure of fun. People did not mean him any ill will, I suppose, but equally they did not want him near them when they were prospecting. The last I heard of him, he had gone off to look for gold in Finland in the far North – just a few days before the big strike in the Klondike.

Now I am telling you this because there is a place named after old Tom Bourke just by the place where we were robbing Kruger's gold. It is a very strange sort of steep gorge in a landscape that already features many deep and precipitous scars and rents in the ground and as you look down into it, you can see the lines in the sandstone cliffs descending to the floor of the valley, all of wonderful colours of cinnamon, red rust, umber, sulphur-yellow, cream, coffee and burned toffee, laid one upon another like piles of multi-coloured paper and shot through with blue streaks like the tears of an elephant in must, and at first glance, the bottom of the canyon does look as though a herd of angry elephants has trampled big holes in a snowy bog but in this case the bog is made of solid sandstone. Then when you look again, you might imagine that it is like a big flint that has been chipped and battered by Bushmen or that the stone has actually been boiled over a great furnace so that it has bubbled and swirled and seethed before curdling and setting into fantastic sweeps and curls and pots and cauldrons. Through this gorge tumbles a cascade of white water that adds to the impression that the stone of this canyon is being cooked up into some gigantic brew; if you are a woman reading this, you might quite naturally think that it looks as though a giantess would use it for doing the laundry for in parts the water almost looks like it has been whipped up into suds. In other parts there are small sandy beaches which look like the sort of places where alluvial gold might be found – Tom Bourke thought so – but no-one has ever found even the smallest nugget here. Hence the name: *Bourke's Luck*. Well, if old Tom had been with us on the day we encountered his canyon, he just might have seen his luck turn; just as ours did.

We had come up with a smaller train of mules, heavily laden with large, hessian covered bales, that was going fast under a sky that was tall and far and peacock blue, and because the Boers guarding it were making it travel fast it took us some little time to catch it. At first Major Willoughby was puzzled at why such heavily laden animals were able to travel so quickly, but when we finally brought the muleteers to a halt and carried out our tin cup trick, he discovered that the sacks were stuffed full of pristine blue bank notes, neatly stacked, still in their wrappers. Only three of the mules were carrying gold coins and it occurred to us that their loads had been specially reduced so that they would be able to keep up with the paper money. This, I found disconcerting, for if Kruger was changing the way he was moving his money, then it was possible – indeed probable – that word had somehow got back to him. In turn, this made me think of Ragwasi's odd behaviour at letting those Maroti boys head south without interference once more, but I confess I was still too baffled to work out what was going on. The one thing that I could be certain of in all this confusion was that Ragwasi would not, *could not*, be in any kind of cahoots with Kruger and had allowed those riders to go back and tell him how and where we were stealing the Treasury of the Transvaal Republic.

Someone had though. We had ambushed the convoy as it was trotting its way along the Mapalagele River valley and Willoughby's plan was to hide it with the headman of Moramela village, who had been recommended as a very capable smuggler of cattle from Mozambique. It was as we were heading there that I first felt the hairs on the back of my neck stand up. I checked my arms and there were goose bumps there too; this was my hunter's instinct and it was never wrong. We were being followed; actually, not just *followed*, but *stalked*. I shot a glance at Ragwasi and saw him cock his head, listening hard, detaching the sounds of the bush and the breeze from the background and I knew his instincts were up too.

'Major,' I said, in a low tone. 'We must just stop for a call of nature, hey?'

'Must we indeed?' he replied, as though the suggestion was improper and then catching the look on my face, understood what I meant. 'Oh, of course. Five minutes. Loosen girths, what?'

I dismounted, handed my reins to Ragwasi and went into the bush as though to do my business but in reality to find a large flat rock on which I could put my ear. It is the oldest trick that a hunter has but still it is a good one because the sound of a horses hooves hitting the ground travels a long way through the air but even further through the ground. It was not difficult to find such a rock because the ground was quite stony in this area and once I had discounted the high pitched calls of the sunbirds and concentrated on the lower, dull pitch that a horse's hooves make, I became quite convinced that there was a troop of cavalry coming in our direction. I could not be completely certain because there was a lot of red hartebeest in this area and they travel in quite big troops too. We had also seen some giraffe in the thicker bush at the bottom of the valleys and there seemed to be no end of springbok, but there did seem to be a steady rhythm in the faint vibrations that I thought I could feel and this was important because although red hartebeest do gallop along together, they don't do it for long and these vibrations were persistent, if distant.

Well, there might have been some cavalry in the far distance, but the ones that ambushed us were a lot nearer than I had banked on. They came charging down on us from a little side valley, scattering startled birds left and right, rifles at the ready and spurs dug right in like a Newmarket race day. I counted a dozen riders at first guess, but I was back in the saddle and riding hard after the mules before I could get a proper look and I was glad that Ragwasi had had the presence of mind to let loose two shots in close succession to cool their enthusiasm a bit and buy us a bit of distance. Major Willoughby was away in front yelling for us to catch the damn mules which had bolted after the first panic had sent a klipspringer flying right under the legs of the lead mule. And mules being mules, they all bolted like crazy, blindly careering off down the valley and braying out mocking laughter at us as though they were in on a drunken practical joke. What made things worse was that Stamford had taken the Major's instruction to 'Loosen girths' literally rather than in the euphemistic way he meant it and so the loads on the mules' backs were already going awry, this way and that way and under the belly and everywhere; within a hundred yards the first of the hessian bales had caught on a camel thorn and the tear allowed the notes to start spilling out; another ten yards and they were fluttering out like pigeons from a loft and pheasants before the beaters; another twenty and even the most hopeless of hunters could follow the trail that was spewing out through the bush. Honestly, I have not seen so much confetti floating free in the countryside since I was on paper chase duty at my old school. And through all this came the *zeep zeep* of bullets cutting through the bush and snapping off twigs and branches.

What a hell of a ride that was! The mules were crashing through the bush, Willoughby was shouting like a maniac, all the time trying to head off the leading mule, while Stamford had his head down, hand on hat and his spurs in. Ahead of us was a clearing and then a fine sward of grass beyond that and as the mules careered towards it, I knew that we were in trouble because the only thing protecting us from those Mauser bullets was the thickness of the bush and the difficulty for our pursuers of getting in a decent shot. Once we were in the clear, they would simply dismount and pick us off like ducks in a little fairground shooting gallery; I could almost feel the bead settling between my shoulder blades and so made a little jink to the right which was fortunate because at that very moment a bullet went past my ear so close that I felt the wind of its flight. A moment later, I heard Ragwasi, riding hard on my heels, take a little thump and give a little grunt and I knew that he had been hit. I reined in in case he lost his seat, but he just shot past me, a grim set to his mouth and I spurred up to follow.

As we burst out of the bush, a couple of white cranes clattered up and set out in a crazy flutter straight ahead and up over the leading mules and then dived down, as though going to earth but it was with a thrill of horror that I realised that this was not what they were doing at all. Rather, they were diving head first into a canyon that lay straight ahead and which now, with only half a furlong to go, suddenly opened up like the crack of doom. I swear, that gash in the land looked like the evil-toothed smile of a big croc I once shot and the thought of disappearing down its throat to a battering ruin below made the blood drain from my face. Willoughby had seen the danger too and was hallooing like a madman, beating his horse with his hat in a last ditch attempt to turn those stupid mules from certain death. Stamford had his head up now and I could see him struggling to control the terrified animal beneath him and then…the first mule went over the lip of the gorge, head first, straight down. The second followed. The third tried to stop but being lashed to the second went over likewise, while the fourth – also lashed to the third but on a longer lead – tried to dig its heels in but too late and was dragged over. The rest broke right and left and were saved but only at the cost of their loads; the boxes came off, cracked on the lip of the gorge and then plunged over, splintering as they hit the jagged rocks below and spilling thousands of gold coins into the pools and riffles below. Tom Bourke's Luck had finally broken; now there *was* gold in the river. Well, almost; the only gold that he was ever likely to see was now being washed downstream at a rate of knots into the Blyde River beyond.

Looking left and right now, I realised to my horror that we were trapped. The arms of the canyon swept back in a semi-circle behind us and to turn would mean galloping straight into those waiting Mausers. My head snapped this way and that as I tried desperately to seek a way out but another bullet whizzed past, this time nicking my horse's ear and making it rear up.

'uPelly,' said Ragwasi through gritted teeth, as I drew up to him. He was hit but I could not see where or how badly. 'Look!'

It was then that I saw Willoughby's proposed solution to the problem of our escape. He was whipping up his horse into a paroxysm of excitement, just like a jockey ahead by a nose against the rails and going into the last fence, and setting it to jump the gorge – all six yards of it. The horse responded by going all out for it like some monstrous great hare with the hounds of hell after it and as Willoughby took it to the lip of the canyon, it gave out a great whinny and jumped.

'He'll never make it!' I called, just as, to my equal horror, I saw Stamford punch his horse to regain control and then launch it towards that terrible edge.

Willoughby rode heavy. He was a big man and the horses he chose were as big as he could get them and so more of the cob than the racehorse, but that big grey did not let him down that day, I am pleased to say. It sailed through the air like Pegasus, head down and forelegs stretching for the nether edge, the Major sitting well forward and then, as its hooves touched the turf on the other side and thumped down in safety, it tossed its head in triumph as though it had carried Bellerophon himself into battle. A moment later and Stamford was also airborne, reins in one hand, hat in the other and leaning back like a rodeo rider as his horse went over the gorge as easy as kiss my hand.

'Let us hope it is possible to cross a river without getting wet,' said Ragwasi.

'Let us hope,' I replied, and we dug our spurs in together.

I have never been especially good at jumping but the one good lesson that I learned when foxhunting was that 'green and green mean black and blue; at least one of you should have a bit of a clue', which means that if you are not experienced at jumping then you should either let the horse take the lead or not attempt to jump at all. So, on that day, I gave the horse its head, let it stretch out and lift off and, keeping a hand in its mane, stood forward and let my weight go down into my heels. Looking down, I saw in that split second a terrible vision of what would happen if the horse did not make it, for the wreckage of the mules broken on the rocks below or swirling in what looked to me like a whirlpool was clearly visible, and then...with a thump and a heartbeat of terror, we were over, Ragwasi touching down almost at the same instant and I could breathe again.

'I say!' called out Willoughby, his big face full and flushed with exhilaration. 'If it weren't for those damn Boers, I might just be tempted to give that another go!'

'Be my guest,' I replied, experiencing a great big thrill of relief myself. My heart was pounding, my breath was coming in great gasps and I was so full of the joy of living that in other circumstances, I might have been tempted to agree with him, but Ragwasi had landed with a heavy grunt of pain and I knew that he must soon be treated for his wound.

'Perhaps another time,' Willoughby replied, with a devil-may-care grin. 'What about it, young Stamford?'

'Count me in,' he called back, laughing with the same relief at surviving this madness that I was feeling. 'Although perhaps another...'

A bullet blew his hat from his head and cut his sentence short.

'Oh! Oh!' he said. 'I'm hit.'

*

We got away and made it deep into the bush before we stopped. Ragwasi grunted with pain every time his horse scrambled up a bank or dropped down onto the bed of a sandy donga but I could do nothing for him because I had hold of Stamford's reins while he lay slumped over his horse's mane, blood streaming from his matted blonde hair. Willoughby, I must say, played up like a gentleman, going backwards and forward and around us, checking that we were not being pursued while scouting out the best and easiest route forward until I declared that we could go no further without treating our wounds. Upon that, he found a narrow gully, with good shade from an overhanging sausage tree and concealed by white pear, a giant fig and a thick tangle of Cyclids – ancient trees like big pineapples and very thick waxy leaves that are poisonous to eat - and a stream of water cascading off the rounded rocks above.

'Leopards,' warned Ragwasi, through gritted teeth, and I looked about confirming to myself that this was indeed just the sort of place that a leopard would choose to inhabit, but dismounted anyway because Stamford was sliding from the saddle like a slow motion avalanche.

'You too,' ordered Willoughby, pointing at Ragwasi. 'Off saddle and let me see your wound.'

'I am fine,' replied Ragwasi, tersely.

'You are not,' declared Willoughby, with finality, and Ragwasi obeyed.

Stamford, I caught and laid down with his back against the rock. He was still conscious, but groggy and half blinded with blood, and as I mopped at his face with a rag and a splash from my canteen I could do no other than fear the worst. Flesh wounds, I could treat; stitches were easy and though bones were harder, I knew how to stretch, set and splint them; but a stomach wound was fatal nine times out of ten and a head wound every time. My hand trembled and my breathing came short as I cleaned away the dust, grime, matted hair and drying blood and I truly dreaded what I would find underneath it.

'More water,' I called out. 'Major Willoughby. I must have water.'

Willoughby was crouched over Ragwasi, who was now also sitting with his back to the canyon wall, and though he too was busy, he recognised the urgency in my voice and at a nod from Ragwasi, came over, took my canteen and filled it from the spring.

'Will he do?' he asked, quietly.

I emptied almost all the contents of the canteen onto Stamford's head, sluicing and flushing away the welling blood in order to get a better look, and then poured the remainder over my own face, in part to refresh myself and in part to sluice away the tears welling in my own eyes. That a boy should so lose his life like this was too much for me to bear, kin or not, and I cursed myself for a fool and Kruger and Rhodes and the rest of those drawing room warriors for stiff-necked villains who did not know how to compromise or make a deal like businessmen and so make money in peace and quiet instead of blood and the thunder of war.

'He may be lucky, yet,' said Willoughby. 'Keep sponging.'

And I did and though I hardly dared hope, it was a grave wave of relief that I saw the wound come clear and realised that it was no more than a scratch. Actually, it was more of a six inch long jagged tear where the bullet had gone under the skin and scraped along opening up the flesh and exposing the white bone but without shattering the skull.

'There,' said Willoughby, comforting. 'He'll survive, though he might need to part his hair on the other side for a while.'

I almost choked at the joke and found myself giving a nervous giggle which slurred into a sob and then I was nodding vigorously and crying and feeling Willoughby's hand patting my shoulder.

'Well done, old man,' he said. 'Now patch him up, eh? Good show.'

Twenty seven stitches I put into Stamford's head, all with a needle like a bodkin and sutures like string and then plastered the whole lot over with comfrey and bacon grease. Stamford took them without complaint, mainly because I gave him some mampoer to make him drowsy, and then, when I had finished and I laid him back against the rock, he gave me a small, wincing wink from out of a face grey with pallid pain.

I would have been less than human if I had not taken this as an opportunity to question him and though I had no wish to take advantage of his disordered mental state, I knew that a head wound, even a scratch like this, was no simple thing to be dismissed easily. I was no doctor and though I had done what I could, there was no guarantee that the boy would survive my treatment. This was the bush, where even the slightest wound could fester overnight and turn into a great bubbling cauldron of septic pus and green infected matter however much carbolic you scrubbed it with. There were any number of insects that would feed on a wound and the first of the flies had arrived before the first stitch had gone in. There could be fever. He might sink into a sleep from which he might not wake. A bullet had hit his head and might have caused an injury internal, of which we were not aware and which might manifest itself only in time. If he was to die, then I felt it my duty to my sister to ascertain whether this was her son or some other man so that I might tell her and lessen the weight of the dull funeral bludgeon.

'Stamford,' I said, quietly, holding up his head and bringing his eyes up to meet mine. 'Does the name *Edgar Smithfield* mean anything to you?'

'Uh?' he replied, letting his eyes slide away from mine.

I gripped his jaw a little tighter and ignored the wince of his pain.

'*Edgar Smithfield*,' I repeated. 'Do you know anyone who goes by that name?'

His eyes came back up to mine. They were red-rimmed and gritted but I could see that there was still intelligence in the well behind them.

'No,' he said.

Then, 'Yes.'

And then, 'Thanks, Uncle,' he muttered.

And with that his whole body slumped into unconsciousness.

*

Ragwasi was looking grey but more, I thought, with fatigue than pain and the reason for this was revealed when Willoughby and I persuaded him to remove his tunic and then his shirt and undershirt. As each layer was peeled off, Ragwasi complained that although he had been hit, the injury was trifling.

'It was a spent bullet,' he protested. 'It has not drawn blood but is only a bruise.'

'Come now, come now,' ordered Willoughby, holding up Ragwasi's tunic and putting his finger through the ragged hole just above the belt on the lower right hand side. 'No false heroics, what?'

The shirt duly came off after a certain amount of huffing and puffing and I could see that despite his protests, he was moving stiffly and thinking about moving before he actually moved.

'What's this then?' said Willoughby, hauling off Ragwasi's undershirt and holding the rather grubby item up. There was no hole that corresponded with those in the tunic and the flannel shirt. 'Where did the bullet go?'

'As I said,' answered Ragwasi, irritated. 'It was a spent bullet.'

'Spent bullet, my eye,' contradicted Willoughby, pushing Ragwasi around and inspecting his lower back. 'A Mauser bullet isn't spent after a couple of hundred yards, old chap. That is for certain.'

Ragwasi turned around to reach for his undershirt but Willoughby spun him back.

'And a spent bullet never made a bruise like that,' he said, peering closely. 'What do you make of this Mr. Pelly?'

I looked; and there on his lower back was the clearly emerging spoor of a large and angry bruise. In places the skin had broken, but not deeply, and there was no need for stitches but there was something very odd about the shape of the injury. To begin with, there was no hole or star-shaped entry wound, but rather a rough oblong about three and a half inches by four, topped with a separate bruise about half an inch square above. I straightened up and gave a long, tired sigh.

'Show me your hip-flask, Ragwasi,' I demanded.

'What hip-flask?' he replied, a look of such guilt spreading across his face that I almost felt sorry for him.

'The hip-flask that Tepo bought for you from Amm's Hardware in Johannesburg three years ago on your birthday.'

'Oh, that old thing?' replied Ragwasi, as though Danish tinned butter would not melt in his mouth at the height of a Lowveldt summer. 'I gave it to my son a long time ago.'

'A hip-flask, you say,' said Willoughby, beginning to smile. 'Was it your *lucky* hip-flask?'

'It is now,' I said. 'Let's see it. Come on. Hand it over.'

Ragwasi huffed and puffed a bit more, then pointed to his saddle bag.

'The left one,' he said, hopping awkwardly from one foot to the other.

Willoughby went over to the horse, rummaged around a little and then produced the silver object that Tepo had spent so much of my money on. It was battered and dented, and leaking a thick brown, gelatinous substance like treacle.

'This it?' he said, unscrewing the top and sniffing. He grimaced. 'I take it this is your own concoction? Not Hatherley's whisky, that's for certain.'

Ragwasi tried to snatch the flask from Willoughby's hand, but I was too quick for him and took it myself. I sniffed and then looked him directly in the eye.

'You've been to that Sangoma again, haven't you?'

'Sangoma?' said Willoughby.

'What you might call a Witch Doctor,' I said. 'And what I call a load of hocus pocus. I thought you had given up consulting that old fraud, Ragwasi?' I sniffed again. It smelled foul, like a mixture of Dr Batty's Asthma Cigarettes, camphor oil, stale hessian and asafoetida and I pulled away as though I had ingested smelling salts. 'What is this?'

Ragwasi looked rather injured and puffed his chest up in defiance.

'It is none of your business what patent medicines I take for my complaints. Do I ask what you take when you have a cold or a touch of the Marthambles?'

'Ragwasi,' I replied. 'Whatever this is, it is not a patent medicine.'

'Yes, it is,' he contradicted. 'And it is every bit as good as *Birley's Phosphorus* or *Hamlin's Wizard Oil*.'

'Come now, man,' said Willoughby. 'What is it called?'

'It has its own special name,' answered Ragwasi, reaching for his undershirt and wincing as he pulled it over his head.

'You mean, it's just some old woman's *muti*,' I said.

'It has a special name – a patented name – which I am not at liberty to disclose, it being a secret remedy,' replied Ragwasi, becoming proud.

'*Arabian Balsam*?' I ventured. '*Urodonal*? Or perhaps, *Mrs Winslow's Soothing Syrup*?'

'What about *Parker's Tonic*?' offered Willoughby, tugging sagely at his moustache. 'Or *Stanley's Snake Oil Linament*?'

'I have spoken,' said Ragwasi, cocking his head back. 'It is a secret.'

'Very well then,' replied Willoughby. 'If you can't tell us the name, perhaps you might tell us its function? A general pick-me-up, sort of thing? You know, a drop of cocaine mixed in with the old sarsparilla?'

'Something like that,' conceded Ragwasi.

'Does it improve mental agility too?' I asked. 'Or reduce the effects of old age?'

Ragwasi sniffed imperiously and reached for his shirt.

'Is it as efficacious as *Bumsteads Worm Syrup*?' asked Willoughby, warming to the task.

'Twice as efficacious,' replied Ragwasi. 'The Sangoma says…'

'So it did come from that damned old quack!' I said, triumphantly. 'How much did she sharp you for this time?'

'She is a wise woman!' protested Ragwasi. 'You white people think that only white medicine is good medicine but this medicine is the best medicine of all because it works when it is supposed to work, in the way that it is supposed to work, uPelly! It is not like that syrup of figs which you think is a good thing to give to children!'

Now it was my turn to protest.

'Syrup of figs *is* a good thing to give to children who have eaten too much meat and not enough vegetables,' I replied. 'But you are only supposed to give them one spoonful, not the whole bottle.'

'So what is it supposed to cure?' interjected Willoughby, before we could go off on a domestic tangent.

Ragwasi took a deep breath.

'It is a preventative measure, for prevention is always better than cure.'

'Hear! Hear!' I said. 'What does it prevent?'

'Death, specifically,' said Ragwasi, striding forward and snatching the ruined flask from my hand. 'The Sangoma formulated it to give protection from bullets.'

Well, there was no arguing with that, I suppose. Willoughby gave a great horse laugh and went to look at Stamford, while I stood there scratching my head, which was itching horribly. And I suppose, it might have been advisable for me to have gone to see that same Sangoma because when Ragwasi stood right in front of me, the last words that I heard were: 'Are you well, uPelly?'

*

Malaria. It has been my constant companion these long years, dogging my footsteps, stalking me through desert, veldt and bush, laying in ambush and striking me down whenever it chooses. And it usually chooses the time that is most inconvenient to me. I can go for long, contented months – years, even – without ever being bothered, but it is in times of stress and endeavour that it chooses to get me in its grip and drags me sweating and shaking to my bed so that whatever battle I have to fight at that time, it feels like I have to fight it twice. At such times, there is nothing to do but to submit, wrap myself up in every scrap of clothing I can find, then wrap around me the hide of a zebra that I keep for just such a purpose, lie down by a fire and simply endure however many long days and nights of shivering cold and thick, hot, heavy sweats until it goes. *If* it goes, that is: with malaria, a man might be healthy at breakfast and dead by midnight. I cursed myself: I had foolishly wished for it and it had duly come.

It is a strange affliction and takes different people differently, I have noticed. Some people rave and have terrible and confusing dreams, while for others it is no worse than a bad head cold. Some people know instinctively when they are about to be attacked or are granted a particular warning signal, like aching teeth or shaking hands; it comes upon me suddenly and without warning, preceded only by a minute or so of intense itching, like small animals are scurrying over my whole body. What is worse is that there seems to be no obvious cause of the disease nor no obvious cure either. Some people say that it is an affliction caused by breathing miasmas in swampy places, but I have known people struck down by it the Kalahari Desert where a swamp would be a welcome thing indeed. Others say that it is caused by the biting of mosquitos, but I was bitten by mosquitos many times in England, the Cape, the Karoo and Kimberley without any serious consequences and it wasn't until I travelled to the line of the Zambezi that I first felt its hand. I know some people who never get it unless they travel and others who never get it at all. As to medicine, well, your guess is as good as mine; some people swear by quinine, but I have drunk gallons and gallons of Indian Tonic Water when ill to no effect whatsoever. Others say that chewing willow bark helps; good luck with that. I absolutely refuse to have leeches put on me, as others recommend, mainly because I need my blood and have none to spare for those loathsome worms, especially as it is getting a bit thin with age. What is certain is that the disease is unpredictable; you can get up and walk about within a day or two, or you can be drained yellow with your skin turned to paper and needing a months' convalescence or you can be dead as a Dodo within hours, depending on its whim or the way the wind is blowing.

As I have said, some people have terrible and confusing nightmares but I am not one of them. Instead, I drift in and out of sleep and sometimes it feels as though I am standing inside a big cave inside my head and I am looking out on the scene as if I was looking out of the windows of my house. It is a curious experience made even more curious by the sense that time seems to get scrambled up like the rocks of the pass through the Groot Swartberg at Meiringspoort so that sometimes it seems like hours pass in minutes and sometimes minutes take hours to pass. When the malady is over, I can remember all these moments very clearly but not always in the right order and, of course, sometimes I am not sure if I have dreamed them or if they have really happened. I suppose I should be thankful for not seeing monsters, hey?

I am telling you this because there were three or four things that came clearly to me as I drifted in and out of this world during those few days. The first was that Stamford, though injured, was not badly injured in the sense that he was incapacitated. I distinctly remember seeing him smile and chat while Ragwasi slapped comfrey over his wound and I am more than certain that he went out on horseback with Major Willoughby at least once in that time. This pleased me because I was growing fonder of that boy by the day, even though he was less than truthful with me. I liked his attitude; he was all zip and zing and get-up-and-go and didn't feel the need to be chattering all day like so many young people today, which was a blessing because I like to hear the veldt as much as look at it. The second thing was that Willoughby himself was away a lot though I did not know what he was up to obviously.

Still, I am clear in my mind that he seemed happy - although being holed up while his schemes had been rumbled by Kruger's Kommandos did not seem to me entirely a satisfactory situation. But then, if nothing else, Willoughby was an optimist. The third thing – which I am absolutely not sure of but I distinctly remember it happening all the same – is that at some stage a leopard *did* make an appearance. I can see it now looking down on me from the top of the rocks, silhouetted against a bright moon, wrapped in its own thoughts and completely unconcerned by the appearance of these squatters in its favourite lair. It looked at me for a long moment, concentrating in that supercilious way that all cats have, gave a big yawn and then sat down to lick its forepaws as though none of us down below were of any consequence at all. Normally, I would have been reaching very slowly for my gun at this point but actually, a strong feeling of calmness came over me and I remembered a tale about an old bergie who had regularly shared the shade of a katjiepeering tree at noon with a female leopard who enjoyed the fine shade and the powerful and delicious scent of its white flowers as much as he did. They had rubbed along together for several years like this, each content in the other's company; why the bergie did not get killed is beyond me; perhaps the leopard thought him too stringy a bit of meat to bother with, but I don't know. That's leopards for you though; they are unpredictable and dangerous, but also can be very content if they have everything they want already. They are not like foxes who will kill everything in the coop and bury the chickens they don't eat straight away for later.

The last thing I distinctly remember was coming to with Ragwasi pulling me up into a sitting position and spooning some hot broth into me. For a moment I had that strange sensation of looking out at the world through the windows of my eyes, but then all of a sudden I was lucid and determined to ask the question that had been bothering me ever since Johannesburg.

'You lied to me, Ragwasi,' I murmured. 'Why?'

If he gave me an answer, I did not hear it for I slipped back into unconsciousness on the instant and when next I reached a state of lucidity, he had been replaced as nursemaid by Stamford, who showed me his stitches and smiled and called me Uncle again. But later, I saw Ragwasi sitting off to one side and I don't think I had ever seen him looking so miserable at any time in all our long friendship.

*

I was in and out of that bout of malaria for a couple more days before I could count myself cured. It had been a particularly bad one and I was weak as water when I finally came out of it. This is the thing about that disease though; it is unpredictable and apt to come and go like a bad tradesman. This time it went as quickly as it came; one minute I was sweating and delirious and the next – well, it was just like getting out of bed after a late night and I took the cup of tea that Stamford handed to me with great thanks. He also fried up a couple of eggs that he had bartered from somewhere which slipped straight down my gullet without pausing.

'Are you fine, Uncle?' he asked.

I nodded and asked him to bring me up to date with the situation.

'The Major is out negotiating for boats,' he replied, making chapattis just as Willoughby had done.

'Fat lot of good that will do,' I replied, hoarsely. 'The rains are a long way off and without them the Limpopo is too shallow to float balsa wood on.'

'Yes, well,' replied Stamford, with a grin. 'He seems confident of being able to overcome that particular obstacle.'

I was about to ask him to explain further when the sound of approaching hooves made me come straight to the alert.

'That'll be him now,' said Stamford, nonchalantly. 'Don't worry. If the Boers had any chance of finding us, they would have found us already.'

I wasn't so sure but on this occasion the boy was right. Willoughby came trotting up and then dismounted from that great, grey carthorse of his while Ragwasi followed him, leading one of the mules on which was mounted one of the strangest attired men I have ever seen.

'What ho?' cried Willoughby, cheerfully. 'Feeling better, are we? Jolly good show! Meet the latest addition to our merry band.'

He beckoned the stranger forward and I took him in. For a start he looked older than Methuselah, being wrinkled just about everywhere that a wrinkle could be squeezed in; honestly, his face looked like a topographical drawing and though he was a black man, he had smeared his face and those exposed parts of his chest and legs that were visible with white ash, which gave him a very alarming appearance indeed. His hair was tangled and matted and would admit no comb to penetrate its thickets and was only held together by a braid of brown beads that he had wound around and around his head. The rest of his attire was no less remarkable, consisted mainly of a breach clout of French blue, heavily embroidered, and a kaross of scarlet cloth, similarly decorated with outlandish patterns and designs. As he dismounted, flipping off the back of the mule by swinging his leg over the mule's head and then pushing himself off with his hands, I saw that his sandals were adorned with silver filigree toe-rings and that he carried a skin bag that rattled ominously when he landed. He strode forward to shake my hand, looking up at me for he was no more than four and a half feet tall, muttered something inaudible, and then proceeded to squat on his haunches and invited me to do likewise. I knew what he was and my heart sunk.

'Meet Khotso,' said Willoughby, announcing him as though he was waving forward the Bearded Lady at the circus. 'The best Rainmaker this side of the Limpopo.'

I looked at Ragwasi: 'Was this your idea?'

His expression was unreadable to anyone who was not used to Ragwasi's unreadable expressions but I knew how to read Ragwasi's unreadable expressions and I will tell you that what was written there was the same mixture of pride, guilt, pig-headedness and defiance that he showed every time he lost money on the Johannesburg Stock Exchange.

'He can tell the future,' said Ragwasi.

'Then why doesn't he tell us the next winner of the Derby?' I replied. 'Then we can make a solid bet and win a fortune?'

'Not *that* sort of future,' replied Ragwasi, holding out his hands in appeal.

'Never underestimate the local Gods,' said Willoughby, coming to his aid. 'More things on heaven and earth than dreamed of in your philosophy, Horatio, eh what? Got to be worth a try, at least.'

'And you expect that finding this…this…' I looked for the right words. 'This *venerable* old gentleman and then paying him to cast a few old bones about will fill up the Limpopo so you can float Kruger's millions down to the coast in a dug-out canoe?'

I sat down, heavily.

'Lord,' I said. 'The country is crawling with Boers, I'm full of malaria, Stamford here is lucky to still have a head to wear his hat on and your only plan is to pay one of these old frauds to make it rain?'

'Not the only plan under consideration,' replied Willoughby, looking hurt. 'But it can't do any harm, eh? Some of those *Saddhus* in India could do some pretty remarkable things. And, why, I once saw a Tibetan monk dry ice cold sheets on his body just by thinking about it and once you've seen the Indian Rope Trick, then you'll not discount these chaps so easily.'

'Indian Rope Trick?' I said, hardly able to contain my disbelief.

'What is the Indian Rope trick?' asked Ragwasi.

'Chap gets his basket of snakes….' began Willoughby.

The Sangoma sat up. Any mention of snake spirits gets the attention of the muti men every time.

'…does the old tootling bit with his snake charming flute whatchamacallit and up comes the snake…'

'Really, Major Willoughby…' I protested.

'And when he's charmed the old cobra into a state of stupor, up comes the rope swaying in just the way the snake is doing, but then keeps on going…'

'*Hau!*' exclaimed the Sangoma, clearly impressed.

'…and up and up it goes until it's higher than your head…'

'This is nonsense,' I said, but to no avail.

'… and then he gets his boy…'

'Where does the boy come from?' asked the Sangoma, a note of temporary suspicion in his voice.

'Oh, he's usually a sort of apprentice, I dare say…' replied Willoughby. 'Looks after the snakes and cleans the stables, that sort of thing.'

Khotso the Sangoma nodded at the essential rightness of this and Willoughby continued.

'So up goes the rope and then, damme, all of a sudden it stops swaying, goes rigid and up climbs the boy…'

'*Hau, hau!*' cried Ragwasi and the Sangoma together. 'This is big muti indeed.'

'Ah, but that's not the end of it,' said Willoughby, his eyes widening. 'When the boy climbs up that rope and gets to the top…he vanishes! Poof! Just like that! Thin air!'

'*Hau!*' cried the Sangoma. '*Hau!* I have seen something similar! This is very big muti!'

'Amazing!' cried Ragwasi.

I shook my head.

'And you saw this with your own eyes?' I asked.

'Well,' replied Willoughby, evasively. 'Not exactly – but the chap who told me about it was an impeccable source. Known him for years. Trust him with my wallet, I would.'

I shook my head again. Everyone knows *someone* who has seen the Indian Rope Trick – but *no-one* I have ever met has, upon close questioning, admitted seeing it at first hand and with their *own* eyes. I looked from Willoughby to the Sangoma and then at Ragwasi and then back at Willoughby.

'You actually believe this chap can make rain?' I said.

'He is a very good Sangoma,' chipped in Ragwasi. 'His muti is strong.'

'His muti is a load of old cock and bull,' I replied, suddenly feeling weary. Ragwasi and I had had this dispute for years and while I was prepared to accept that some of their herbal remedies were efficacious, the charms and fortune telling that they always tried to add on to the bill was, in my opinion, just the same old flummery that the Gypsies at Dines Hall peddled. Ragwasi, having once sold his soul to the Mamlambo, a snake-woman water-spirit, was apt to disagree. 'How much did you pay him?' I asked.

'Two gold coins only,' replied Ragwasi.

'And a big cash bonus if it rains within forty-eight hours of him casting his spells,' added Willoughby. 'Also, I bought some tobacco off him. Fancy a cheroot?'

I looked to Stamford for support, but he was grinning: 'Voodoo,' he said, and pulled a horrible face.

I looked down at the old gentleman, who was busy rolling a dagga cigarette.

'Are you sure those are cheroots?' I asked, looking at the cigarette.

'No,' answered Willoughby. 'But they ain't Indian hemp either, so far as I can tell.'

I took one and surrendered yet again.

The Sangoma flipped open his match holder, struck one and held it up for me.

'Don't worry, *yase Ngilandi*,' he said, looking confident. 'My name is Khotso and I'm good at this.'

'I bet you are,' I replied. 'I just bet you are.'

*

Over the next couple of weeks or so, Willoughby kept us hard at it. Our problem was to gather up all the gold and cash that we had deposited with the Moramela people and move it up to a suitable spot on the Limpopo which was discrete enough not to be not noticed by the Boers – and by now, the British also – but also with enough water to float the boats that Willoughby was counting on. In finding such a spot, Willoughby chanced upon the knowledge that the Limpopo was perfectly navigable all the way to sea from the point where the Olifants River flowed into it and as this river was considerably nearer than the Limpopo, his hopes rose that his plan might be executed much more quickly than he had expected. So it fell to us to ride out to all the places where the Moramelas had hidden the mules, gather them up and move them to a rendezvous at a place called Timbavati, which the Sangoma informed us, was haunted by the spirits of lions that had fallen from a comet and so were white. I accorded this information the respect it deserved – none - and concentrated on lugging those stubborn mules through the hundred and thirty miles of dense bush thereabouts until finally we collected up all two hundred of the wretched, bad tempered creatures.

We kept a sharp look out, of course, but the Moramelas who came with us knew this area like the back of their hands and what they did not know about smuggling across the Mozambique border was not worth knowing. The bush here was so thick and the grass so high that unless a herd of elephants had not gone through first, there would have been no tracks to follow whatsoever. Fortunately, there were plenty of elephants to blaze a trail for us to follow; what was not so fortunate was the number of cobras that slid across our paths, flickering their tongues, raising up their hoods and so looking at us with their black beady eyes that I wished for Willoughby's Indian snake charmer; I also noted that our formidable Sangoma always gave them a wide berth rather than cast a charm on them that would keep them away. Sometimes we saw - or heard rather – the sound of other mule trains for Kruger was still sending the remainder of his gold away and at times I thought I saw the old gambling instinct cross Willoughby's face again. This time, however, he was content to stick rather than twist and though he scouted a couple of those columns, he resisted the temptation to risk just one more lift.

Finally, when all the mules had been gathered together, we and the Maromelas moved them in one great herd down to a spot just before the confluence of the two rivers and unloaded all the loot into one great stack which we then covered with branches so that it looked like a rather untidy oblong hut. Willoughby paid off the Moramelas in a mixture of cash and silver coin and bestowed the mules on them as a sort of tip which pleased them greatly and Ragwasi even more, for those beasts had been as difficult as they always were and he had no liking for them at all. And then we sat down on red earth so red it was almost like a pomegranate or a blood orange and, in places, so red it was almost purple, while up above the sky was pale blue above a wash of lemon watercolour, the finest of beaten brass and the thinnest of gold leaf. It was a beautiful end to a tough couple of weeks. All we needed now was some rain.

'The boats will come down as soon as the water level gets up to here,' said Willoughby indicating the middle of his thigh. He was standing ankle deep in a trickle of water that ran through the centre of a wide flood plain. 'All we have to do is wait.'

'*Ja*,' I said, trying to keep the exasperation out of my voice. 'Except the rains are not expected for another month or more – and don't say anything about Sonny Jim, here.'

Khotso the Sangoma was lying on a comfortable sand bank smoking dagga. Ragwasi was taking the opportunity to bathe. It was hot and the journey had been trying, what with the dust that those mules kicked up.

'Have faith, old boy,' replied Willoughby, striding out of the water. 'I say; do you think there might be crocodiles in this river?'

'Absolutely,' I said. 'But Ragwasi will probably find them first.'

Ragwasi said something that I did not quite catch.

'Ah well,' said Willoughby, lighting a cheroot and standing tall with his hands on his hips. 'I suppose we should take an inventory while we are waiting for Khotso to earn his pay.'

'Inventory?' I said.

'Yes,' he replied. 'We should at least count our ill-gotten gains while we have the time. Make sure it's all there, what?'

'Oh, I'm sure it's all there,' I replied. 'All three hundred and something boxes – not to mention the sacks.'

'Aren't you curious?'

'I'll be interested when it rains and the boats show up. Until then it's just heavy metal and waste paper.'

*

Well, we did count it. We prised open every one of those boxes with a crow bar, wrote down what it contained and then nailed the lid back down again. Stamford and I emptied the sacks and counted the bundles of notes while Willoughby totted things up in his notebook with a pencil that lived behind his ear when it wasn't scribbling figures. Ragwasi spent most of the time patrolling or keeping a look out while Khotso, who clearly felt himself to be above manual labour, maintained his mysterious aspect by constantly touching up his face paint, smoking a lot of dagga and periodically casting a set of gnarly old bones onto a leather apron that looked like it had been thrown out with the rubbish from the back of a Masonic Lodge. This routine he varied with brief periods of muttering and longer ones of what he claimed was communing with his ancestors in the spirit world but which looked to me like being plain old drunk. In the end, what with checking and double checking, it took us the best part of two days to establish the inventory. I still have my copy of it, which Willoughby insisted on; we all had to have our own copy 'for the sake of fair dealing' he said.

Precious Metals, Monies, Specie and Assorted Items of Value

Liberated from the Treasury of the South African Republic (ZAR)

by Forces Operating on behalf of Her Majesty Queen Empress Victoria of Great Britain, her Colonies, Dominions, Overseas Territories and Possessions Various.

'Does that sound about right?' asked Willoughby, composing.

'Oh, right on the button,' I replied, trying hard not to laugh at the *operating on behalf of* bit.

'Righty ho,' he continued.

Item One

1680 Bars of Gold divided into 210 Boxes containing 8 Bars each. Each bar is estimated at 400 Imperial Troy Ounces (give or take). Estimated price per oz is £10 Sterling so each bar is worth £4000 Sterling.

Total value of bullion £6,720,000 give or take depending on market prices.

'Not bad for a start, what?' said Willoughby, with a wide smile. 'And certainly better than the miserable thirty odd bars that Cunningham bilked us of, eh?'

Item Two

60 Boxes Gold Kruger Ponds at ¼ oz. Each box contains 12,800 coins.

Total Value £768,000 at face value, but might be worth more.

20 Boxes Gold Kruger Half Ponds at 1/8oz. Each box contains 3200 coins.

Total Value £32,000 at face value, but might be worth more.

Total Value of Gold Coins £800,000 give or take.

'Hardly worth the effort of counting it,' said Stamford, laughing.

Item Three

20 Boxes Silver Coins Mixed Half Crowns, Shillings and Sixpence pieces.

Estimated Value £10,000 give or take.

'Not worth counting at all,' said Willoughby. 'Anyone want to dispute the estimate?'

We all shook our heads.

Item Four

Forty Sacks of Paper Currency Mainly in £50 notes issued by the Pretoria Government.

'Worthless,' said Willoughby. 'Light your cheroots with them. Waste of time now.'

Item Five

Ten Sacks of Paper Currency of Mixed Issue and Denomination. Mainly £50 notes but also some US Dollars, some Mexican Dollars, some Reichmarks and some others.

'I think we'll just stick with the Fifties,' suggested Willoughby.

We all nodded our agreement while we sucked at the paper cuts on our fingers.

Value of Pounds Sterling £1,250,000

'Everybody happy?' said Willoughby. It was more of a statement than a question. 'Right then.'

Item Five

Total Value of (counted) Liberated Funds

£8,780,000

It was an absurd amount of money.

'Which means,' said Willoughby. 'That split four ways…'

'Count me out,' I said. 'That money will get you hanged if you don't hand it over to the government.'

'Oh really, Mr Pelly,' replied Willoughby, a little piqued. 'Show a little imagination. And as I've already done the calculation, I shall proceed.'

Total Value of One Equal Share (minus sundry expenses of £300,000)

'What sundry expenses are we talking about?' chipped in Ragwasi, using that tone he has when he fears he is about to be bilked.

'The charter of a ship and the necessary *douceurs* to make this money disappear, amongst other things,' said Willoughby, nodding at the Sangoma, who was rattling his bones again and pretending not to hear what was being said.

Ragwasi assented.

Total Value of One Equal Share (minus sundry expenses of £300,000)

£2,120,000

'Not bad for a couple of month's work, what?' said Willoughby.

Stamford nodded in enthusiastic agreement. Ragwasi looked equally pleased.

'You forget,' I said. 'I want no part of this.'

'Very well,' said Willoughby, scribbling figures again. 'Are you *sure*? Well then…'

Total Value of One Equal Share (minus sundry etc etc)

'There are a devil of a lot of sixes in that calculation and the job isn't finished yet, Major,' I said. 'It's a long way to the coast.'

'Oh? I didn't take you for a superstitious man, Mr.Pelly. The Number of the Beast, eh? 'Cept that's *666* and not 66666. And I'm sure we'll be fine once the boats arrive,' said Willoughby, directing our attention towards the Sangoma.

At that moment, Khotso stood up, took a huge lungful of dagga, held his breath for what seemed an eternity, then gave a long low moan as he blew out the blue smoke and fell over backwards.

And a big fat raindrop came out of a cloudless sky and exploded on the top of my head. You had to hand it to Willoughby: he had the Devil's own luck.

Chapter 7

Limpopo.

I suppose I should have known to expect that something unexpected would happen for this is the way things are in Africa and all Africans know this thing even if sometimes they forget it. I remember when I first came to the Cape, when everything was still new and every day was a new adventure, when I went from farm to farm working as a journeyman labourer, earning my keep and working towards redemption, that unexpected things were to be expected all the time. There was one time – it was on a big wheat farm down near Bredasdorp, I remember – that a young man came looking for work and it being harvest time, the farmer took him on straight away for there is always more work for more people on a farm at harvest time. His name was David Frey and he was no more remarkable than any other of the young men who had torn up their roots from England and were wandering around the Cape looking for work, life and the possibility of a future, except insofar as he carried with him a small guitar on his back which in the evening he would play. We farmhands would gather under the oaks or on the steps of one of the square whitewashed shacks that were our homes and for an hour or so, he would play and we would listen and I would wonder at how I had missed the sound of music since leaving home, for in England there was always a fiddler at the pothouse or a penny whistle on the green. Here in Africa, the sound was precious for mostly music was confined to church on a Sunday and the Dutch religion did not really take to hymn singing as much as the Church of England and we were usually a long way away from anything that might resemble a pub where someone with a German flute or a squeezebox might tootle out a jig or a homely song.

Well, I did not know if David Frey was rated a good player or a bad one but it seemed to my ears that he was good enough for Covent Garden and when we sat there listening to him strum and pick and sing songs from near and far, like *Daar Kom Die Alibama*, *The Recruiting Sergeant of Rochester* and *The Wild Rover*, it seemed that his voice was golden, the oaks under the sun were golden, the harvest was golden and the world was a good place to live in indeed. And when the sun went down and only the glow of the fire was left to light along his tunes, it seemed to me that sparks flickered from his fingers making the embers clatter like clog dancers and the fireflies whirl like waltzers. That such a talent was possible in such a man, I thought marvellous, for he was ordinary in all other ways.

All other ways, bar one; he believed that a pack of cards was a guide to life. Now, in this I was wary of him because I had ended up in Africa because of a fondness for cards and the dream of quick wealth that they brought and so it was my habit to avoid or deflect any conversation that came within a country mile of them. Still, he was convinced of the rightness of his theory and one night, when the guitar had been laid aside and the Cape Smoke bottle was near empty, he lit up a hurricane lamp and I, fogged from the brandy, decided to listen to him lay it out.

'This,' he said, holding up the King of Diamonds. 'Is the Great Deception, for though we all need money, we need not diamonds. Chase him, challenge him and you will soon meet his right-hand man.'

He produced the Knave of Clubs.

'Not the *Knave*,' he corrected, his dark eyes passionate in the yellow glow of the lamp. 'The *Knight*; for the Knight of Clubs is the mailed fist who serves the King of Diamonds, protecting him from those who would take his wealth and taking wealth from those who's wealth he desires. The King of Diamonds and the Knight of Clubs are the curse of the poor man, tempting and taking away, awakening greed and justifying it with violence. For a man to live a righteous life, he must draw no more than the Ten of Diamonds and no more than the Seven of Clubs; sufficient wealth to live by; sufficient force to defend it.'

'*Moderation in all things* is your motto?'

'Quite,' he said, shuffling the deck and then fanning the cards out with a twist of his thumbs that any sharp would be proud of. 'Choose two cards and lay them face down on the floor.'

I plucked first one, then another and put them face down on the packed earth floor.

'Now turn them.'

First, the King of Diamonds stared up at me, and then the Queen of Hearts.

'Which would you choose?' he asked, looking directly into my eyes.

'You have warned me against the King of Diamonds,' I shrugged. 'So I must choose the Queen of Hearts.'

'She is always your best wager,' he said.

'I no longer wager,' I replied sharply. '*That* lesson, I have learned.'

'Life is a wager,' he countered. 'And though the King of Diamonds may buy all other Hearts in the suit, he cannot buy *this* Queen. So always choose the Queen of Hearts over the King of Diamonds.'

I pondered this for a moment and drew a conclusion.

'Diamonds, Clubs, Hearts,' I said. 'Wealth, Force and Love?'

'You understand,' he replied, drawing in the cards and shuffling once more.

'And Spades?'

'Draw,' he commanded, the cards fanning out once more, but I knew even before I had touched the proffered deck which card would come into my hands.

The Ace of Spades.

Drawing that card in a Newmarket gambling hell had bust me, nearly bust my father and bust the Stockwell family, who had been evicted from their holding so that it might be sold to pay off my debts.

'Luck,' I said. 'Spades represent Luck.'

'*Bad* Luck, Pelly,' he corrected. 'Spades only bring bad luck. When first the pack of cards was handed down to the Three Wise Men by the Ancients for our guidance and instruction, there was no suit of Spades, just one for each of those Magi. Only later was it added.'

'By whom?'

'By the Fool,' said David, picking up the Ace and shuffling. 'By the Fool, who slipped it into the pack while the Wise Men were busy worshipping the infant Jesus.'

He handed me the cards and I took them, shuffling them in turn and then fanned them out for him to choose one.

He drew the Ace of Spades. I gave a wry smile and shuffled again.

He drew the Ace of Spades a second time.

'Coincidence,' I said, taking the card and putting it back into the deck. 'A man's fate is governed by his own actions – his folly sometimes, true – but not by a pack of cards. Draw again.'

For the third time, he drew the Ace of Spades and though my head knew this was all nonsense, a thrill of uncertainty ran through my gut.

'Are you sure?' he said, his head cocked to one side, his eyes limpid, intense. 'Are you sure?'

Well, I never was sure after that because the next day, David Frey was killed by a scythe that fell from its place against the barn wall and cut through an artery in his leg. He bled to death before anything could be done for him.

*

It took an hour for the rain to arrive properly and when it did come, sweeping down from the escarpment like the swish of a theatre curtain, we were left in no doubt at all that the rains had broken early that year. As we huddled under what cover we could wrest from the brushwood piled up around the treasure boxes, we saw wave after wave of grey water come sizzling out of a blue-black sky that seemed to contain all the water in the world and all we could do was pull our hats down a little lower and lift our feet a little higher out of the puddles already forming. The thirsty earth drank up that thunderous first deluge as quickly as it could, but there was more behind it and soon the puddles began to stretch out beneath our feet and almost immediately the river began to rise and spread. There was no hope of starting a fire, so there was no chance of a warming brew of tea and less chance of anything hot to eat and as the rain soaked into everything, dribbling off the brims of our hats and trickling down our necks at every opportunity, we were soon shivering and wishing for a mouthful of even that dreadful army tinned mutton. All we got though was biltong – and smug looks from Khotso.

We spent an uncomfortable night made worse by the crackle of lightning around the horizon and the great, flat, white sheet lightning that boomed like the drum of a vengeful God. Somewhere in the rocks, the lions were raging too, roaring and wuffing, their voices carrying long and terrible through the night so that at times we thought they were close enough to touch and dreading the lightning that might reveal their faces to us at any moment. The only consolation to this dismal night was the thought that anyone in pursuit of us would be similarly hunkered down and that all spoor of those hundreds of donkeys would now be obliterated.

When the red dawn came, the rain let up long enough for the sun to light up an angry sky and for Khotso to get a fire going. Willoughby was pleased with the rise of the river and said so as he took off his shirt and wrung it out, as though this small addition might make it rise a little further and bring the boats a little quicker. I was not so pleased, for if those boats did arrive and allow for Kruger's gold to be transhipped into Portuguese territory, I feared that this would put us completely beyond the pale. If we were apprehended now, or turned north west towards Rhodesia or some other British territory, we might still be able to claim that we were a latter day Robin Hood and his Band of Merry Men robbing Sheriff Kruger to give to the rightful king – or Queen Empress in our case. Once we took that money over the border though, no-one would believe we were anything more than common criminals or freebooters. Khotso handed tea round – after first ensuring that he had filled his own mug to the brim – and Ragwasi went to stand sentry on a raised point sheltered by a fig tree; Stamford shook out all our soaked blankets and spread them over some bushes in the hope that they might dry before the next deluge; they were heavy and smelled of horse.

'Do you know any Portuguese?' asked the Major, whipping up soap in a small cup and readying his razor.

I did not.

'Perhaps young Mr. Holtzhausen can teach you a little?' he replied. 'It might come in handy.'

I could see where this was going and I did not like it. I had been to Mozambique; imagine a country three and half times bigger than England, Scotland and Wales combined, mostly covered by deep bush, with only one railway and no roads to speak of and either sweltering under a searing sun or flooded out by torrential rain which makes the soil impassable to anything on wheels; a country with wide swampy areas full of the biggest mosquitos on earth interspersed with arid areas where a pint of water is more precious than a pouch of diamonds. It's a place where a man rots with things much worse than malaria, is constantly tormented by insect pests and watches his animals die off wholesale from the tsetse fly; where you see your porters taken by crocodiles and lions – and there are hundreds and hundreds of lions – and your boats battered by hippopotami; where the giraffes pull down the telegraph lines, elephants wreck everything and black rhinos charge anything that moves; and don't mention the bees – I am telling you, they come in black and brown varieties as well as yellow and I have seen them put elephants to flight. So no; I did not want to go back to Mozambique. I am a man for the veldt and the deserts of South Africa, not that infernal place.

'Major Willoughby,' I said, determined on one last attempt to make him see reason. 'You know, you could hand this money over to the government and claim a reward under the Treasure Trove laws. That way, you would still be a rich man and keep the hangman off your back.'

'Poppycock,' replied Willoughby, plastering on the soap. 'Under the law, treasure is only *trove* if no-one knows who it belongs to - and that certainly isn't the case here. Also, there is the question of *animus revocandi* which, as I am sure you are aware, means that the treasure must have been buried by someone who intended to come back at a later date and dig it up. So, unfortunately, the law that you are referring to doesn't apply here.'

'Is there any law that does?' I said, berating myself for acting the clever lawyer when I am clearly no such thing.

'Well, I suppose, we might expect a reward in prize money,' he said, with a sniff, before commencing to shave. 'But it would hardly be comparable to what we have now. And Lord knows how much of it would go missing between handing it over and waiting for the pittance that those Treasury misers would remit. No, Mr.Pelly. Fair's fair, eh? Fortune of war and all that? Finders keepers?'

He had a point: I never saw any good done by handing money to the government.

'So, while we're waiting, you might like to get a few Portuguese phrases under your belt,' said Willoughby, looking at the rising river. 'They might come in handy.'

Already the rain was coming on again, spitting like bullets with a promise of shrapnel to follow so I decided that I would dispense with persuasion and look for a bit of shelter. I reckoned that we would be here for another day at least because this rain was not the rain that would lift the river; this stuff was already gone to the sea; what mattered was the rain up beyond the escarpment in Rhodesia and further on because it was that rain that would drain into the river and send it rising down to us.

'What do you plan to do with Khotso?' I asked, just as an afterthought.

'We'll pay him with a sack of Transvaal notes and then he can wait here a bit with the horses in case something goes wrong down river and we have to beat a bally retreat.'

'Another eventuality planned for, Major?' I tried not to sound impressed.

'It pays to be thorough,' he replied, skimming soap from under his chin with the razor. '*Prior planning and preparation prevents poor performance*, what? That's what I learned at the Shop and it always seemed to me to be a jolly good lesson.'

He had an answer to everything, it seemed, and I mooched off feeling damned hipped, cold and weary and wondering whether my malaria was on its way back. The sky above was grey-blue with the coming rain and it was sultry beneath it, breathless almost, as though the air had soaked up as much water as the land. For a moment, the sun blasted out from a rent in the clouds a hand's breadth above the hills to the west turning the underside of the clouds an angry scarlet and dashing any lingering hopes I had that the rains would ease off and leave Willoughby stranded long enough for me to find a British patrol and bring them down on him.

This had been a thought that had been growing in my mind since I had come out of my fevers and I had pondered on whether it was time to leave Ragwasi and Stamford to their follies in favour of the greater good. Needless to say, I still could not resolve this conflict between loyalty to country, friend or family but I had come to a vague resolution that the Mozambique border was somehow a limit to my procrastination and that I would have to decide one way or the other before the boats arrived.

Stamford, I feared, was lost. If a bullet to the head could not convince him to use that thing that the bullet had just missed then there was little that I could do to persuade him; sister Hattie would just have to accept that her boy was a rascal and a rogue. Furthermore, if I did approach him then I ran the risk of him telling Willoughby and that niggle I had about the man was growing and growing in me. It was only a gut feeling but there was something, well, *immoderate*, in the man's character; I had been a gambler, of course, but the sums of money involved in this caper were beyond reason. Cunningham and the others had been, on balance, much saner in taking only what they could carry and could reasonably dispose of; a third share in this mad enterprise was too great not to be noticed unless released only little by little; Ragwasi and I knew this from experience, but somehow, I could not imagine Willoughby confining himself to a modest competence in the Home Counties. Rather, I saw him buying up a castle and a deer park and inviting every swell in the district to dinner twice a week and a ball on Saturday, all of it reported by the local press hounds; that sort of wealth would be noticed and questions would be asked by inquirers more perspicacious than a scribbler for the local penny dreadful. For a moment I thought of gunning him down, but then I would surely find myself in a worse predicament; I would have murdered a British officer on no evidence but my own suspicions with no reliable witnesses to back me up. It would be the hangman's noose for me, no question.

Could I confide in Ragwasi? It shames me to say that I could not. The madness that was on him made him unreliable in my eyes and though it pained me to admit it, the plain fact was that after all these years, he seemed to have dispensed with any need for me and so I must reciprocate. Previously, I had always clung to him like a raft in a gale and he had never let me down; but things had changed. I resolved to be a character witness at his trial and would refuse to give evidence against him; but I could not condone this greed anymore.

There was a low rumble in the sky, like a wagon wheel grumbling down a bad road, and I saw the clouds begin to roil preparatory to loosing another deluge on us. Ragwasi, wet, damp, miserable, came down from his sentry post pointing up to the heavens and jerking his thumb over his shoulder.

'There are riders behind the storm, uPelly,' he said.

'Ours?' I asked, hopefully.

119

'Who are 'ours'?' he replied.

So I came to a resolution. I would make my escape, take a horse and ride for Tom Smith and Mike Rimington and tell them what plans were being made to dispose of Kruger's millions. When the boats came, or at some other convenient point, I would desert my friend and my family in favour of my country.

*

The sky stayed as grey as a Burberry Gabardine and didn't we just wish for one of them throughout that drenching? For most of the morning there was no let up from the rain, only variations in intensity. It hissed on the river, spattered through the trees, rattled like loose teeth in a tin box when it turned momentarily to hail and absolutely crackled on any attempt to get a fire going, even under the rough shelter we rigged in the hope of gaining some small respite. We took it in turns to ride out a little way to scout out the land but the horses were as discontented as we were and would often dig in and protest like mules. When one of them started to whinny and shy at the merest suggestion of a saddle, we gave up and drew damp straws for the miserable duty of sitting up against a tree wrapped in a soaked blanket and staring into the opaque distance. Even Willoughby's spirits seemed dampened.

The rise in the river came by the evening though. The water had at first been crawling sluggishly through channels in the sand but gradually the sandbanks submerged, the channels converged and there was one, dirty-brown river before us. Then it spread out, wider and wider across the flood plain, doubling and tripling in width without adding anything much to its depth; Willoughby strode thirty yards into the flood without the water coming above the middle of his calves and would have gone further if Ragwasi had not alerted him to the danger of crocodiles. It took some hours for the first sign of real force in the flow to arrive; then the twigs became branches and the branches became logs and soon after it was possible to see the water in the centre of the channel speeding up and tearing away from that held up by the drag from the banks. And almost with the last of the light came the boats.

There were four of them, broad pontoons constructed from rough cut timber and floated on canoes that had been securely lashed together with strong hessian ropes and steered from the rear by long oars that moved in a rolling pattern like the tail feathers of the sakubula bird. Each boat was crewed by two Marotis, who waved and called and then steered for the beach with grave skill, swinging the square platforms around and across the current as though they were ships' biscuits spun across a flat sea.

'This is not an African boat,' said Ragwasi, watching as the mate of the first pont dropped from his post at the prow and ran ashore with the rope and mooring stakes. 'Perhaps it is an Indian thing.'

'Chinese actually,' said Willoughby, with a smile and a self-satisfied sniff. 'Shallow draught but very stable. Just right for heavy loads on flood waters. Sent them the design myself; scribbled it on the back of an envelope. Done a good job too, I say.'

'Four boats?' I said. 'Do we need so many?'

'Ordered four because I rather expected to have a little more than what we have,' he replied. 'We only really need two now, but as they have been ordered, so they must be paid for. It's only fair. And good business too. Never know when you might need to deal with the Maroti again.'

'Just how long have you been planning this, Major?' I asked.

'Since before the war, of course,' he replied, and strode off to meet the Maroti skippers.

'*Prior planning and preparation...*' I said to myself. 'Well, it is certainly a performance.'

'uPelly,' said Ragwasi, quietly. 'Will you go to Mozambique?'

'I will not,' I replied and left him.

*

Willoughby wanted to get going straight away but the Maroti captains would not hear of this on account of the rocks and rapids that lay ahead, so he contented himself with having us load all the boxes and sacks onto two of the pontoons so that we could leave as soon as there was light enough to steer by. Two of the captains, he paid off with the Transvaal notes and possession of the boats themselves which, though being provided with masts, would have to be physically hauled upstream against this wind and current. I wished them good luck; I suspected that they would cannibalise the pontoons for the wood and rope and then construct more practical canoes with what was left, for such craft would not be much use at all further up either the Oliphants or the Limpopo Rivers.

It was, I calculated, only a morning's travel down to the Limpopo and the Portuguese border - actually, the border was some way along the Oliphants but no-one ever counted themselves over the border properly until they came to the Limpopo on account of the difficulties of navigating in the dense bush – and so I determined to go thus far and no further, more in the hope than the probability that something might turn up at the last minute to halt this madness. So the next morning, pushing off and then accepting a helping hand from one of the Marotis, I squatted down amidships alongside Stamford who had his boots off and was dangling his feet in the water like he was cooling his toes in the Thames. Ahead, Ragwasi was standing at the stern of the lead boat chatting with the helmsman, while Willoughby perched on top of the pile of loot boxes and smoked a cheroot, looking complacent.

'*Ja*,' I said, to Stamford. 'You shouldn't hang your feet over the edge of the boat. Not in Africa, at any rate.'

'Why not, Uncle?' he replied.

'Crocodiles,' I replied, and smiled as he pulled them straight up and out.

'I thought they only attacked on the bank or in the shallows,' he replied, drying off his feet.

'That's normal,' I confirmed. 'But you don't know how deep this water is.'

He looked down at the turgid brown of the muddy water, glowing golden like coffee in the early morning light and raised his eyebrows. The captain was steering for the middle of the river where the water ran quicker and more smoothly and we quickly picked up speed and began to spin. The captain dug in his steering oar, moved it in a gentle figure of eight motion and checked the spin so that we were facing square on to the river again. The light was coming up quickly now and the gleaming river revealed more and more of itself as we drifted along it a pace faster than a man could run. Along the banks, the fig trees were full of monkeys squealing and bickering while below the last of the buck to drink were finishing up, grateful for surviving the night and turning their thoughts to the day's grazing. There was a family of giraffe, too, full eleven of them, loping along slowly, oddly graceful and wearing supercilious expressions on their faces; I could see now why Kruger thought they were a species of camel, because they have that same look about them. Somewhere, further into the bush, I heard the trumpet of an elephant, perhaps a lone male or a matriarch calling to a stray calf.

'And there are hippos too,' I said, standing up and indicating what looked like a series of smooth round rocks fifty or sixty yards ahead. There was a snort and a massive head appeared above the water. 'See?'

'Thanks Uncle,' he said, pulling on his boots and peering. 'I don't know what we would have done without you. You've been really helpful on this trip.'

'*Been*? I said.

At that moment there was a sharp cry from the boat in front and I saw a splash as Ragwasi went head first into the water.

'Man overboard!' cried Willoughby.

'Quick!' I said, turning towards the load and looking for something suitable. 'Throw something that floats! Ragwasi does not swim well.'

'Sure thing,' answered Stamford.

I felt a sharp jerk on my shoulders and the next moment I was in mid-air and then in the drink myself, flailing around and gulping up river water. By the time I came up for air, the pontoon was already fifteen yards away and gaining and the last thing I saw as I went under again was Stamford, hat in hand, waving farewell.

Chapter 8

And They All Lived Happily Ever After.

It is a very strange and unusual thing that Africans in general and Zulus in particular are not very good at swimming. When I first taught Ragwasi to swim, I noticed that he was very reluctant to put his head under the water and just relax and allow himself to float so I explained to him that everyone floats naturally, even in a vertical position, and that the water will come past their eyes to about the middle of the forehead but no further. He found this difficult to accept, even when I demonstrated it several times and when he tried it he always went straight down like brick in a bath tub. This was very puzzling and I put it down to the fact that he would not relax and so gave up this method. Instead, I got him to float on his back, which was something he managed to do for a while when he was not panicking and sinking, and it was then that I noticed that he lay a lot lower in the water than I did. I thought it might be because he was a bit fat but then I remembered that I had seen a lot of fat men swimming over the years – and some fat ladies too, although they did not appreciate it at the time and belted me with parasols – so there must be some other thing at work. In search of an answer to this conundrum, I looked up Archimedes Principle in a big, thick book of facts and *Eureka*, I found the answer. It was because Ragwasi was denser than I. I do not mean by this that he was less intelligent – though he has his moments, I will admit – but that his body has more weight squashed into a smaller area than mine, so it takes a lot more water to make him float than it does me (I think). Ragwasi was much happier when I had explained all about this and so was much more relaxed and so much easier to teach and soon he was floating and splashing about like an otter in a trout stream in no time.

Swimming in the sea was another thing altogether though. Ragwasi would not entertain the idea at all because he was afraid of the surf and in this, I have to admit, he had a point. In a dam, he was happy because he knew exactly what the water was up to, where it came from, what was in it, how deep it was and so forth; in a river he was less happy because he quite rightly feared ambush by a crocodile; only a fool swims in an African river; unwary children are taken very often by crocs. For him, the sea was another kettle of fish altogether; the ocean was unpredictable (true), tasted different (true) and was full of sharks (true); and in these views, he was not alone. It was only when he pointed it out that I realised that I had never seen a sea going boat in the whole of Zululand, the Ciskei, the Transkei and anywhere in the whole of the Cape outside Cape Town and False Bay, that was owned, managed or commanded by an African. Not a dinghy, wherry nor a smack.

'Where do you get your fish from?' I asked, rather stupidly.

'From out of the river,' he replied.

I put this reluctance down to the Zululand surf. Actually, the surf anywhere along the coast as far as the Cape is pretty big and powerful and it is also very cold and never gets warm; this is something that I ponder a lot on because the weather in South Africa is often very hot and if the sun is so hot, why doesn't it heat the water up like it does in England? On the West

African coast under the equator, the water is like a warm bath and very many Africans swim and have boats there – to see a surf boat shooting the roaring, green breakers under a pastel blue sky is a fine sight indeed. It is my belief that Ragwasi, who was born a Zulu, never learned to swim because the water was too rough and too cold at the seaside and too full of crocodiles inland, while he himself, being solidly built, was too dense to float properly long enough to get his confidence. (It took a long time before I managed to persuade him to even try eating sea fish). What I am saying is that Ragwasi, even when I finally taught him to swim, was not really a strong swimmer; more of a doggie-paddler, is how I would best put it. So this is why I was concerned about him when Major Willoughby pushed him overboard into the Limpopo river that morning.

When I finally coughed out that brown soup of a river and got my bearings, it was really too late to catch up with the boats but I started out after them anyway because unless Ragwasi had the good sense to swim for the bank across the current straightaway, he would be washed further and further downstream until he was either drowned, eaten by a croc, snapped in half by a hippo, dashed to death on the rocks or washed out to sea to be eaten by sharks. I took a breath and started crawling down, trying to get some purchase on the flowing stream and all the while looking out to see where Ragwasi was. At first this was very difficult because a big mass of duckweed lay between me and the Major's boat obscuring the view but then I saw some splashing off to the right and realised that perhaps Ragwasi was trying to make it to the shore after all. This thought was confirmed when Stamford's boat went past something in the water and he raised his hat to it; this meant that it was definitely Ragwasi in the soup because not even that rascal of a blasted boy would raise his hat to a croc or hippo. I put my head down and swam for the point indicated, glancing diagonally along the stream so that I would not run the risk of shooting past Ragwasi in my haste and all the while aware that the muddy banks were full of the slide marks that told the spoor of crocs entering or leaving the river. Oh Lord! How I hoped they were leaving it! I know that some people eat crocodiles and they say that their tails are very tasty; very good; people eating crocodiles is fine by me; it is as it should be, for the other way round is not good; not good at all.

I must have been no more than ten yards from Ragwasi and no more than ten yards from the right bank of the river when I saw them. Six or eight round grey shapes lying like smooth boulders in the river thirty yards to our front; big, dumb, dangerous hippos; docile enough if you leave them alone, but they have the nervous little eyes of someone who will lash out ferociously in defence if they feel threatened with the full intention of getting their revenge in first and to hell with the consequences. And I would say that careering straight head first on into a bloat of them was about the best way of provoking an attack. I raised my head and my panicking heart lurched when I saw there were calves among them too and a split second later a big, big mouth opened, bearing teeth like tusks, and snorted a warning. But Ragwasi, flailing about and splashing like a Mississippi side-wheeler did not seem to see them and I thought him lost, for a hippo will snap a man in two without thinking.

'Ragwasi!' I spluttered, waving frantically. 'Ragwasi!'

The river was still strong even though there were reed beds now to slow it down and I was certain that, short of a miracle, it would not be possible to save Ragwasi from the fate that lay in store for him twenty yards ahead. He was turning in the water and trying to swim back upstream, his eyes wide, but his face determined still as he clawed his way against the current. For a moment, he made headway, but then the river took him and though I put on another spurt I could not get to within grasping distance of him.

And then, he just stood up. He stood up like Neptune emerging from the sea, hauling himself to his feet and standing with his hands on his hips.

His feet had somehow found a rock and instinct had done the rest. And a moment later, I was with him and up on that rock too, gasping and swaying as the river tore at my knees.

'Thank God,' I said, grasping on to my old friend. 'Thank God.'

'We are not out of the river yet,' he replied, panting and jerking a thumb at the hippos. 'And I do not trust these reed beds either. I see the spoor of crocodiles on the bank but I see no crocodiles in the water. So…'

'Does your revolver work?' I asked, pulling out mine. It was full of water, grit and sand and I could not trust the ammunition.

He checked his too, emptying the water from the barrel, then breaking it open to wipe off the bullets.

'There is grit in here but the action is fine,' he replied. 'Shall we risk it?'

'Wait,' I said, raising my Webley and pointing it into the reed bed. 'Just in case.'

I pulled the trigger and was gratified to hear the report and feel the pistol kick in my hand. I fired once and then twice more into the reeds. Downstream, the hippos scarpered in short order, much to our relief, while there wasn't so much as a ripple in the reeds.

'Nothing in there,' I said. 'Or it would have moved.'

We left our rock, sinking into the water and finding our feet in the mud, then waded into the reed bed, parting them with one arm while keeping our pistols ready in the other. It was only a short way to go, no more than a few yards, but when we emerged onto the muddy bank, the unmistakeable slide marks of crocodiles were everywhere, alongside the big, dinner plate prints of hippos and we were careful to keep going until we were twenty yards away from the bank and could sit in something like safety.

We undressed and lay our soaking clothes out on a thorn bush to dry for we neither of us relished the prospect of a long walk back up river with chafing clothes. Willoughby, Stamford and Kruger's millions were gone now and there was no prospect of catching up with them that I could see. Even if we dashed for our horses and then gave chase, we would not catch them on the river and we could not be sure where they were headed because we could not be sure just how much smoke or false scent Willoughby had laid to cover his tracks. He had said he was going to Xai Xai but that and all the talk of learning Portuguese could not be relied upon. The truth was that he could be heading for the Mountains of the Moon, the Zambezi or the pyramids for all we knew.

'It looks like I have been double-crossed,' said Ragwasi, looking ruefully downstream.

'You are not alone,' I agreed.

'I am glad to hear that uPelly,' said Ragwasi.

*

Well, for the next couple of hours, we occupied ourselves in removing the leeches that had fastened on to us in the reed bed. This we did by getting a finger nail under the sucker and flicking them off; leech bites bleed for hours so there wasn't much we could do to stop our shirts from getting bloody once we put them on again because our medical supplies were in our saddlebags and our saddlebags were on our horses and our horses were a long way back up river. Once this chore had been completed and we were as dry as we might expect to be, we set off on our trek, both feeling very miserable. Ragwasi, I reckoned, would be feeling the loss of all that filthy lucre while I was weighed down by the prospect of giving some explanation to Colonel Tom Cole as to what we had been up to without handing him a rope to hang us by. What was worse was the ignominy of being double-crossed by Stamford; how on earth I should break the news to Hattie was a question that I could not right then answer and I could only hope that some inspiration would be given to me before this last long march was over. Perhaps the only consolation to me was the thought that with the money gone, Ragwasi might come back to his senses and our old friendship might be renewed.

We walked in silence, following an elephant track through the bush and keeping a wary eye out for leopards. Once, we disturbed a pair of serval cats, nocturnal creatures with big ears and big eyes and which trot like dogs rather than lope like cats; they remind me of foxes back in my native East Anglia and I was immediately drawn back to the time when I went home to apologise to my father. This long walk back to Colonel Cole felt like that long walk up the drive to Dines Hall; all I could hope was that it would turn out better, for that meeting had been cold and unsatisfactory. I had apologised then, and been forgiven, but there was too much distance between us to return to any warmth of feeling and I dreaded losing the good opinion of Tom Cole after so many years.

'Riders,' said Ragwasi, cocking his ear. 'On the strand.'

I peered out of the bush towards the river and was rewarded a few moments later by the sight of a half troop of Rimington's Tigers, led by Mike Rimington himself, and hauling along four spare mounts – our mounts. He saw us at the same time and reined in.

'Well, here's a pretty kettle of fish!' he called out. 'Pelly and Ragwasi blundering about the bush without rifles or horses and making enough noise to wake every Boer sentry between Pretoria and Rhodesia! We have been looking for you chaps. Colonel Cole is just behind and he is *particularly* interested to hear the explanation for your – what shall we call it? *Furlough*? Cook's Tour? Family outing? I suppose that sounds about right.'

My heart gave a sudden lurch at that and in every hanging liana I saw a hangman's noose; but then he grinned and jerked a thumb over his shoulder.

'Here he comes now.'

Colonel Cole appeared on the instant at the rest of the troop and pulled up short. He was hot as hell and hard as rhino hide and I could see from his face that he was in no mood to bandy pleasantries.

'Where's Willoughby?' he barked, without bothering with a greeting. 'Where is the damned fellow?'

'Gone, I'm afraid, Tom,' I said, rather weakly and wishing that I had called him 'Colonel'.

'Damn it all!' he replied, tugging on his reins. 'Mr. Pelly – make your report to Major Rimington. Ragwasi – with me, please.'

This I thought rather odd, for reporting separately seemed to me a little too much like being questioned separately, which is what police detectives do to their suspects. Cole dismounted and led Ragwasi a little way off to one side, a concerned and quizzical look on his face. I looked at Mike Rimington as he slid off his saddle and handed his reins to one of the troopers; the trooper had the look of a Peeler too.

'So what's it all about?' I asked.

'Rather thought you'd fill us in on that, old boy,' replied Rimington. 'Rather mysterious, you and the Major disappearing into thin air like that.'

'How much do you know, then?'

'Not much more than what that dreadful Cunningham chap babbled out when we caught up with him,' said Rimington. 'Something to do with a robbery?'

'You arrested Cunningham?'

'Not exactly,' replied Rimington, with a grimace. 'We found him with a bullet in his guts some way outside Pretoria, babbling away, rotten with the fever. He only lasted long enough to tell us that he'd been attacked by Zulus and robbed blind. Two of his mates were beside him in the hut; both dead. I recognised them.' He shook his head. 'Waste of good soldiers. But that was some scheme of Willoughby's, I'll admit,' he said, looking up. 'Robbing a bank. Who'd have thought it? Did he get away with the money? Cunningham seemed to think that you were too late.'

'Cunningham was right,' I confirmed. 'Most of the money had been removed before we got there. What was left was substantial but Willloughby wasn't satisfied. He wanted it all.'

'Did he indeed?' said Rimington. 'And how did he propose to pull that off?'

I decided to come clean, although without drawing too much attention to Stamford's role in the affair; I couldn't keep him out of it and he damn well did not deserve to be kept out of it after shoving me overboard, but I still could not give up on family; and so, I told how we'd blown the train and then lifted the mule trains and then paid the Marotis to smuggle them down to the river prior to putting the loot aboard the boats.

'Well,' said Rimington, putting his hat back on his head and looking down river. 'Willoughby seems to have done his homework alright. Do you think Xai Xai is where he's heading?'

'He could be heading anywhere,' I shrugged. 'But I should think he'll use the river as far as he can.'

Rimington agreed. 'Problem is,' he said. 'We're already over the border and we daren't go further without risking diplomatic complications. Damn touchy, the Portugoosers, you know.'

I knew.

'Well,' he said. 'The best we can do is send someone back to the nearest telegraph and get them to warn the Admiralty. Maybe they can pick him up offshore.'

I thought that the interview was over, but then Rimington fixed me with his hunter's eyes, all kindness gone out of them now.

'And Stamford Holzhausen?' he said. 'He's with Willoughby?'

I nodded; I could not lie.

'Why?' he asked. 'I know why Cunningham and that crew went with the Major. I know why Ragwasi went and I can guess why you went: but him? I recruited him to my troop and I count myself a fair judge of character and he was no bad hat. So what would a boy like that be doing with a rogue like Willoughby?'

I pursed my lips and decided that if he did not know about Stamford's safe-cracking abilities then I need not enlighten him.

'Why do you think *I* went?' I asked, trying to deflect the conversation away from Stamford.

'I would guess that you went out of loyalty to your friend,' he replied. 'Or perhaps for family reasons.'

Did he know about Stamford being my nephew? My mind reeled; I could hardly credit it but before I could enquire further, Cole and Ragwasi joined us.

'Well, that's that then,' said Colonel Cole, swatting at his leg with his hat and looking vexed. 'As I thought, Willoughby is a cad and now he's escaped with a fortune and we can't follow. Still, at least I have the satisfaction of having warned High Command about him. No blame can come this way.'

He lifted his eyes and met mine. 'And I owe you an apology Pelly, for not letting you in on the business from the beginning.'

'I beg your pardon?' I said, for this was the second baffling development in as many moments. 'What business?'

'About Willoughby,' said Cole, pursing his lips. 'Damn bad show.'

I looked from Cole to Ragwasi, who had also pursed his lips and had his hands behind his back, looking guilty.

'We had a communication from Scotland Yard asking us if we had any knowledge of the whereabouts of a Harry Willoughby, wanted in connection with a series of jewel thefts from various country houses. It seems that Willoughby had been a guest at these houses when the articles went missing and the Yard wanted to speak with him. Well, the War Office wouldn't have any of it. As far as they were concerned, Major Willoughby was an officer and a gentleman employed on active and dangerous service while the police were just a bunch of flat-footed boundahs out for scandal. Fortunately, my principals in the Intelligence Branch thought it wise to keep an eye on him and so when I saw the chance, I had him attached to me.'

'You mean, you knew Willoughby was going to steal Kruger's gold?' I was aghast.

'Not at first,' replied Cole, shuffling. 'That's when Ragwasi came in. I asked him to stick close, gain his confidence and then follow him into whatever it was he had in mind.'

I could hardly speak. Ragwasi was Tom Cole's spy?

'But...but....' My mouth opened and shut like a goldfish in new water.

'Yes, I'm sorry,' said Cole. 'But I couldn't let you in on the secret in case family loyalty got in the way. I know you for a man of high character, Pelly, and I could not risk putting your integrity to the test.'

'Family loyalty?' I said, completely confused by now. 'You mean you knew about my nephew?'

'*Cousin*, surely?' said Cole. 'Even if he is on the distaff side, so to speak. I say, it gave me quite a start when Scotland Yard told me that you and Willoughby were related.'

'Willoughby and I are related?' I cried. 'How can this be? I have no knowledge of this!'

'Really?' said Cole. 'But Major Harry Willoughby is your cousin. His father is your uncle, John Pelly.'

'Uncle John?' I cried, once more. 'He lived in Rutland. I distinctly remember! He never went near Leicestershire in his life.'

'Actually, he did, old boy,' said Cole, dropping his voice. 'It seems he had a bit of a liaison with the wife of old Baronet Willoughby and young Harry was the result. Well, the Baronet took the view that to avoid a scandal, it was better to adopt the boy as his own and hushed it all up. Trouble was, your Uncle John couldn't –well – restrain himself - and Lady Willoughby being – ahem – rather younger than the Baronet and keen on – ahem – country sports - they ended up making a – well – *irregular* arrangement – and John Pelly got the use of part of the East Wing for as often as he cared to visit as long as he was discrete. When the old boy passed on, he stepped into his shoes and took over the Baronetcy – quite irregular of course – not even sure if it was legal, but well, it was Leicestershire – some damn funny things go on there, I hear.'

I was aghast. Uncle John a Baronet? It was simply not possible.

'Fraid it's all true, old boy,' said Cole, embarrassed. 'Best authority and all that. Thought you knew. Family secrets, what?'

'I deny it absolutely,' I said. 'It's ridiculous. Uncle John lived in Rutland. I distinctly remembered visiting him there when I was a child.'

'Harry Willoughby was born in 1865,' said Cole. 'We have his registration.'

I thought back to 1865; I would have been ten years old or thereabouts. Just about the last time I remember going to visit with Uncle John. Of course, no-one had told me and in 1873, I was packed off to South Africa and so would never have found out on my own. And it came back to me how Willoughby had laid a stress on the *Leicestershire Willoughbys* when we had first met back in Colesberg, giving me a signal that I was supposed to pick up but didn't. That's why he didn't let me in on his plans, I suppose.

'Sorry, old man,' said Cole. 'Bit of shock, what?'

Rarely have I felt so stupid or so utterly duped. It was as though I was back in those Newmarket gambling hells being sharped rigid by coves who knew how to fleece a new boy, yet I was a grown man with years of experience! I should have realised! I should have known!

And then it came rushing in on me that I had treated Ragwasi appallingly. I had thought ill of him, ascribing to him motives of greed when all this time he was engaged in carrying out a particularly difficult duty with dedication and skill.

'The mules,' I said, slowly raising my hands to my thick skull. 'The riders that you sent off without Willoughby's knowledge after we lifted the mule trains, Ragwasi. You were sending messages back through the Marotis. My God, I owe you the deepest apologies, Ragwasi. I should have known....'

'You owe me no apologies,' replied Ragwasi, looking rather miserable. 'For I deceived you in this matter, uPelly, when I should have ignored Cole uLootant and trusted you. It is I that should apologise to you.'

'Here, old chap,' said Cole, handing me his hip flask. 'Pass it around. For good fellowship's sake, eh?'

Colonel Cole, it seemed had anticipated this moment.

*

So there it was. *Cousin* Harry Willoughby had disappeared of into the wide blue yonder with Kruger's millions accompanied by my nephew, Stamford John Holzhausen, safe cracker, con-artist and a man in possession of a cynical hardness and lack of sympathy that a decent chap had no business learning before he had been cheated, robbed and maltreated by nature, fate and his fellow man over very many more years than his fresh face had yet seen. It was a lot to swallow and difficult, I'll say, making humble pie seem like ice cream by comparison and I chewed on that gristle all the way back up to the highveldt and on to Pretoria, where we made our official report. After that, as a consequence of our wounds, sickly state and general dilapidation, we were granted leave and allowed to return to Kuruman and rest up for half a season – what we had swallowed in that river kept us within dashing distance of a privy for longer than I care to remember. Tom Cole and Mike Rimington bade us farewell before galloping off to chase those Boers who had taken to the country at Kruger's behest to begin the guerrilla war and so we were back to being just Ragwasi and I once more.

We did not speak about what we had done for both of us were unhappy that our mutual trust had been strained like this and though I could forgive Ragwasi's deception as a military necessity, it still rankled. That said, I still knew my unspoken accusations of criminality and greed and my generally 'holier-than-thou' attitude throughout rankled with Ragwasi and I could see no point in opening up a pandora's box of explanations, excuses and the inevitable recriminations that would follow by breaching the subject. You cannot cross a river without getting wet and we had both been in too many rivers lately so we stuck to everyday matters and kept our upper lips stiff.

Then, one day, just after dawn, we came over the low sandy ridge that marked the boundary of our farm and saw the small boys with little sticks driving the cattle out of the thorn bush enclosures and onto the veldt to graze. They shouted and whacked as the sleepy cattle stumbled along waking the dim figures emerging from the thatched bomas and making the women who were drawing water from the wind-pump trough call out in irritation. Beside them, men were already gargling water and rinsing their faces and heads, pulling on trousers or winding loincloths and jamming down caps onto their heads before heading out to work. A couple of dogs came out to bark at the crows and then shot straight out towards us like furious bees until they saw us, recognised us and began to yelp in greeting.

'We are home, uPelly,' said Ragwasi, straightening in his creaking saddle. 'Let us leave the evils of war here and not take them any closer to our home.'

I held out my hand and he took it and we shook in the African way, with a shake, a bind and a twist and we let our distrust blow away with the breath of dawn off the cinnamon land.

'This is all we got of Kruger's millions,' I said, reaching into my saddle bag and pulling out the three rolls of gold coins that Cunningham had tossed at me in the State bank strong room. 'I think that there is probably just enough for one each for the children.'

'And they can play Ducks and Drakes with them in the dam,' said Ragwasi, smiling. 'For do we not have enough wealth already?'

I flicked one out of the roll and held it up to examine it closer. It was heavy, solid and Kruger's old troll of a face peered grumpily over a '9' stamped below and wondered for a moment if that stood for the nine lives he seemed to have enjoyed. If it was lucky for Kruger, I decided, then the best place for it was in the dam. I nodded in agreement; it would be fun and somehow fitting to see the gold that had brought so much trouble to South Africa skipping and splashing out of the children's hands and on across the water. It might bring a little laughter to put in the balance against all the tears.

All I had to do now was tell my sister Hattie that her son was a rogue.

*

There are areas in the north of Zululand that are so close in appearance to Northumberland or the Yorkshire Dales that if you could forget about the heat and the flies for a moment, you might catch a hope of a dream of Bamburgh or Harrogate. There are ferns too, just as you would expect to see in Thetford forest. If you ride out to Hlobane mountain in January and climb up to the Devil's Pass, you would be no more surprised to see a Roman legion marching along there than if you stood on Hadrian's Wall and saw a Zulu impi coming, for the landscape is just like the Border country or the Pennines. It's cold too, which often surprises newcomers to Africa because they always expect to be broiling under a fierce sky with only a palm tree for shade or admiring great spaces washed with sun while supping on a cooling peg. Ha! You should try Kimberley in winter when the wind is a flurry of sleet and your teeth are chattering on the edge of your tin mug of tea like a giddy skeleton playing on a washboard!

I am telling you this because these are just some of the things I thought about instead of thinking about the exact way and the precise words that I must use to put in a letter to Hattie and send off to Mijnheer Cronjie in Cape Town who would then send it on to Montevideo or Buenos Aires or wherever she was sitting and waiting for news of Edgar Smithfield, who had changed his name to Stamford John Holtzhausen for reasons which it was my duty to confirm as nefarious. It is a good job my head is not made of wood because otherwise I would have scratched several notches into it just then and then spent the next two hours being scolded by Tepo as she took out the splinters. And a bottle of Cape Smoke and a good cupful of mampoer (my son had inherited the family talent for concealing the still in places unfrequented by either Tepo or Botuimela) gave me a temporary inspiration and for a while the words flew off my pen like sparks, faster than old Coleridge scribbling away at Kubla Khan but then, like old Coleridge, I was forced to break off to hide the bottle from Tepo and when I came back to my desk, all inspiration had fled from me. I also knocked the ink over and spoilt what I had not already smudged and got into even more trouble for making a mess in the house. It must be a terrible life, being a writer.

Fortunately I was spared much more of this, for on the fourth or fifth attempt, a shout went up from outside the house and a rider appeared with an express letter, which had come up from Cape Town via Kimberley for me. It was from Mijnheer Cronjie and in it was enclosed a letter which bore a postage stamp from Argentina. It was news from Hattie.

Dear Nicholas, I hope you are well and that you have not been put to too much trouble in the search for Edgar –

'Tepo,' I said, on reading this. 'I must have my bottle of Cape Smoke.'

I said this because it is a well-known fact of life that when someone hopes that *you have not been put to too much trouble*, they know full well that you have; and it is also a well-known fact that when people know full well that you have been *put to too much trouble*, they mean to tell you that you should not have bothered putting yourself to *all that trouble* because they have since found out that they have put you to all that *trouble* for *no good reason*.

I have stamped on my hat again.

It appears that there may have been a certain amount of misunderstanding –

Tepo came back with the Cape Smoke just in time.

Edgar is safe and well –

'I bet he is!' I roared. 'Sitting on a mountain of gold and laughing to himself over the best champagne Kruger's millions can buy!'

He has seen the error of his ways and has promised to reform –

'Reform!' I spluttered. 'Reform? You might as well expect a scorpion to give up its sting!'

He is to enter the Church –

'As a fully-fledged Arch-bishop no doubt, complete with a newly built and paid for cathedral to sit in!' I cried. 'Poppycock! Fiddlesticks!'

He came to his senses after an unfortunate incident in South Africa, which played upon his conscience –

'*Unfortunate incident*? Which one?' I nearly choked on my Cape Smoke and Tepo had to slap me on the back before I could continue. I swear, I had to take a break or I would have died of apoplexy then and there. 'Deserting the Queen's Colours? Bare-faced robbery? Safe-cracking? Blowing a train sky high? Jumping that blasted canyon and getting a bullet in his head? Or nearly drowning me in the damn Limpopo? Lord knows he's got a variety to choose from!'

He understands now what it means to lose one's rightful property –

'Aha!' I cried once more. 'Serves him right! Willoughby bilked him too, did he? Got him half way down to Xai Xai and then dropped him in the drink too? Well, serves him out right! Cheers!'

I downed another mouthful while Tepo rolled her eyes and muttered something about 'buffers' and 'puffing Billy'. I could only think that she wanted to go on a railway herself, but I cannot be one hundred percent sure of this thing.

He was not aware of just how attractive to the criminal classes the Cape is –

'It bally well drew him to it, Hattie!'

And understands now that it was <u>foolish</u> of him to adopt a nom de guerre *–*

'Is that what he calls a false identity? Outrageous!'

Especially when the papers which he was relying on to give substance to this boyish <u>prank</u> –

'Prank? Prank! Putting a drawing pin on the teacher's chair is a prank, Hattie! Dropping a mouse down the back of a fat washerwoman's dress is a prank, Hattie! Stealing diamonds in the company of a fake Countess and then skipping the country does not come under the appellation of *prank*! Lord above!'

- were stolen from his hotel room by a <u>dastardly young villain</u> with a <u>deceptively innocent</u> face who seems to have been a <u>master criminal and safe cracker</u>. I am therefore delighted to inform you that he has been back in the bosom of his family at Dines Hall after a stay of only one week in Cape Town and has reverted to his given name, Edgar Smithfield. I do hope you are well.

Yours, etc

Hattie.

Pass me the mampoer. What a fool I was. The person I thought was my nephew turned out not to be and the person I thought was no relation turned out to be my cousin. Well, it just goes to show, I suppose; but I'm not sure what. Anyway, that is often the way with real stories; they are supposed to end very nicely and neatly but never really do. All I can say for a proper ending is that of Major Harry Willoughby, I never heard nor saw sight nor sound of and neither did anyone else. Where he went to and what he did with Kruger's millions if he did get away with them, no-one knows. There are those who say Kruger got the bulk of his money out through Portuguese East Africa and put it in a bank in Germany and those who say it is buried somewhere below the escarpment at God's Window but no-one knows for sure if these stories are true or if Cousin Harry is sitting in the Casino at Monte Carlo to this day, trying to break the bank there. He could be anywhere although you'd think a chap as big as him would be hard to miss. It wouldn't surprise me if he was a cattle baron in America or Australia, or if Captain Scott or that Norwegian chap find him at the South Pole. It's possible he got eaten by crocs or torn apart by hippos but, as I say, no-one will ever know probably, because he would be in serious trouble with the law if he ever broke cover.

As to Stamford, well, a chap called John Holzhausen was arrested for stealing horses back in 1905 and claimed that he actually knew where the millions were buried. He claimed that he and two other chaps had buried it fifty miles north of the Blyde River but he busted out of jail and disappeared and was never heard of again. I can't vouch that this was *the* Stamford because I only read about it in the papers a year later and there wasn't a picture. So maybe he's sitting at the tables of the Casino at Monte Carlo too, wondering what the best way to get at the safe is. Like I say, most real stories don't have a neat ending. I suppose that the only proper way to tell the ending is that we did take our share of Kruger's millions, gave them out to the children and spent a good fifteen minutes seeing how far we could spin them across the dam until they were all gone. Now and again the children dive for them when the sun glints through that dappled water and lights them up but most of them are gone, buried in the mud now. No doubt that a long time in the future someone will dig them up and think they have found the long buried hoard of a long gone king. Ragwasi thinks so, at least.

Author's Note

In 2016, the value of each incredibly rare 'Single 9 Gold Pond' coin was estimated at £750,000. The whereabouts of Pelly and Ragwasi's dam is not currently known.

16015563R00078

Printed in Poland
by Amazon Fulfillment
Poland Sp. z o.o., Wrocław